# JUST LOVE

by

## PRESCOTT LANE

# TABLE OF CONTENTS

# PROLOGUE
## PRESENT DAY

### RHETT

I'M A GOOD liar. Always have been. I could convince my mom I didn't eat that cookie before dinner with a single look. *The dog ate my homework* actually worked for me.

My lies were always meant to help myself. Never to hurt anyone else.

But the best lies I tell—those I reserve for myself.

The lies we tell ourselves are the most important we tell. You can lie to your boss, your partner, your friends—keep things to yourself, not share the whole truth. You want the day off, so you phone in sick when you're not. You say you'll call somebody, knowing you won't. Conveniently forget that party you were supposed to go to, but didn't really want to attend. The list is endless.

All those are crappy, but it's the lies we tell ourselves that define us, hold us hostage, give us excuses for doing what we do.

Those are the lies that keep up the facade. The ones that keep our lives going. The lies I tell myself—those are the tape holding everything in place, and once you start to pick at it, it can all unravel.

She's better off. That's what I tell myself.

Ass in the chair, fingers tapping my leg, my eyes burn a hole in my phone. It's the same every day. Every day since she left. Correction, every day since I forced her out of my life. Every day, I fight the same damn fight.

Call her.

Don't call her.

Falling in love is easy. Holding on to that love—well, that's the real bitch.

There's two sides to every love story. The how you fell in love, and the how you fell apart.

# CHAPTER ONE

## EIGHTEEN MONTHS AGO

I can't remember not loving you.
A. Rose

### RHETT

"THERE ARE WOMEN you should never, ever have sex with: your boss' girlfriend, your secretary, a married woman, your friend's ex, but the holy grail of women you should never screw is your best friend's baby sister."

I look at Sadie, my golden retriever mix, for confirmation, but she simply licks my hand. "I'm a total lunatic," I say, giving her a good scratch behind the ears.

Ainsley is off limits. There are lines you don't cross, and fucking your best friend's little sister is one of them. But all I've been able to think about since I heard she was moving back to Charleston was the way she looked last time I saw her, her strawberry blonde hair flowing, her bright smile, and blue eyes.

No matter how much I scold myself, tell myself it's wrong, I know I'm thinking about her way too much. She's a beautiful woman. I'm a healthy, red-blooded man. It's just physical. That's it.

Bullshit.

Fucking lie.

Sometimes it's best to lie. Like now.

The lie of the day is: Ainsley's sexy as hell, and my dick knows it. That's all this is.

Yep, that's my story, and I'm sticking to it.

And now she's back in town, living one floor below me in her brother's old place. Brody's condo and mine have the exact same layout. Two bedrooms connected by an open concept kitchen and living area. The only difference is, mine is one floor higher. Located in one of those great old buildings that used to be a chocolate factory or something before its conversion, it's been a perfect setup, walking distance to our vet clinic right off the historic district in Charleston.

But a few weeks ago, he and Skye bought their dream house and moved in together. They're only here now to celebrate Ainsley's move to Charleston.

I'm completely screwed. God has a sick sense of humor some-times. I am literally living right on top of her, which is exactly where I want to be—on top of her naked, making her moan, screaming out my name, her nails digging down my back, until her legs are trem-bling and . . . Jesus Christ, I have to stop this.

Slipping on a pair of shorts, I head out of my condo toward the elevator. "Come on, Sadie."

"*Little sister, little sister, little sister,*" I repeat over and over again, drilling it into my thick skull, tugging at my hair.

The elevator doesn't move slow enough for my dick to under-stand that I'm supposed to think of Ainsley as my little sister, not my next screw. For God's sake, I've known her for well over ten years, since I met Brody, her brother, our freshman year in college. Ainsley was only around twelve at the time, still flat-chested, wearing braces. Oh, how times have changed.

Standing outside Brody's door—well, I guess it's Ainsley's door now—I close my eyes then look down at Sadie. "Little sister," I tell her one more time, opening the door.

"It's about time," Brody says as his fiancé Skye hops up off his lap.

They are the ideal couple. Everyone envies them. They've been dating since undergrad, and Brody finally asked Skye to marry him. The wedding is just around the corner. Not sure what took him so long. Aside from one brief breakup while we were in veterinary school, they've been inseparable. Skye is like a sister to me.

"Nice date," Brody teases, cocking his head to Sadie. "Best looking woman I've seen you with in a long time." I affectionately flip him the bird. "Sadie's the longest relationship you've ever had with a woman. In fact, she might be the only woman in your life besides your mommy."

Brody's right about that. And it's by design. Settling down, getting married, not something I've ever looked for. College, vet school, starting our own clinic—that's been the priority for me. Besides, I prefer to keep things carefree with women. I'm only thirty-one. I grab Skye, easily twirling her petite body around and dipping her. "What about this fine little thing?"

"What about me?" Ainsley asks, coming out of the bedroom, wearing tiny black shorts, knee high socks, and a fitted Atlanta Braves t-shirt. Her hair is on top of her head in a messy bun. She's the whole package—blue eyes, that strawberry blonde hair, funny, smart, curves for days, and an ass that is so perfect that it's almost obscene.

*Little sister, little sister, little sister.*

"A. Rose!" I say as she wraps her arms around my neck, going in for a full-frontal hug. Having her tits pressed against my chest isn't helping, but Christ, she smells good.

"When are you going to stop calling me that?" she asks, her bottom lip pouting out just slightly. I shouldn't be noticing that, but if it keeps my eyes on her face and not her gorgeous tits, then I figure it's the lesser of two evils.

"It's your name," I say simply. "A" is her first initial, and "Rose" is their last name. It just fits her and has stuck.

Ainsley bends down to pat Sadie, who has rolled over on her back, panting heavily in demand for Ainsley to pay her some attention. Ainsley looks up at me from under her lashes, and I hope I don't start panting, having her on her knees right in front of me.

"Game's on," Brody announces, turning up the television for the Braves game, and pulling Skye down onto his lap. "Beer's in the fridge."

Ainsley looks over at Skye and her brother smiling at each other. Skye fits perfectly in his lap. They look so in love, their brown eyes gazing at each other. I hear Ainsley sigh wistfully. She catches my eye for a second then gets up, taking a seat on a chair, and pats it for Sadie to jump up with her.

"No dogs on the furniture," Brody says.

"You don't live here anymore," Ainsley says, patting Sadie with even more affection.

"Don't be such a hard ass," I say to her brother then pat the chair, too, encouraging Sadie. "She's older now. She has arthritis."

I still remember the day I found Sadie. It was Freshman year of undergrad. At the time, I thought I was going to be an attorney like my dad, so I was taking a criminal justice class. One of the class requirements was to do a police ride along. We got a call about some disturbance in a trailer park on the outskirts of Charleston. I wasn't supposed to get out of the car, but I was eighteen and thought I knew best. Turned out in this case, I did. In the middle of an old tire, I found the saddest, skinniest runt of a puppy whimpering as she cuddled next to her dead mother. She was so small at the time I don't think she could've gotten herself out of the tire. I picked her up, smuggled her into my dorm, and managed to keep her hidden there for the rest of the year. Feeding her with bottles and taking care of her made me want to be a vet.

Ainsley Eskimo kisses my dog. Lucky bitch. "You're still my sweet puppy-wuppy, aren't you, girl?" Sadie's normally flopping ear sticks straight up in the air.

"Boner," Skye calls out.

"What?" I turn toward her, afraid my own dick is showing.

"Sadie's got an ear boner," Skye says, laughing.

"She's a girl," Ainsley says, flopping Sadie's ear back down. "You've been a nurse at the fertility clinic too long. Now you're imagining boners."

Brody's eyes flip to Ainsley. "Watch your mouth."

Brody may be my best friend, but the dude rides his sister way too hard. Ainsley is the sweetest looking girl you'd ever see, but she can hold her own. She has a bit of wild child in her, although she doesn't come out to play very often. I could do something about that.

I know Brody means well. They lost their parents our senior year of undergrad.—house fire over Christmas break, leaving Brody the sole caretaker for Ainsley, who was only fifteen at the time. I'll never forget that phone call—my best friend in tears. Guys don't cry, especially in front of one another. I drove through the night to get to him. Brody wasn't just my college roommate, but my best friend. We are like brothers. So there was no question that I would stand by him during that tragedy, even if that meant moving his little sister into our college bachelor pad. I wasn't going to let him leave school, move home. We had plans. The vet clinic was one of them. I made a promise to him. Skye did, too. The three of us would help him raise Ainsley. And we did. So, Ainsley isn't just my best friend's little sister. She's so much more.

"Seriously, Brody, I spent my teenage years with you and Rhett. Every morning for years, I was greeted with morning wood," Ainsley says.

Skye elbows Brody in the side. She and I are constantly reminding him not to be so overbearing. He stills sees Ainsley as that teenage girl who cried herself to sleep for weeks after their parents died. He protects her with the love of a brother, but also the love of a mother and father. Most of the time, Ainsley lets it slide. They're all they have left of their "real" family, so he can take it to the extreme. Another reason for me not to touch his little sister.

I see Brody glaring at her, and Ainsley glares right back. Time to help her out.

"How was your drive in from Atlanta?" I ask, motioning around the condo which is littered with boxes and huge plastic containers. "What's all this stuff?"

"Beads, lace, fabrics," Ainsley says.

"You must have hit every estate sale on your drive in," Brody says.

Ainsley is wicked smart, scored a perfect thirty-six on her ACT. I credit myself for helping her through Honors Biology II. But beyond being book smart, she's got a creative side to match. She designs wedding dresses for a living. Her creativity and brains earned her a full scholarship to the Savannah College of Art and Design. It was hard for Brody to let her go away to school, but ultimately knew it was best for Ainsley. Before moving back to Charleston, Ainsley's been working in Atlanta. Her dream is to own her own shop. She loves to take beading and lace from vintage dresses, and use them in her work. No one designs dresses like her. She hand-stitches every bead herself.

"I can't wait for you to get started on my dress," Skye says.

"I've already got some things sketched out," Ainsley says.

Wedding dress talk? That's my cue for a beer, getting up to grab some cold ones out of the refrigerator. I take out three and hand one to Brody. I offer one to Skye, but she shakes her head. "Still trying to lose those last five pounds before the wedding," she says.

I roll my eyes. Skye is always on some sort of diet. In the years that I've known her, she's been every size under the sun, but Brody loves her no matter what. I hold out the beer to Ainsley, who takes it with a smile.

"Thanks, Rhett," Ainsley says.

Brody's eyes dart to me. "Don't give her . . ."

Ainsley's in her mid-twenties. Brody is really overdoing it today. "Sorry, I forgot. Can I see your ID, miss?" I snark. Ainsley busts out into a huge laugh, popping her top and taking a long sip, smacking her lips for good measure.

"Got to love a woman who likes beer," I say then bite the corner of my mouth, realizing that was a slip of the tongue.

Skye elbows Brody again—harder this time. "Sorry, sis," Brody says, and Ainsley throws him a smile.

That smile. Her smile could melt any guy's heart. I want her to smile at me like that. To make her smile like that.

I try not to stare at her, but the combination of her shorts and those knee-high socks has me struck stupid. I can't help myself. It doesn't hurt to look, right? Truthfully, she isn't dressed provocatively. She looks more like a college girl, but the curve of her neck seems to call to me. The way her lips linger on the bottle is driving me crazy. Something about the way she moves makes me unable to concentrate.

"Where's the pitching? You call that a slider!" Ainsley scolds the television. Skye looks at her like she's an alien. "What? I spent my formative years with these two," Ainsley says, pointing to me and Brody.

"We raised her right," Brody says, raising his beer to me.

"Beer and baseball," Skye says, smiling at Ainsley. "And a wedding dress designer. Interesting combo."

"That should be my personal ad. Hopeless romantic who likes beer and baseball . . ."

"What personal ad?" Brody asks.

"You better not be on some dating app," I add, a wave of heat shooting over my body. "I don't want to hear about you swiping right!"

"She was kidding," Skye says, smacking us both this time. "Ainsley, I don't know how you survived being raised by us."

"The Three Stooges," Ainsley says. "I laughed a lot. And snuck around."

"Don't tease your brother," Skye says. "He may have a heart attack. And I'd like to finally walk down the aisle after over ten years together."

Ainsley smiles again. She's one of those people that smiles easily. Even after all the pain in her life, smiling is as natural as breathing to her. Smiling while hurting is a talent she and I have in common, only she does it to make the world a better place, and I do it to keep the world from looking too closely.

The truth is, Ainsley was a good kid. Living with two twenty-one-year-old guys couldn't have been easy, but it was often funny. Thank God, Skye had been there to provide a female influence. Brody was the hard ass. And I was the fun, laid-back one, who protected her from Brody. The three of us are bonded for life over raising Ainsley. My parents were a big part of the process, too. Brody and Ainsley became a feature at all my family gatherings. My parents love them both.

Ainsley went to high school while we finished college and vet school. The day Ainsley left for college was bittersweet. I went from seeing her every day to only seeing her on the holidays, and somewhere in between all that, she went from being a girl to a woman, at least for me.

Brody and I opened our vet clinic in Charleston, and Skye became a nurse at a fertility clinic. Life just moved on, no longer about who was carpooling Ainsley, who could help with her calculus homework, or teach her how to drive.

"I'm so glad you guys are finally getting married. You are so perfect together and college sweethearts. It's so romantic," Ainsley says.

That's my cue. Time for another beer. This is when Ainsley looks younger than her age—believing in a happy little fairytale marriage. She hasn't outgrown the notion that one day she'll meet her prince. I guess we did something right with her, if she can still believe in love like that.

Turning back, I find Ainsley's blue eyes right on me. She gives me a small, reassuring smile like she can read my mind. I smile back at her. She had her heart broken recently, so maybe she needs reassurance that everything will be alright. I know for her it will be. She breaks our gaze and turns her attention back to the game.

Sitting down on the floor next to her chair, I pat Sadie, who promptly licks my cheek, her own little reassurance. Ainsley reaches over and pats Sadie, too. I can't resist. I gently glide my finger over her pinkie, just one time so she'll assume it's an accident.

She doesn't squirm. She doesn't blush. Still, I see tiny goose-bumps on her pale skin. My eyes wander down to Sadie's fur, where both our hands are patting her. My hand is as close as it can be to hers without touching. Time to test the waters. I move my pinkie slightly, but her voice stops me.

"How about you, Rhett? Still seeing that girl from Christmas, Meghan?" Ainsley asks.

"Who?" I ask, no clue who she's talking about.

"Meghan, stunning, long-legged flight attendant."

"Nah," I say, wondering what made Ainsley think of her.

Skye rolls her eyes. "She was perfect for him. Out of town a lot, no big commitment."

"Until she used the *love* word," Brody piles on. "Kiss of death."

"Yeah, like after two weeks," I say, the ridiculousness of that conversation coming back to me.

"Here's the thing, Ainsley. Now that you're living here, you should know—don't ever set Rhett up with any of your girlfriends because they'll all end up hating you," Skye says.

"Got it," Ainsley says, flashing me a smile.

That smile? I wonder what's behind that smile.

# CHAPTER TWO
## PRESENT DAY

### AINSLEY

AT LEAST I'M not counting the days in my head anymore. Counting the minutes, hours, and seconds since Rhett broke my heart. That's progress.

Heartache sucks. I've gotten good at pushing through the days, losing myself in work. I'm the poster girl for the phrase *Fake it till you make it.*

But the nights are the worst. I dread the sunset. It only brings another night without the man I love.

I miss him.

It's hard to decide what I miss the most.

His arms around me.

The way his breath sounds when he sleeps.

The feel of his body pressed to mine.

The way he looks at me.

There's not one specific thing. It's the whole Rhett package that I miss. If Rhett were here, he'd make some sex joke about me missing his "package." Yeah, I miss his sex jokes, too.

There are two types of people in the world—those that have a thousand unopened email messages on their phone, and those that have to look as soon as the little number pops up. I'm the latter. I also keep my ketchup in the refrigerator and believe cabinet-ketchup people are insane. Another thing: you're either a morning person or night owl. You can't be both.

There are people that think with their heads, and those of us that think with our hearts—I'd wager a bet that heart thinkers end up more heartbroken.

Then there are the people who believe in happily-ever-afters, and those who don't. I used to believe. Now, not so much.

How much heartbreak does it take to get it right? It's like that old Tootsie Pop commercial, where the owl asks how many licks it takes to get to the center. I'd rather know how many heartbreaks it takes until the heart gets it right.

Heartache has a life of its own. It comes without you knowing, and you have no idea how long it will last. You can't cure it. You can't will it away. The life expectancy of a woman is about seventy-eight years in the United States. The life expectancy of heartache is unknown. And mine's been hanging around for almost a year now.

My life's taken a dramatic detour since my heart got broken.

Rhett.

It's been hard. Movies, books, songs—they all paint love as this amazing experience. I know deep down it is. I had it—the butterflies, the tingles, the hopes and dreams that love promises. *Had* is the operative word.

The thing that those songs and movies don't tell you:

*Love isn't always a good thing.*

There, I've said it. Love can feel good, but be bad for you—like that donut I ate this morning. Was good at the time, but when it's gone, you just feel blah! Love has left me blah.

It's funny. I design wedding dresses for a living. Creating wedding dresses is my passion, the bright spot in my day. A person's wedding day is one of the happiest days of their lives. I love being a part of that. I basically sell the fairytale, but deep down, I wonder if it's all bullshit.

I sunk every penny I had into opening my own wedding dress design studio. Keeping busy helps. Distraction is the only thing that keeps me moving.

My heart starts remembering Rhett—time to sew. My head floats into a memory—time to sketch.

That's why Skye and I are grabbing a drink after work today, I need the distraction. But she's running late. I should've just met her at the bar, because now I'm surrounded by the hope of offspring in the air. I want to have babies, be a mom, but there are no potential fathers in sight. Then again, I am standing in a fertility clinic.

Waiting at the nurse's desk for Skye to finish up, I flip through a pamphlet on fertility options. Who knew there were so many ways to conceive? My momma only warned me against one.

"Excuse me?" I hear a smooth voice say from behind me. "Can I help you with something?"

Dropping the pamphlet to the floor like I was caught looking at a dirty magazine, I stammer, looking up into his smile, "Um . . . No, I'm waiting for Skye."

He bends down and picks up the pamphlet, handing it back to me. "She's in with a patient. Can I help you with something?"

I search his lab coat, trying to see around his stethoscope, looking for a name. "No, thank you."

His head tilts, and he smiles again. He's very nice looking, but I can tell he's much older than me—a touch of gray on his temples. But he's sexy, nonetheless.

"It's perfectly normal to be nervous. Why don't you let me put you in a room?" he says, and I feel his hand go to my back, encouraging me to move.

"There's some mistake," I say, stopping and looking back at him.

"You're not an egg donor?" he asks, furrowing his brow.

An egg donor? Do egg donors have a certain look? And what about me would make him think that? "Uh, no."

Red rises to his neck, and he starts fiddling with his stethoscope. "I apologize. We don't get unmarried women in here very often, especially ones that are . . ." He pauses. "I just assumed you were meeting Skye to . . . I apologize for my error."

"Hey, Ainsley," Skye says, coming out of a nearby room. "Doctor, everything is fine in room two now."

"Thank you," he says, giving me a little nod and grin. "Ainsley."

As soon as he's out of earshot, Skye booty bumps me. "Dr. Hottie has eyes for you."

"No, he definitely does not. He thought I was an egg donor," I say.

Skye laughs out loud then covers her mouth. "No wonder his face was so red. He's smoking hot, though."

"You've already got yourself a hot doctor."

"Yeah, but your brother only knows about animal anatomy." Skye nods her head in the hot doctor's direction. "He's an expert in women. Mmm, mmm, mmm."

We both start to giggle as we leave and head to a local watering hole a few blocks away. Despite being close to the water, Charleston is hot much of the year. I swear I can almost hear my pale skin sizzle as soon as the sun hits it.

"I'm sorry I kept you waiting. Today has been insane," Skye says. "First, this really, really pregnant lady falls into the toilet."

"What?" I ask, almost falling over from laughter. Skye always has the funniest stories to tell and her delivery is classic.

"I know, right?" Skye laughs. "Poor thing, someone left the toilet seat up, and she fell right in, but she couldn't get back out."

"No way."

"Yep," Skye says. "That's *so* not in my job description. Then this crazy lady comes in with some of her boyfriend's sperm she pulled out of a used condom. She tells me she told him she was pregnant even though she wasn't and wants us to use the sperm to get her pregnant for real."

"That's crazy."

"Yep, you haven't heard the best part," Skye says. "She bought a positive pregnancy test off the internet to convince him."

"Someone is selling positive pregnancy tests?" I ask.

"Yeah, fifty dollars a pop," Skye says, eyes wide. "I throw that shit away every day. I guess I should be selling them."

It's good to be with Skye. She is the trifecta of female support, acting as my sister, friend, and mother when I need one.

She opens the door to the bar. It's still early, so the place isn't too crowded, mostly tourists and a few business types, throwing one back after a long day. We grab a seat at the bar. Seems like Skye had a rough day, so I let her order. I'm slightly surprised when she orders champagne. I'm even more surprised when the bartender cards me. I pull out my license and flash it to him, thankful that my recent heartache hasn't taken a toll on my face. He gives me an apologetic smile.

"Are we celebrating?" I ask, putting away my identification.

"Nah," she says, grinning. "It's the lowest drink in calories."

That's good to know. There's not a bride I've worked with that hasn't been on some sort of diet. It's a little crazy. You have the ring, the man obviously loves you. Own it!

"Have you heard anything from . . ." Skye asks, treading lightly.

"You can say his name," I say. "No, I haven't heard from Rhett."

Rhett is the last thing I want to talk about. I'm here to avoid all the memories—the site of our first date, first kiss, where he proposed to me. We should have been married by now, happy. There's just something about Rhett. His eyes are the palest blue I've ever seen, and his brown hair is always slightly messy like he just fucked someone hard. Rhett's got handsome down pat.

It's the details of a man that make him sexy—the stubble on his face, the v-cut, the blue of his eyes, the veins in his hands. Rhett has it all. He just might be the perfect man. There's just one problem, he's gone.

I can't forget. Did I mention the way he kisses? He kisses me like he means it, like kissing me is one of his basic human needs. I wonder if any man will ever kiss me like that again.

No matter what's happened, Rhett still gets my knickers in a twist, but I guess there are certain attractions that just burn too bright to fade.

"Maybe that's for the best," Skye offers.

Resisting the urge to ask if she or Brody have heard from him, I down my drink. After all, the calories aren't going to kill me. The memories might, though.

Skye's phone dings. "It's probably Brody," she says with a snipe of attitude, digging through her purse. "Telling me he's working late again."

With that, I motion for another drink. Things between Skye and my brother haven't been great lately. There's tension between them that wasn't there before. Brody has yet to hire a replacement for Rhett. It's long overdue. I'm not sure why. We don't really talk about it. My breakup didn't just happen to me. It happened to all of us, but none of us want to talk about it. Maybe that's why Brody is working like he is. Must run in the family. He and I both seem to think if we work hard enough, we won't have to feel so damn much.

Skye waves the bartender away. "It's not your brother." Turning the phone to me, she raises an eyebrow. "Dr. Hottie wants to know if you're single?"

There's not a ring on my finger. I haven't been on a date in God knows how long. I check the single box on my taxes, my medical forms. Yes, I'm single. It's just my heart still feels very much attached. I blow out a deep breath and fake a smile.

Single girls have more fun, right?

"He's a little old," I say.

"Experienced!" Skye says, winking at me.

"What else do you know about him?"

"He's a rich, single doctor who is sexy as hell," she says. "What else do you need to know?"

"My last relationship was with a rich, single doctor who was sexy as hell."

She places her hand on top of mine. "I'm pulling rank here. It's time."

# CHAPTER THREE
## EIGHTEEN MONTHS AGO

You've always been my measure of what a real man is.
A. Rose

### RHETT

SADIE LOOKS UP at me with her leash dangling from her mouth, reminding me that I missed her evening walk. Attaching her leash to her collar, we walk out to the elevator. It was a hell of a day, having two emergency surgeries pop up back-to-back. One dog made it—the other didn't. It always drains me to have to tell an owner their pet died. I'll never get used to it. Being in the room as a living thing takes its last breath isn't something most people experience in their life. Being the one who couldn't save them? Having to look in a child's eyes and tell them their best friend went to heaven? That's the shit that keeps me up at night.

The elevator stops one floor below mine, and my breath stops with it. "A. Rose, where you off to?"

"Need to clear my head," she says, her voice soft.

She had a breakup recently, so I suppose that's what her somber mood is about. It's part of the reason she moved to Charleston. I think she did the breaking, but apparently, he moved on real quick. I never actually met the guy. I don't have all the details, but I don't need them. You hurt Ainsley, I hurt you. That was the motto Brody and I had for years.

"Want to walk Sadie with me?" I ask.

She steps inside, briefly glancing at me. "I'd like that."

She looks so sad. Her usual smile, gone. I can't remember the last time she and I were alone together. The most recent times I've seen her have been holidays, so Brody and Skye were always there, too. It wasn't always that way. When she lived with us, I spent lots of time alone with her. Of course, that was before she'd turned into this bombshell. But even then, I'd always liked her. She was fun to hang around with and always made me laugh. I never resented her living with us. She made it fun. She cramped my style a little bit in the dating department, but she was a teenager. She wasn't doing it on purpose.

We used to spend hours on the couch watching some show she was obsessed with, talking and hanging out. Of course, she loved any show about weddings or wedding dresses. Every Super Bowl Sunday, she made me watch the entire puppy bowl with her, and she loved all the awards shows like the Oscars and Grammys, asking me what I thought of the dresses, the shoes. Brody usually refused to watch, but I indulged her. She had me wrapped around her little finger, even then. But I don't mind. Ainsley's the type of person that can make anything fun, even fashion.

It's strange how, even after all this time, we can fall back into that place. Back in the day, she walked Sadie with me, or for me, all the time. Sadie moves a little slower now than she did then.

Ainsley leans over, rubbing Sadie's coat a little. "Remember how she used to pull on the leash, chasing other dogs?" I ask.

"And acting like squirrels were her arch nemesis?"

The hair on the back of Sadie's coat stands up at the mere mention of her rival. "She still hates them," I whisper.

A small smile crosses her lips, and I hope that means she's feeling a little better. She raises an eyebrow at me. "You really shouldn't make her wear the poop bags around her neck. She's probably embarrassed, like all the other dogs are making fun of her."

Sadie rubs up against Ainsley's leg like she appreciates her humiliation being addressed. But that little contraption that holds the bags and attaches to her leash is a life saver. Sorry, Sadie. This time Ainsley breaks into a full-on grin, making my heart miss a beat. How can talking about poop bags and the bowel habits of my canine do that?

Charleston is a romantic city by anyone's standards. Tree lined streets echo with the sound of horse hooves from the private carriages, and certain times of the year, the city is painted pink with camellia blooms. Romance lives in the streets here, so it probably isn't the best idea for me to be walking around with a woman that is totally off limits. Too much temptation. Everywhere we turn there seems a couple making out, holding hands, fondling each other on a bench.

"So what are your plans now that you're back?" I ask, hoping for a nice, safe conversation.

"I'm not sure," she says.

I know Brody's letting her live in his place rent free. He says it's in exchange for her making Skye's wedding dress, joking he's getting the better end of the deal, but I know he'd never take a dime from her.

"I've got some side jobs making veils and things. I've got some savings and my portion of the money my parents left me. So I have a few months until I have to decide anything." She stops for a second. "I have applied with some designers in New York and Paris."

"Does Brody know that?" I ask.

"No, but it's a long shot. I'm not sure Charleston is right for me. I'm just keeping my options open. I'm here at least through the wedding. We'll see what happens afterwards. I'm also thinking about looking for space for my own wedding dress boutique. If I stay in Charleston, that's what I want to do." She looks up at me with those blue eyes of hers. "Please don't mention any of this to Brody."

This isn't our first secret from her brother. I'm the one who let her have her first sip of beer. She was eighteen. Never told Brody that. "He'll flip his shit if he finds out you might be leaving," I say. "He was so excited when you told him you were moving here."

"I know," she says.

"He still worries about you like you're fifteen," I say.

"He needs to get it under control. He put his life on hold for me, all three of you did."

"He never thought about it like that. You were never a burden. He wanted you with him back then," I say.

"I'm sure he'd rather not have been raising a teenage girl. I'm sure you and Skye would have preferred to be young and having fun," she says.

Her parents' funeral flashes in my mind, Skye and I flanked on either side of her, and Brody with his arms around her from behind, resting his head on top of hers. Thank God, Ainsley wasn't home that night, or we could've lost her, too. Brody was home for Christmas break, and the two of them were out at a late movie together. Any other night and . . . I can't even think about what might have happened.

Those first few days after his parents died—I've never seen Brody so torn up. I patted his shoulder and asked when we were taking A. Rose home to Charleston. That was it. We all knew that we'd do it together, no questions asked. He wanted her with him. He needed her with him. Skye and I just gave him the support. Don't get me wrong, we were all scared shitless. We were so unprepared, walking into our tiny two-bedroom apartment. Brody slept on the couch for months until we got a bigger place.

"Brody insisted we meet every Sunday night to talk about your week, your schedule. He didn't want you to be alone too much. And when you started dating, my God, he'd drone on and on about supervising you and scaring your dates. You are his family. My point is, Brody never thought of raising you as putting anything on hold."

"It's so weird to be thinking about all this again. It seems so long ago, but at the same time, it doesn't. You know?" she asks, looking up at me from under her lashes. I give her a nod. "We had some good times. All my friends were jealous. You guys were so cool. Well, you and Skye were. Brody was a typical overprotective big brother."

"He used to drive Skye nuts. He wouldn't ever let her stay over unless you were sleeping at a girlfriend's house. He said it was inappropriate."

"He should have told you that," she teases. "I caught you making out with girls quite a bit."

I was really hoping she'd forgotten about that.

"Brody used to get so mad at you, but you were always there," she says, looking up at me.

I'm still here for her. Always will be.

My step falls right back in line with hers. When I was younger, my mom used to point out when she'd see couples walking, the man ten feet in front of his woman. It's a pet peeve of hers. She made me swear never to walk in front of a woman I was with.

"There's a great ice cream shop around the corner. You up for it?" I ask, and she smiles.

Walking past a colorful row of houses, each is bigger than the next. The sounds of horse drawn carriages fill the air. There are very few cobblestone streets left in the city, but that might be the only charm Charleston's lost in its history. Modern day offices, stores, and even ice cream shops are housed in old buildings that you just know have a story to tell, a secret buried deep inside its crevices. From the outside, everything looks charming. It's only when you take the time to look a little closer you see the cracks, the tiny threads barely holding everything together—much like the earthquake bolts on the old buildings here. Yes, South Carolina has had earthquakes. Strange, but true. They are a telltale sign of the disasters of the past, and a warning of what could come.

I hook Sadie's leash under the table leg and walk inside the ice cream shop to order. I don't have to ask Ainsley her favorite. I already know. I know everything about her, except how she kisses, how it would feel to have my arms wrapped around her, or simply hold her hand.

Ordering, I glance out the window, seeing Ainsley leaning over, patting, and talking to Sadie. Sadie's a dog, so she can't talk, but it looks like they are having a "real" conversation—tail wagging, head tilting, eye contact. People should take some communication skills from dogs. Sometimes all you have to do is listen to the person. Often, we are so busy thinking of what to say next, we forget to really listen to the person, to pick up on the little clues in their mannerisms, their voice.

I get the cones and walk back out to her. To anyone else, this would look like a date, but it isn't. It never can be. Never.

Sadie and Ainsley look up at me, both smiling. "I can't remember the last time someone bought me a cookies and cream ice cream cone—my favorite!" Ainsley says.

I wonder if she remembers the first time I bought her ice cream. It was only a few weeks or so after she moved in. The memory is still fresh in my mind.

*I was asleep in my bedroom when I heard the softest knock on my door. The only reason it woke me was because Sadie barked. I opened my bedroom door, and Ainsley was standing there teary, asking if I knew where Brody was. I knew he was taking a big exam and Skye was working.*

*"I need my mom," Ainsley said, sobbing.*

*Not sure what to do with a crying fifteen-year-old girl, I offered to call my mom for her. My parents had really stepped up, helping us out with Ainsley, having us over for dinners.*

*But she didn't want my mom, she wanted hers.*

*"Do you know where Skye is?" she asked.*

*"Working," I say, tilting my head to try to make eye contact with her. "What's wrong? How can I help?" She tried to tell me but couldn't get any words out. "I can't help if you don't tell me what's wrong, and your brother will kick my ass if he finds out I didn't help you."*

*She smiled at the ground, whispering. "It's my time of the month."*

*"Oh!" This was definitely out of my job description as roommate and best friend. Way above my pay grade. In no universe does a fifteen-year-old girl want*

*to discuss her monthly visitor with a twenty-one-year-old guy, and vice versa.*

*"I don't have anything to use."*

*I grabbed my keys. "Okay, the store is right down the street. I'll go for you."*

*There is nothing more confusing than the feminine hygiene aisle. Pads? Tampons? Super? Lite? Regular? Liners? Cardboard or Plastic applicator? Jesus Christ! I had no idea. I grabbed one of every kind, knowing she was waiting. I passed the frozen food section on the way out and tossed some ice cream in my cart. I've had enough girlfriends to remember ice cream helps everything. The store clerk looked at me like I was some sort of deviant, but that was only slightly better than the look Ainsley gave me when I walked in with a dozen bags. I just shrugged as she dug through and took what she needed before disappearing into her bedroom.*

*I could've used a drink, but it wasn't even ten in the morning. Reaching in the bag for the ice cream, I opened the freezer to put it away, but something stopped me. The tears. She was so upset. I had to check on her.*

*I took the ice cream carton and grabbed a spoon, knocking on her bedroom door. She didn't answer, but I could hear her crying, so I pushed the door open slightly, seeing her head buried under the pillow. She needed her mother—or at least some female person—and her brother's best friend was a terrible substitute.*

*Sadie jumped up on the bed with Ainsley, and I lightly touched her leg. "I brought you ice cream."*

*"What kind?" she sniffled.*

*"Cookies and cream."*

*Her eyes peered up over the pillow. "That's my favorite."*

*I held out the entire carton for her, and after a moment, she came all the way out from under the pillow, tearing off the lid and digging in. I sat and talked to her about her mom and dad for a long time. Long enough for her to finish the whole carton. Then she curled up next to Sadie.*

*"Why don't you get some rest?" I said before slipping out her bedroom.*

*I closed the door slowly behind me, and then Brody's eyes met mine, a flash of fury shooting out. It looked so bad to be sneaking out of her bedroom—the look on Brody's face will forever be etched in my brain. Ainsley was just a kid.*

*"She's been crying all morning," I said, and Brody moved to go in. "I think she's asleep now."*

*"What the hell was wrong?" he asked.*

*I motioned to the bags. That was explanation enough. "Dude, I had no fucking idea what I was doing. There's like a thousand different options. I just bought them all. She was embarrassed. I was embarrassed. I wasn't about to ask her regular or super strength."*

*Brody laughed again. "Thanks for being there for her."*

"What?" Ainsley asks, wiping her mouth and bringing me back to the present.

I realize I've been staring at her too long, so I shift my gaze to Sadie. "Just thinking about the first time I bought you ice cream."

Her pale skin blushes, remembering too. "Oh, God. I was hoping you didn't remember that. One of the most embarrassing moments of my life."

"Mine, too."

"Really? You seemed so cool about it."

"I was sweating bullets. You should have seen me on the aisle reading all the boxes and debating. It was ridiculous."

"It was sweet," she says, glancing at me, but only for a second. "I should get back."

We don't talk a lot on the walk back. The building where we both live isn't far. We took a lot longer walking before, turning down side streets, enjoying the slightly cooler temperatures, but I know it's dangerous to be alone with her for too long, so the short route home is best.

Stepping inside the elevator of our building, I push the buttons to both our floors. When the door opens to her floor, I step out with her. Why the fuck did I do that? This isn't a date. I'm not going to get a goodnight kiss. But Sadie certainly is. Ainsley bends down and nuzzles my dog's nose, and Sadie licks up her entire face.

Ainsley laughs out loud. This has been a deal breaker for me more than once. If a woman doesn't like dogs, or freaks out about Sadie licking them, game over. Ainsley long ago passed that test. Too bad she's off limits. We're friends. That's all we can ever be. She unlocks her door and turns the knob.

"Thanks for the walk and ice cream," she says over her shoulder.

"Same time tomorrow?" I ask without thinking.

"Sure," she says, flashing me that incredible smile of hers.

# CHAPTER FOUR

## PRESENT DAY

### AINSLEY

I KNEW THE kind of guy Rhett was. I knew serious wasn't his thing. I knew using the word *love* usually sent him running for the hills. I knew it, and I did it anyway.

But he wasn't that guy with me. He and I were different. I know he loved me.

I've loved that man since I was fifteen years old. How could I not? Forget the abs, the tan skin, those pale, sexy blue eyes. Forget the fact that his voice sends shivers down my spine. The first time we kissed, I felt my whole world shatter and fall into place at the same time.

I tried to pretend to be "that" girl. The kind that can kiss a guy just for fun, screw a man and not imagine a life with him. I tried. I failed. The hopeless romantic in me wasn't having it.

My heart should've known better—but my heart was no match for Rhett Bennett.

When Rhett and I fell apart, I broke up with social media. I have to say, that breakup was a lot easier. No hashtags, no emojis, no memes to post. Some people use social media as their therapist. I've seen people post play-by-plays of their divorce, or explain every detail of their latest illness or drama. I probably could've attracted a lot more followers if I chronicled the demise of our relationship. It's the stuff of soap operas.

But instead, I broke it off with Facebook, banned Instagram, and boycotted Twitter.

Today, Facebook and I are having one last romp. Relationship status update: Single.

That's it. That one little change. I have to start somewhere. Skye's right about that.

The one part of being single I have embraced is the diet. The single woman diet consists of basically any breakfast food for dinner, coffee, and alcohol. I've gotten so good at it, I no longer need a grocery cart when I shop. Quick tip, don't get a cart at the grocery store, only buy what you can hold. It's good for the budget and the waistline. Unfortunately, that rule doesn't work so well at clothing stores.

My hands full of cereal, bagels, orange juice, and the champagne Skye introduced me to, my overloaded arms tell me my shopping is done for the evening. I step up to the self-checkout. There's something about sliding my items across the scanner that takes me back to being a kid. I think all little kids dream of one day making that little *beep beep* sound.

The ding of my phone from my purse doesn't give me the same feeling. When Rhett and I were together, I loved when my phone dinged. It was almost always a sweet message from him or something funny to make me laugh. Now the dings are either work or Brody worried about me and checking in. I'd love a pic of Sadie right about now. I think about her almost as much as I think about Rhett.

I don't want to be this woman. The one who can't let go and move on. The one that others feel sorry for. I know Rhett wouldn't want this for me, either.

Grabbing my grocery sacks in one hand, I muster a smile, re-membering Rhett trying to carry all the groceries inside in one trip. He'd have bags lined up his forearm, both hands holding at least eight bags each. Crazy man! It's little things like that. Just when I think I'm moving forward, something tiny like that will pop into my mind, and I'm sucked back in.

I make it to my car. Thank God for keyless entry! Getting the handle is hard enough with my arms full, I can't imagine if I had to dig through my purse for my keys.

First world problems all the way.

Tossing my bags in the passenger seat, I glance out the back window to make sure no one is waiting for my parking spot before fetching my phone from my purse. It's the worst when you are waiting for someone to pull out of a parking spot, and they are taking their sweet time. I refuse to be that person, so I make sure no one is there before checking my cell.

*I hope you don't mind Skye gave me your number.*

That's as much as I need to read to know who's texting me—the hot, older doctor from her clinic. My stomach does a somersault. A new man should be a new beginning, but instead, it only makes things feel more final. Suddenly, I wish someone was waiting for my parking spot. Staring down at my phone, I realize Rhett's name is no longer on the home page of my messages app. It's been too long, too many other people have messaged me. He's buried beneath a sea of people far less important than he is to me—even still.

Tossing my phone back in my purse, I start my car and pull away. I didn't actually open the message, so I know that little number one will be taunting me from my message app, daring me to answer. Of course, I could always delete the message. That might put Skye in an awkward situation, but I'm sure she'd understand.

I glance at my purse then back to the road, realizing now I've missed the turn home. You might think I wouldn't want to continue living at the condo downstairs from Rhett's place, but it's been fine. It took me a little while to accept that he wouldn't be knocking on my door to walk Sadie or that I wouldn't roll over and find his handsome face sharing my pillow. My heart isn't going to forget Rhett, so it doesn't matter where I live. He's not even living at his condo anymore, so it's not like I'm going to run into him.

Besides, I can't really afford to move right now. Even if I did, it wouldn't be away from Charleston. Skye, Brody, and I need each other more than ever these days. So, I sunk every dime I had into opening my own storefront. *A Rose Wedding Dress Designs.* That store has saved my sanity.

When I just don't want to face life, I escape into my designs, where everything is perfect. The right pearl placed just to catch the light, the right crystal to highlight the neckline, those things can make me forget the world.

I think that's what sets me apart as a designer. At least I hope so. I don't just go online and order crystals and beads. Each one is a story, a hunt, a treasure. I've ripped dresses apart I found at yard sales or the Goodwill just for five or six perfect pearls. Some brides come in with their mothers' or grandmothers' dresses. They want me to use bits and pieces of each to create something new and unique for them. I certainly do that, but there are women like me who aren't fortunate enough to have their mother's dress, and I want them to feel just as special. So I hunt around and do whatever is needed to make it happen.

I've used christening gowns, handkerchiefs, old corsets. Heck, once I used an old dishtowel in a dress. It was the one thing that made this particular client think of her mother. To see a bride's face when she realizes a part of her mother is going to walk down the aisle with her, well, that's why I do what I do. That's why I love designing dresses.

I love taking things that others discard, things that anyone else would think of as ugly or outdated and giving them new life. Ever see a broken glass bottle, the way it catches the light and casts a rainbow? Beauty in imperfection, that's what I'm about as a designer. I guess that's what I'm about as a person, too. My parents took me to pick out a puppy once when I was very little, and I picked the runt of the litter. Not because it needed me, or because I felt sorry for it, but because to me, it was the cutest.

Not everyone can find beauty in ugly.

Rhett included.

# CHAPTER FIVE
## EIGHTEEN MONTHS AGO

This is me handing you my heart.
A. Rose

## RHETT

THERE ARE NO *how-to* manuals on avoiding bedding your best friend's baby sister. I'll have to wing it. Daily dog walks probably aren't part of the manual. I need a plan.

Step one of my plan—preventative jerk off.

No offense to Sadie, but man's other best friend is his cock. Men have been beating off since the beginning of time. I bet Adam whacked one off in the Garden of Eden. Sure, we do it because we are horny, but it's not solely about pleasure. We jerk off to relieve stress, help us sleep, or just because we're fucking bored, so why not do it for preventative measures?

So begins the pattern—work, jerk off, evening stroll with Sadie and Ainsley, sometimes ice cream, say goodnight before my boner comes back. I always end the evening at her door.

My plan works for the next week or so.

This time, feeling my preventative beat-off subsiding, I move to push the elevator button behind me. "I'll see you at my parents' house this weekend," I say, reminding her of the little welcome home dinner my mom and dad are having for her.

"I can't wait to see them," Ainsley says then starts chatting away about Skye and Brody's upcoming wedding. Sadie seems to be getting bored because she nudges Ainsley in the ass. Ainsley pats her head, a half-attempt at affection. Normally, Sadie's mellow, lazy, and arthritic, which is why I didn't expect Sadie to jump on Ainsley's back, knocking her into my arms.

Dropping the leash to the ground, I can't even scold Sadie. All I can manage to do is stare into Ainsley's perfect blue eyes and try to stop from combusting at the heat coursing through my veins. Her breasts are pushed against my chest, and her skin is so soft and warm. For a split second, I forget she's my best friend's little sister. I forget I'm supposed to think of her as *my* little sister. She's simply a beautiful woman in my arms, and somehow my lips fall to hers, and my hand goes around her waist, pulling her tighter.

It's a soft, tender brush of lips, nothing more, but God help me, the sweetest little moan falls from her lips. I'm done for. I push her against the door, pinning her arms over her head, feeling her nipples harden. I want to take her right here in the hallway. Her tongue meets mine, exploring my mouth, and I can't believe she isn't slapping me away. She wants this, too. How did I not know that?

We slow a bit, no longer frantic for each other, falling into a rhythm of pure pleasure. Slow and sweet with an intensity I could never have imagined. Her hands slip through my hair. Mine slip to her perfect ass, pulling her tighter. In that instant, I'm addicted.

I'm not sure which one of us pulls away first, but when we finally do, she gives me a coy smile, her eyes holding the sexiest look, and I know we aren't just friends anymore.

I look down and swear to God, Sadie is smiling, too, totally pleased with herself. When I look back up at Ainsley, the magnitude of what just happened, what I wanted to happen, hits me. I take a step back, watching her eyes change from delight to dread. "I shouldn't have done that" are the words that come out of my mouth, but every part of my body is screaming otherwise. Her eyes gloss over, and I know she's holding in tears.

She reaches for the doorknob and says, "I'm sorry you feel that way."

"Ainsley? It's just, I mean, Brody trusts me," I stammer. "I can't do this to him."

Her head whirls around so fast I worry she might hurt herself. "I'm a grown woman, for God's sake. I'm not a little girl anymore."

"He's my best friend, my business partner."

She doesn't look away or nod that she understands. Instead, she takes a step toward me, placing her hand on my chest. She's so close I can smell her shampoo. Leaning forward, her soft lips press to my cheek. I suck in a deep breath, using every ounce of self-control in my body not to turn my lips to hers.

I DO THE only thing a good best friend can do—keep my distance. No more walking Sadie with Ainsley. It's best to stay away from her for a while until things calm down. I can avoid her the rest of my life if I have to. I'm lying. I actually have to see her today; my parents are hosting that welcome home dinner for her.

It feels like it's been a helluva lot longer than the week it's been since that kiss. I miss her—her smile, her scent, her laugh. Taking those walks with her were the best part of my day.

But I've resisted every urge to call her, to text her, to knock on her door. Seeing Brody at work every day is enough of a reminder why nothing more can happen with Ainsley. We're lucky no one in the building saw that kiss. Brody still has other friends that live there, and patients, too. It could've easily gotten back to him. That's why keeping my distance from Ainsley is best. I'm trying to do the right thing here, but honestly, it sucks.

I wonder if she's avoiding me, too. I haven't run into her on the elevator or even caught a glimpse of her coming or going. It's possible she thinks she's the one avoiding me.

I'm not the only one suffering from withdrawal. Sadie's not been herself, either. The past few nights, she's walked even slower on our evening strolls, stopping and sitting down halfway around the block and refusing to go any further. Not even the promise of sharing a steak for dinner could perk her up.

I'm a vet, which means I give advice all day long to people with obese pets about the dangers of table food, but Sadie's geriatric by any standards, so I figure she should be happy in her old age, but nothing could cheer her up the past few days. I know how she feels.

I tell myself it's no big deal to be at my parents' house for a barbecue. They love Brody and Ainsley like their family. My parents knew Brody and Ainsley's parents just from he and I being roommates and friends. My mom and dad told me that if anything ever happened to them, they'd want someone to make me a home cooked meal and invite me over for Christmas. They saw it as doing for Brody and Ainsley what they would want someone to do for me. The Bennett family Christmas went from hanging three stockings to five.

So it's natural for us all to get together. I just wish it had happened before I kissed Ainsley. Things are bound to be awkward. I just hope I can look at her and not think about the way her lips felt on mine.

My parents' house is something out of a magazine, resembling an old, antebellum mansion. It's built in the Charleston single style, popular for the area. Basically, the house looks sideways from the street—one room wide, but several rooms deep, designed that way to save valuable land space and maximize breezes through open windows. Blue with green shutters, it's located about twenty minutes outside Charleston in Mount Pleasant. Pictures and keepsakes from my childhood line the shelves and walls. My old basketball hoop still hangs over the garage. My dad and I used to spend hours out there. Most of our big father/son talks happened while shooting hoops. There's a huge backyard, which Sadie loves, so I always bring her with me when I visit. My parents love her just as much as I do.

I'm late, and I have no good excuse why. Work ended on time. Traffic wasn't horrible. The only thing keeping me from getting here on time is that I didn't want to risk getting here when Ainsley might be the only other guest. I wanted to make sure that Brody and Skye would be here before I arrived.

I walk through the door to my parents' house a good half hour after my mom said to be there. I'm not usually late. My mom's a worrier, so my dad and I always try to be on time. I doubt she worried today, though. Too much excitement over Ainsley's return to Charleston.

This house never changes. Sure, my mom updates the decor, but the feel of the house never changes. It always feels like home. I'm not sure how my parents pull that off, but they do. It makes me smile even on the worst days. Come to think of it, being around Ainsley usually makes me feel the same way.

I bend down to give Sadie a hearty scratch behind her ear, just the spot she likes. When I look up, my eyes land on a pair of long, lean legs, the ones I've fantasized about having wrapped around me more times than I care to admit.

Standing up straight, I look through the house, seeing Brody and Skye are outside by the barbecue. I can hear my parents in the kitchen and smell the cookies my mom's been baking.

"You're late!" Ainsley whisper-shouts.

"So?"

"It's not normal for you to be late."

Honestly, I'm not a dumb guy, but sometimes female logic couldn't be figured out by the president of Mensa. It's a whole lot easier to understand what a dog is thinking than a woman. A dog is happy, its tail wags. When a woman's ass shakes, does that mean she's happy? When your pet is mad at you, you might find poop in the house. When your woman is mad at you, you might hear about it for decades to come. Of course, you can always tell your dog to sit and stay. If you want to see tomorrow, I advise you never order your woman to sit and stay.

She throws her hands up a little. "Brody can never find out what happened between us."

"Agreed."

"So, if you don't want Brody to get suspicious, you need to act normal."

"Being late isn't exactly a big ass clue that I kissed you," I say. "I'm totally fine."

"Good, because it was just *one little kiss*," she says, taunting me.

"Right, didn't mean anything," I say, heading inside as she flinches as if I've struck her.

Why did I say that? Why did I lie? What a fucking disaster. I couldn't tell her what that kiss did to me, that I haven't slept through the night since, thinking about her soft lips. That wouldn't help either of us. It wouldn't change the fact that she's still off limits.

Still, I know I hurt her feelings. I feel horrible, but it's better off this way. It's the way it has to be. It's better to hurt her a little now than to have a bigger heartache later.

I walk into the kitchen. Sadie takes her spot on a fluffy rug, and I take mine at the island beside my dad. My parents both kiss me on the side of the head. It doesn't matter how old I get, they never miss a chance to kiss me or each other. Yes, I have *those* parents. The ones that smack each other's asses and have a sex drawer next to their bed that I'm not supposed to know about.

My dad is one of those rare attorneys that actually loves his job. He doesn't practice as much anymore, preferring to spend his days forming the legal minds of tomorrow by teaching Criminal Justice at The Citadel. My mom stayed home with me my whole life. When I went to college, she decided to get her real estate license, and has made a name for herself in the Charleston area.

My mom holds up a plate of cookies, and I take one. My place was always the hangout spot when I was in high school. These cookies are part of the reason why. Everyone loves them. My mom calls them "Marry Me" cookies. Supposedly baking them for your boyfriend guarantees a proposal. Guess it worked on my dad.

Ainsley walks in, snatching the cookie right out of my hand, takes a huge bite, and licks her lips. The little tease. I know that look in her eye. She's about to teach me a lesson.

"You always did make the best cookies, Diane," Ainsley says, giving my mom a hug.

"So sweet of you," my mom says, giving me a little wink.

My dad gets one arm around Ainsley, lifting her slightly in the air. "Cliff," my mom playfully scolds him. "Put her down."

Ainsley gives him a huge hug, and my dad says, "It's been too long. What have you been up to? Rhett says he hasn't seen you much, either."

So I left out the part where we walked Sadie together every night for days and days. To her credit, Ainsley doesn't miss a beat, telling them about her hopes to open a store one day, and that she'll be designing Skye's wedding dress in the meantime.

No matter how hard I try, I can't seem to tear my eyes away from her. The way she smiles as she talks—there's no ignoring that. I don't know the first damn thing about silk or pearls or sequins. I couldn't tell you the difference between Chantilly lace and Venetian lace to save my life, but the passion with which Ainsley talks about it all makes me care. I think I could care about anything she's talking about if she's smiling like that.

"Maybe you could help me look at some options for a storefront, if I decide to open a store here in Charleston?" Ainsley says to my mom.

I know my mom wouldn't take a commission, either. Ainsley is family in her book.

"Oh, I'd love to," my mom says.

They continue to chat and catch up, but I might as well not be in the room. Ainsley hasn't addressed me, asked me a question. She's barely even glanced my way. My dad looks at me then back to Ainsley. I can see his lawyer mind spinning like he's getting ready to cross examine a witness, preparing to lay a trap for them to unknow-ingly stumble into.

"So any dates since you've been back, Ainsley?" my dad asks, his eyes glued on me. "Must be someone special."

Damn! He can tell something is off. Ainsley and I haven't said two words to each other. Normally, we talk, joke around. My parents aren't used to this silent treatment, and neither am I.

"Not really," Ainsley says, glancing at me.

"Oh, come on," my dad says, eyeing me again. "Pretty girl like you, they must be standing in line."

"I think Brody scares them all off," she says, giving me a sweet smile.

"That reminds me," Skye says, walking into the kitchen. "Ainsley, Rhett, are either one of you bringing a date to the engagement party? I've got to get the final numbers in. It's tomorrow night."

Ainsley's blue eyes find mine. I haven't firmed up any plans for the party. I know I should bring someone, but the only person I want to take is staring at me, and I can't ask her. Still, I can't bring myself to play with her that way. "Going solo," I say.

"Everyone lock up the bridesmaids," Brody says, walking in and tossing his arm around Skye's shoulder.

"I'm a bridesmaid," Ainsley says, halting Brody's laughter.

He tips her nose with his finger, like he used to when she was younger. "Everyone knows not to mess with my sister."

"Where's my phone? What's the name of that new dating app? I'm sure I can find a twenty-something year old guy to hook up with on there," Ainsley says.

Skye busts into a huge laugh. Brody looks at me, frowning. "It was easier when she was sixteen," Brody says then turns to his sister. "I'm going to do better about smothering you."

What the fuck! I can hardly believe what I'm hearing. He chooses *now* to stop acting like his sister's personal bouncer? I nudge Brody. "You really gonna let her swipe right?"

"Hell, no," Brody says, giving his sister a look. "I have my limits."

Ainsley looks like she's about to knee him in the groin. Right as she opens her mouth, Skye interrupts her. "So no plus one for you either, Ainsley?"

Her question is met with silence. Ainsley's eyes look everywhere but at me, like she's searching for the truth.

"Maybe Rhett should bring Ainsley?" my dad suggests, cutting the silence with a knife.

Ainsley's and my eyes both dart to him. What the hell? My mom kicks his leg a little.

Brody looks like one confused motherfucker right now. "Um . . ."

Trying to salvage things, my dad offers, "I'm just saying, it might help keep Ainsley from getting hit on all night."

Brody laughs. "That's not a bad idea. Rhett?"

Before I can answer, Ainsley bites out, "I have a date!"

"Who?" I ask, my voice sounding more than a little pissed.

"Why didn't you say?" Brody asks Ainsley.

"I can't deal with this," she says, waving her hands around then storming out.

Brody looks at Skye then me and my parents, asking, "Did I overdo it again?"

We all nod in unison. Brody starts to follow his sister, "I better go smooth things over."

"Give her some space," Skye says.

"Why don't you and Skye go out to the yard?" my mom says to Brody. "Get some fresh air."

The house sits on Charleston Harbor. Even though we're barely out of the city limits, it feels like a vacation spot. It's a daily occurrence to see boats passing by, enjoying the fishing, but it's the sunsets that make this spot special. My mom says that God is an artist, and Charleston sunsets are his canvas, painting the sky with hues of pink and orange. But I always liked the thunderstorms out here the best. The way the lightning bolts look like they are disappearing into the water, the way the thunder seems to boom extra loud always fascinated me. I used to love to open my bedroom window when a storm was coming. Storms have a certain smell, like the oxygen is more pure. I don't get to enjoy the rain too much anymore. Sadie hates storms, hiding under the bed. I've tried everything from aromatherapy for dogs (yes, there is such a thing), to this straight-jacket type thing, which was an epic fail. I've even resorted to giving her drugs to calm her, but nothing works.

Skye and Brody head out of the kitchen, and I start to follow them. But my dad places his hand on my shoulder. Calling out to Brody and Skye, I say, "Give me a sec."

As soon as they're out of earshot, my mom starts, "What's going on with you and Ainsley?"

"I don't know what you're talking about," I say.

"Come on, Rhett," my dad says. "You look like someone slugged you in the gut."

"I just had too many of Mom's cookies," I lie, but even I don't believe that one.

"How long have you been feeling this way about her?" he asks.

My parents have always had a sixth sense with me. The thing is, I'm an only child, so my parents had no one else to focus on but me. We've always had a pretty open relationship with each other. They know who my first kiss was, and I suspect they know when I lost my virginity, although I tried to keep that one secret. I've never brought home a girlfriend to meet them, so I'm sure they know that I've been more of a player than the committed type. We talk about most things. So this line of questioning is par for the course with them.

Still, that doesn't mean this is any of their business. "You guys, please . . ."

"Rhett," my mom says, laying her hand on top of mine.

That's all it takes. I don't want to lie to them. Besides, it seems like the cat is out of the bag, at least where my parents are concerned. "She's Brody's little sister, I can't go there. No matter what I feel. He's my friend and business partner. If it went badly with Ainsley, it would ruin everything."

"So you have feelings for her?" my dad asks. "It's not just a phys-ical thing?"

"Oh hell, I'm not discussing this with you guys anymore," I say, the screech of the stool my exiting bell.

Walking into the den, I find Ainsley on the sofa, all alone. Today is supposed to be a celebration—a happy day, but instead, she looks sad and lonely. All I ever want is to see her smile. She looks up at me, and the feel of her lips on mine flashes through my mind.

She stands up, biting her bottom lip. "I hope we can save our friendship," she says. "It's important to me."

I take Ainsley by the elbow, leading her down into a little hallway for some privacy. The last thing we need is to have someone overhear. "You have a date?"

I don't think I've ever spoken to her in this harsh tone before, but she looks prepared to give it right back to me. Her hand finds her hip. Someone needs to do a study on why women's hands fly to their hips when they're pissed or annoyed with men.

Her silent glare increases my level of pissed off tenfold. "Do you feel this with him?"

Pulling her close, I don't kiss her. I just let her feel the heat pulsing between our bodies. She doesn't answer, but I can see her mind spinning. But there's only one thing on my mind.

"Fuck it," I say, slamming my mouth to hers, claiming what is mine and trying to erase any memories she might have of any other man. From the way her hands are sliding all over my body, I'd say I'm pretty damn successful in my efforts.

My hands slide down to her hips, pulling her closer. Neither of us seem to care that we're in my parents' house, that Brody and Skye are just outside. It's not the thrill that we might get caught driving me. It's simply the thrill of being with her. I can't stop. I've been wanting her for too long.

Her hips grind against me, her heat calling me. Daring me to take this further. I hear the back door open and close, the commotion from the party stopping me.

Ainsley pulls back and straightens her hair, gasping. Her tits rise and fall as she tries to catch her breath. The first time we kissed, we were both in shock it actually happened. This time, we both know this won't be the last time.

I hear Skye's voice asking where we are. Ainsley takes a few steps in that direction. I know she needs to go before we get caught, but still, I whisper, "Wait."

She saunters off, throwing me a smile over her shoulder. "I don't have a date."

# CHAPTER SIX

## PRESENT DAY

Did I tell you enough how much I love you?
A. Rose

### RHETT

*SINGLE*. SHE CHANGED her status to single? I still remember the day she put *in a relationship*. She was so cute about it, showing me her page, all smiles. It shouldn't come as a shock that she's changed it. It's been long enough.

No other updates. No new posts or pictures.

I scroll down her page, finding not a single photo of us. It's like we didn't even happen. Our relationship was a secret for so long, she couldn't exactly post pics of us together. They say if you put something on the internet, it lives forever. There's no record of us in cyberspace. Nothing to prove how much I love her.

Nothing except . . .

I reach for the chain around my neck—her engagement ring resting on my chest.

When an engagement goes south, a guy only has a few options for the ring. He can return it, sell it, or keep it. I think most men probably want their money back. I mean, why keep it? It's not like you can give it to someone else down the road. Well, I guess if you don't value your nuts you could.

But that's not why I kept Ainsley's ring. I kept it as a reminder. A reminder of what my anger cost me. Every time I start to feel angry, I reach for it.

It's like I'm reaching for her.

Sadie comes and rests her head on my legs. This is one reason I'm a dog person. Dogs are sympathetic pets. Even though I brought this whole situation on myself, Sadie doesn't care. She doesn't judge. She knows I'm a miserable asshole and loves me anyway. I haven't been able to push her away like I did Ainsley.

Not that Ainsley went easily. She put up one helluva fight. I may have won that battle, but I lost her.

"It's for the best. It's the best thing for her. I know it is," I say to Sadie.

# CHAPTER SEVEN
## EIGHTEEN MONTHS AGO

Most of my happy memories, you are there.
A. Rose

### RHETT

SHE'S NOT A good liar, yet she fooled me. Just that brief second of thinking she had a date with someone else was enough to make me realize that she's mine. She needs to be mine. Jealousy isn't often painted as a positive emotion, but in this case, it was just the kick in the ass I needed. The idea of her hand in some dick wad's hand, her lips on his, his arm around her, made me crazy. What's even crazier is that I'm no longer conflicted.

Brody will have to be dealt with, but that can wait. Maybe he doesn't even have to know. We can have a little fun together, and no one will get hurt. That delusion fuels my desire, ignoring the parts of myself that know this isn't just a little fun, and never could be.

Right after Sadie's morning walk, I head to see Ainsley. It's barely nine in the morning, but I couldn't get her alone again at the party. I wanted to see her last night, but it was late when I finally escaped my parents' house. And texting her just didn't seem like the right move. Ainsley opens the door yawning, dressed in only a t-shirt and boxer shorts. Is there anything sexier than a woman dressed in man's clothes? I'll take her in one of my shirts over a tight nightclub dress any day.

"Rhett," she says, pulling her hair on top of her head in a messy bun. "Now's not the best time. I'm . . ."

Sadie comes alive, bombarding Ainsley with kisses. Immediately, I'm jealous of my own dog, who currently has her nose in a place I wouldn't mind being buried.

Smiling, Ainsley motions for us to come inside. I remove Sadie's leash. Ainsley sits on the floor and lets Sadie give her a dog hug, wrapping her neck around Ainsley. "You know all my secrets, don't you, girl?"

I bend down, pat Sadie's head, and ask Ainsley, "What secrets?"

Sadie whacks me with her tail like she's telling me it's none of my business.

"Sadie got me through a lot of rough days those first few months after Mom and Dad died. I soaked her fur with tears more times than I care to remember."

I don't want to think about those times. It's a reminder that Ainsley should be off limits, that I'm supposed to be protecting her from guys, not leading her into the dark side, about to encourage her to lie to her brother. But that's exactly what I'm going to do. I take her hand and help her to her feet, running my fingers down her arms and feeling her quiver at my touch.

The wait has been long enough. My eyes land on the curve of her neck, and I lean down, letting my warm breath tickle her. I swear she wobbles, weak in the knees. Lightly trailing kisses down her neck, I let my tongue linger, tasting her sweet skin.

"Rhett," she says breathless. "You have to go."

"You really want me to go?" I ask, continuing to kiss her neck.

"No, but . . ." Ainsley moans, gripping my shirt and pulling me tighter into her body. Sadie runs to the front door barking, and Ainsley steps back, putting her hand on my chest. "Skye's coming over this morning to look at wedding dress sketches." I groan, and she shakes her head at me, smiling. "We can talk later."

Talking isn't what I had in mind. "Can you lie to Skye and Brody?" I ask.

"Do I *need* to lie to them?" she asks. Her lip pops out in an adorable little pout, but no matter how cute she is, it doesn't change the fact that whatever this is can't get back to Brody. She needs to know that. The last thing I want to do is hurt her. It's best to be honest about what this is. What this can only be.

"I think we can have a little fun together. I don't think Brody needs to know about that," I say.

The door flies open. No knock, no doorbell, nothing. I guess Skye's used to this being Brody's place—where she came and went as she pleased. Ainsley and I both take a few paces back from each other, and Skye's eyes dart to me. I'm not about to look away. That's as good as admitting guilt. I keep my eyes fixed on her, and Skye holds my gaze while kissing Ainsley on the cheek.

Skye turns to me and asks, "What are you doing here so early?"

"The kitchen sink was clogged," I say quickly. "I was just on my way out."

"Let me go grab my sketches," Ainsley says, wringing her hands together.

Jesus, she looks so guilty. We're going to have to work on her acting skills. She disappears into her bedroom, and I grab Sadie's leash to make a quick escape.

"You better stop this right now," Skye whispers harshly.

"I don't know what you're talking about," I say, putting on my best innocent act.

"Bullshit, anyone can see you are attracted to her." Her judgmental eyes slide down to the bulge in my shorts. "You are putting me in a difficult spot with Brody."

"Again, I don't know what you're talking about."

"Fine, you want to play dumb and innocent, go right ahead. But you are jeopardizing your friendship with me, Brody, her, and your business." Skye shakes her head. "You know her, how she is. A hopeless romantic. She wants the fairytale she has in her mind of her parents. Hell, what she thinks of Brody and me. The white knight, everlasting love. She designs wedding dresses, for goodness sake! And you know that she deserves it, so you better think long and hard about what you're doing here."

"Skye, I don't know what you think, but the sink . . ."

She points her finger in my face. "I suggest you back the hell off before you break her heart. I won't cover for you with Brody."

Ainsley returns carrying her sketchpad. "Everything alright?"

"Fine," I say firmly then walk out the door with Sadie.

Who the hell does Skye think she is? What Ainsley and I do in our private lives is none of her damn business. I pound on the elevator keys, knowing I'm lying to myself again.

The lies we tell ourselves are the ones that become our truths.

Hardcore truth—whatever I do with Ainsley will affect Brody and Skye.

I take Sadie off her leash and open the door to my condo. "Hey, dude, where you been?" Brody asks from my kitchen island.

Note to self: change locks on both my condo and Ainsley's condo, so these people can't just let themselves in. "I took Sadie for a walk and then went down to Ainsley's place. Kitchen sink was clogged."

"Glad you're around to help her out with things like that," Brody says, opening the refrigerator. "But why didn't she call me?"

"She didn't want to bother you," I say. "It's not like you live two minutes away."

My stomach lurches, and I swear Sadie shakes her head at me. It's just a little lie. But it's yet another one. Damn, they're really piling up.

Brody looks at me, his forehead wrinkling up. "Dude, you really look like shit."

"Didn't get much sleep."

Brody leans against the counter, untwisting the cap of his water. "Who is she?"

My throat tightens. This isn't going to be as easy as I thought.

Trying to play it cool, I say, "You're about to get married, have sex with the same woman for the rest of your life. You don't want to hear about my nights as a bachelor."

"Lucky bastard," Brody says.

"That's what you get for dating the same girl for ten years."

Brody smiles. "Want me to tell you the upside to marriage and committed relationships?"

"Nope."

"Too bad," he says. "The sex is a guarantee. So you might get lucky once a week, but I can have it every night."

Brody plops down on the sofa, all proud of himself.

"I'm not sure that's accurate," I say as I look down at Sadie with her tongue hanging out like she's laughing at me. "I've always heard marriage is the death of sex."

Brody is wrong thinking I have a once-a-week thing. I gave up on random hook-ups years ago, opting for something steady until the girl got too serious. But currently, there's only one woman I want in my bed. My best friend just has no idea it's his little sister.

DOES ANYONE EVEN like engagement parties? I mean, besides the couple getting married. Thank God, there's an open bar. The hotel ballroom is busting with people. It seems ridiculous to me to have so many people at an engagement party. What's the wedding going to be like? How could it top this?

I haven't ever thought about getting married, but if I did, it wouldn't be a circus or a show. Skye wants the whole deal, though. After ten years of being with Brody, I guess she figures they deserve it.

Beer in hand, I try not to stare at the door. The room is full of women, Skye's friends and future bridesmaids, but there's only one woman whose arrival I'm waiting for. Ainsley's been MIA all day, helping Skye with last minute details for tonight. I have no idea whether she scrounged up a date at the last minute so Skye and Brody didn't catch her in a lie, or if she made up some excuse why her date cancelled.

I look to the door as she floats in. Her strawberry blonde hair moves as she walks, and she's smiling. The peachy pink color of her dress matches her skin, and the sweetheart neckline frames her tits perfectly. I have to force myself to look away.

At least, she walked in alone.

THE NIGHT PASSES with well wishes, drinks, and food. I do my best not to stare, but Ainsley is beating me at my own game. Not once have I been able to catch her eye. Not one glance, smile, or hello pass between us.

Things with Ainsley have been simple in the past. Our friendship was an easy one, but as soon as we flipped the switch from friendship to something else, things changed. Now, neither one of us seems to know how to act around each other, at least in public. If we were alone, I'd have her in my arms, we'd be talking and laughing, and kissing. It's as if we talk now, everyone would be able to see right through us, somehow know that we kissed. But avoiding each other probably raises more of a red flag.

Pulling out my phone, I send her a text.

*Meet me on the patio.*

I watch her from across the room, seeing her pull her phone from her purse. She reads my message and her eyes dart up, scanning the crowd in search for me. Her smile is my answer.

I wait a couple minutes before I join her. The warm Charleston breeze greets me as I step outside. I can feel Ainsley's presence before I even see or hear her. It's like a wave of heat over my body.

When she turns to me, her blue eyes are darker than usual. "Just fun," she says, and I'm not sure if she's reminding herself or me. "That's all this can be."

She walks to the edge of the patio, hidden in the shadows behind some trees. She gets this look in her eyes like she's daring me to come get her.

In the game of truth or dare, I always did take the dare. It's always easier than the truth.

Her lips crash into mine. She's full of surprises. I always knew she had a little wild child in her. I just never got to be on the receiving end. I turn, pinning her up against the wall, and meet her tongue.

"Now," she whispers, undoing the zipper on my pants.

I get the feeling it's now or never. She'll lose her nerve if she thinks about it too much. Thank God, it's dark and we're a few floors up; otherwise, we'd be putting on quite a show, and probably end up on the internet somewhere.

"Christ," I whisper, reaching up her dress and sliding her panties off. I'm pretty sure I just lost my mind—I'm going to have sex with my best friend's baby sister on the patio of his engagement party. I lift her up, and she wraps her legs around me as I slam into her.

We both groan loudly then say "Shh!" to each other at the same time.

I hold her there for a second and smile. She's so wet for me, and she looks so beautiful and feels so warm wrapped around me. I want all of her and not fast and furious, but slow and savoring, but that will have to wait.

"This is going to be quick," I moan through gritted teeth, thrusting into her hard and fast.

I watch her face as her eyes clench shut, and she bites her bottom lip. Her nails dig into my shoulders. I can feel her tightening around me. I told her this would be quick, but not so quick that she doesn't finish. I don't believe in that shit.

She lowers her head onto my shoulder and bites down, screaming my name as she finishes. Her body coils tightly around me, then releases, and she makes this sound—this breathy little satisfied moan. Something inside me knows, that sound—that simple little sound will break me.

"Good girl," I say, not wanting this to end, but a few more hard thrusts into her and I'm there, groaning her name.

Her name. I've said it a thousand times. But it's never felt like this.

She lifts her head, and I lower my forehead onto hers as she smiles. We wait for our breath to return to normal, then she lowers her legs to the ground.

She flashes me a smile. "That *was* fun."

Trying not to laugh, I say, "More than a little."

Reaching up, she touches my cheek. "Better get that sex smirk off your face."

This time, I can't control the laugh that escapes. Ainsley glances toward the patio door, suddenly aware that we've been gone too long. Zipping up and snatching her panties off the ground, I reach under her dress and wipe her gently, and she shakes her head, clearly embarrassed.

"Better go to the ladies' room," Ainsley says. She smooths my tie, brushes off my jacket, and fixes my hair. "See you in a few minutes."

She starts back inside, and I grab her hand, pulling her into a lingering kiss, my tongue slowly circling hers. I move my hand to the back of her neck as I draw her closer, memorizing the feel of her mouth. She puts her hand on my chest, giving a sexy smile before walking back inside.

Trying not to make eye contact with anyone, I head back into the party. I don't dare look at Brody or Skye. I know Skye will know immediately, and I'm not sure how to face Brody, given I just screwed his little sister in public.

So I do my best to mingle, as I catch the smell of her mixed with the smell of sex on me. I hold my breath as visions of her coming flash in my mind. She's more than I ever imagined, so beautiful and totally uninhibited. I hadn't expected that.

Lost in my memories and future fantasies, I see Ainsley emerge from the ladies' room. But her "sex smirk" is nowhere to be found; instead, she looks white as a ghost. She's having regrets?

I know I need to reassure her so I start her way, but Brody and Skye approach her first. My heart jumps in my chest. What if she can't lie well enough? Brody turns and meets my eye. Holy shit! She wouldn't just tell them, would she? At their engagement party?

My legs start to move, and I realize I'm walking toward them, unable to stop. I will accept what's coming. I reach them and stick my hand in my pocket, feeling her panties.

"Ainsley's not feeling well," Brody says to me. "Could you get her home?"

"I'm fine," Ainsley says, not making eye contact with me. "It's your engagement party. Please don't worry . . ."

"Your skin is all flushed," Brody says, holding his hand up. "Are you sweating? Do you have fever?"

It's all I can do not to bust out laughing. Of course, he thinks she's sick, not that she just had sex in public. Thank God, Brody still thinks of Ainsley as a child.

"Brody's right," I say. "I'll take you home."

Skye kisses her cheek, glancing at me. "We'll check on you tomorrow."

We walk to the parking lot, managing not to touch or say a word to each other. I get her car door, feeling her tremble next to me. As soon as I'm safely inside, I reach for her hand, stroking her skin with my thumb. "Hey."

I can see her trying not to lose it. I'm sure she's never done anything like this before. Reaching up, I run my hand across her cheek. "I don't want to be something you regret."

"I don't. I couldn't," she whispers. "But that was reckless."

"I was there, too. You don't get all the credit for the incredibly hot sex."

"I guess I don't, but what about the incredibly stupid, unprotected sex?"

Fuck! When she initiated things, I just assumed she had it taken care of. Normally, I use condoms, but this is Ainsley. I trust her.

"You're not on the pill?" I ask. She shakes her head.

What the hell! I'm always careful. My palms start to sweat, but no matter how freaked out I am, Ainsley's more upset. I have to fix this for her. "When's your period due?" I ask.

"A few days. A week maybe. I'd have to look at my calendar."

"It will be fine. If I've learned anything from Skye's crazy stories, it's that standing up is not a prime position for conceiving," I say, making her giggle. "You should be past your ovulation, too."

"How do you know about ovulation?" she asks.

"I went to med school."

"Animal med school," she says.

I grin. "Primates have a similar cycle to . . ."

She slaps me playfully. "You did not just compare me to a female baboon."

My fingers graze her cheek. "We'll be more careful from now on." Her cheeks heat, apparently looking forward to the *from now on* part, I hope.

We drive back to our building, her fingers intertwined with mine the whole time. Are you supposed to hold hands with your fuck buddy? Is that what she is? I've had fuck buddies before. A girl in vet school was my exam fuck buddy. We'd only hook up during exams. She was a good stress reliever. There've been others, too, but it's never felt like this.

We get back to our complex. I open her car door, but don't hold her hand or wrap my arm around her. She gives me a little smile, letting me know she understands. We can't exactly be seen in any romantic way together. It might get back to Brody.

I push the elevator button for my floor, and she moves to push hers, but I catch her hand. "I thought you could stay with me tonight," I say.

I see the words twisting in her brain, searching for what to say. I take her hand. "I'm not proposing marriage, just a sleepover."

She releases my hand. "I don't think that's a good idea. Just fun, remember?"

"WHY WOULDN'T SHE stay the night with me?" I ask Sadie, my current drinking partner. Only hers is out of a water bowl, and mine's a whiskey bottle.

I wish I could blame the fact that I'm drunk off my ass for the reason I'm consulting my canine about the fairer sex, but it's not. Before you judge me, there are all kinds of studies that say only highly intelligent people carry on conversations with their pets. Having said conversation over a bottle of whiskey? Well, that must mean I'm a fucking genius.

It's past midnight. I'm sure the engagement party is long over. Hopefully, it went well. I know it did for me. Ainsley? Every time I close my eyes, she flashes in my mind—the way she bit her lip, the feel of her smooth skin, her smile. I'll never forget the moment I slipped inside her. I knew in that moment nothing would ever be the same. I want more.

I take another long drink. The thing about alcohol is it makes you break your silence, things you wouldn't normally do or say suddenly seem like a good idea—like calling the girl you just hooked up with. Or the time Brody and I thought that ramen noodles on top of meat lover's pizza would be the best concoction ever.

Ainsley answers the phone in barely a whisper.

"How could you possibly be sleeping?" I ask, talking louder than normal, but unable to stop myself.

"Rhett," she says. "Are you okay?"

"I'm having a drink," I say. "Want to come have a drink with me?"

"Are you drunk dialing me?"

"More like booty calling," I say, making her laugh. "I wanted to go slow and savor every bit of you. The patio was too fast. I'm better than that, I swear."

"I thought it was pretty good."

"You were so fucking hot. I had no idea my A. Rose was so naughty. I still have your panties."

"You're drunk."

"You're beautiful and sweet and sexy and funny, and I didn't get to see you naked. I can still smell you on my skin. I'm never going to shower again. I want to smell like sex and you forever."

"You're *really* drunk," she says.

"I miss you."

Silence. I say her name, but it's quiet on the other end. Did she hang up? Did my phone die?

"Bring Sadie and come sleep with me. I'll unlock the door."

Thank fuck! Usually, drunk dials don't end up with a positive outcome. Hanging up, I head toward the door. "Come on, Sadie." She looks up at me, her tongue hanging out like she's laughing. I don't bother with clothes, wandering down the single flight of stairs in just my underwear.

Opening the door to her place, it's totally dark. Good thing our places have the same layout. Even with several drinks in me, I make it to her bedroom without bumping into anything. Sadie curls up in the corner of the room like she belongs there.

Slipping in beside Ainsley, I wrap my arms around her and whisper, "Good night, my rose."

"BE RIGHT BACK," I whisper, disappearing into the bathroom to rid myself of the condom we were careful to use this time. This time?

This time put the patio to shame, which is saying a hell of a lot. Maybe it's because I slept all night with her in my arms. Maybe it's because there's something special about morning sex. Or perhaps it's because this is the first time I've ever seen her naked. I've fantasized about her enough times, but she's sexier than I even imagined. I look over at her from the bathroom door. She's on her stomach, her face turned away from me, the sheets bundled around her waist. She has the most flawless, peachy-pink skin.

She has me tied up in knots already. This is just supposed to be fun. That doesn't include lounging around together all day, but that's what I want. I don't care that I'm breaking my own rules. This is what I asked for—no commitments, but this is Ainsley. I'm used to hanging out with her, talking, laughing. It feels wrong to not do those things just because I've seen her naked.

Her head turns to me, and she holds out her hand. There's no place I'd rather be than in bed with her, but I know Ainsley. I know she's never done anything like this before. She's a relationship woman, which should scare me off, but my dick is driving this train.

Slipping in beside her, she rests her head on the pillow, facing me. Honestly, I can't believe this is my life right now.

Her mouth opens slightly but no words come out, so I plant a sweet kiss on her lips to coax them out. "Why does it feel like I can't talk to you now?" she asks.

I tuck a loose piece of hair behind her ear. "I don't want you to feel that way."

"I don't know how to do this. I only ever had sex while in a relationship." She blushes with her confession, but I suspected as much. She motions between us. "I didn't think this meant sleepovers and snuggling. You said just fun."

"I regret saying those words to you. You seem to be obsessing on them, and it's getting in the way. What did you think? That I would fuck you and go?"

"Isn't that how these things usually work?" she asks.

"Is that what you want?" I ask. "Because honestly, I would hate that."

"Me, too," she says with a smile. "But I don't know how to act. I'm trying to be all casual, and I'm coming off like a crazy person."

She cracks me up. Cupping her face, I say, "It's not hard. We just have to be honest with each other about what we want."

I know she's got more to say. Some girls are made to have this kind of relationship, and some girls aren't. Ainsley's not. She's trying to be, but she's not.

"I wish you weren't my brother's best friend."

"Me, too," I say, pulling her into my chest.

And that's where she stays the entire day, except for when I'm forced to get up, like to take Sadie out. Other than that, we spend the day in bed. We shatter my personal record for how many times I've had sex in a day. And when night falls, there's no discussion about me sleeping over.

It just happens, even though I have work in the morning. Sometimes work is the perfect excuse to get the hell out after a fuck session. "I've got an early morning" or some shit like that always works. But this morning, I'm searching for any excuse to stay in bed with her curled in my arms. I feel like this is payback for all the lame excuses I've given in the past.

I find none, and I can't have Brody asking questions. I hate the idea of her waking up and finding me gone, but I don't want to wake her, either. She looks so peaceful.

I reach for her sketchpad, which she keeps by the bed. I'm no artist, but since I don't have the real thing, this little drawing will have to do.

# CHAPTER EIGHT

## PRESENT DAY

### AINSLEY

"CAN YOU PUT on your sister hat? Forget you're married to my brother," I ask Skye.

Whenever I need to talk to her about something private, I invoke this privilege, knowing it won't reach my brother. We've talked under our sister hats many times before: about sex, birth control, etc. But never about something that directly effects Brody. I won't ask Skye to keep a big secret from Brody. That wouldn't be fair, but I do need some solid advice.

She fakes changing her hat before plopping down on my bed. "I have a date," I say, my face crinkling up at the word. She starts screaming like a wild banshee. You'd think I just told her I won the lottery, not a date with a doctor. "Can you *not* tell Brody? I just don't want to make it a thing. I'm only telling you because it's that doctor from your office and . . ."

"Brody will be happy for you!" she says.

Exhaling, I say, "I just don't want a thousand questions."

"Okay," she says, sticking her bottom lip out before she visibly sobers. "Rhett's gone. He's not coming back."

"I know."

"I love Rhett, too," she says. "He was the closest thing Brody had to a brother. We all miss him." She gets up, taking my hand. "No one misses him more than you. I know that. But this is long overdue. I won't say a word to Brody until you're ready."

"Thanks."

Shaking my hand to loosen me up, Skye says, "Now, where are you going, and what are you going to wear?"

PAUSING ON THE sidewalk to scan my dress one last time before I go inside the restaurant, I take a deep breath. I didn't want him to pick me up at the condo. It seems more casual, and less awkward, to meet him at the restaurant than have him come to my door.

I suddenly have second thoughts. Why did I let Skye talk me into wearing a dress? Skinny jeans and a cute shirt would've been more appropriate, more me. I tell myself things will be okay, that at least my boobs look good—thanks to my new padded pushup bra, which was also Skye's suggestion.

*False advertising!*

Rhett Bennett, get out of my head.

When you are with someone, you have inside jokes. Things that mean something to only the two of you. One of those things for Rhett and me was padded bras. He used to tease me that my padded bras were false advertising. He thought he was getting a woman with a full C, and it turned out I'm barely a B.

My response was always the same, *"No going back now."*

Then he'd pick me up, kiss me, and say, *"How about going down instead?"*

He loved his stupid sex jokes. And I love a man who can make me laugh. Because of him, I'll never look at bras the same. It's hard to move on when even your boobs remind you of your ex.

Still, this is what I'm supposed to be doing. I'm a single, twenty-something. I should be dating, trying to find "the one." The only problem is—I found him already.

I hate that I think about him so much, but I'd hate it more if I didn't.

But now's not the time to be thinking about my ex. Standing on the sidewalk, I look up at the sign, moody lighting cascading on it. I've never been here. It's pricey and considered one of the most romantic restaurants in Charleston. Seems like a lot of pressure for a first date. Shouldn't we have gone for coffee or something first? This guy obviously wants to impress me, and I can't fault him for that.

Okay, this is it. Take a deep breath, open the door, walk inside. Nothing to it. One, two, three, here goes nothing. Before I can actually step inside, I hear my name.

I turn to find my date. He's tall with a good build. I remember him looking older, though, a touch of gray at his temples, but tonight the age difference doesn't seem as big. Maybe out of the doctor's garb and dressed in a nice suit has made him look younger. He flashes me a smile. It's that awkward moment when you aren't sure if you should do a side hug, quick hug, handshake, or kiss on the cheek hello. Instead, I do nothing but say, "Hi."

He grins at me again. This man must be easy to please. "I'm so happy you could . . ." I don't hear the rest of what he says because he holds up a long stem red rose.

My chest tightens, my skin rushes with heat, and a stream of tears immediately rush down my cheeks. I cover my mouth in an attempt to contain my cries then rush down the sidewalk away from him.

All I can see is the poorly doodled picture of a rose Rhett left me on my nightstand after our first weekend together, remembering his sweet good morning message.

*A rose for my rose. One morning soon, I'll have to have the real thing. Hoping to see you again tonight. Sorry I won't be there to kiss you good morning.*

"Ainsley," he calls after me, catching me by my elbow. "Are you alright?"

"The flower," I choke out.

He glances at it then tosses it to the ground. "Sorry, your last name is Rose. I thought it would be cute to . . ."

"I'm sorry," I say. "Obviously, I'm not ready for this."

"Skye warned me that you just got out of something pretty serious," he says.

"She warned you?" I ask.

"She didn't give me details," he smirks. "More like she told me she'd have my balls in a vice if I hurt you."

That makes me relax slightly. "Aren't you her boss?"

"On paper," he jokes.

Wiping my tears, I say, "I'm sorry."

"You said that already," he says. "It wasn't necessary either time."

I feel my lips start to curve into a smile, but stop myself. I don't want to smile at another man. All my smiles belong to Rhett. Even after all this time, all the pain, all of me still belongs to Rhett. I think I always will. Most woman have one—the man you wonder about. The man you can't get over. Either because you aren't sure why it ended, or because you wonder what could've been.

"I should go."

"I'll see you to your car," he says.

Giving him a little nod, I turn around, realizing in my fit, I'd gone the wrong way. Before turning back towards my car, I stare down at the cracks in the sidewalk, the old kids' rhyme echoing in my head.

*Step on a crack, break your mother's back.*

"What's this other guy's name?" my date asks.

I know he's trying to be nice, but it's none of his business. "I try not to talk about him, or really think about him," I lie.

"Maybe that's the problem," he says.

I stop at my car door. "What do you mean?"

"Maybe you can't move on until you talk about him. Holding everything in is holding you to him," he says. "Let yourself talk about it."

He makes a good argument, but maybe he also has his own agenda. Most men do.

I shrug, and he continues, "What's the point in fighting it? You're the one losing." He flashes me a grin, opening my car door for me. "I hope someday you can enjoy roses again."

"Me, too," I whisper.

# CHAPTER NINE

## EIGHTEEN MONTHS AGO

You are my answered wish.
A. Rose

### RHETT

A CAT OWNER who insists his feline is anorexic started my morning, and it's been non-stop since. People love their pets. Their pets are like their children. I get it. I love Sadie, so I try to keep that in mind with all my patients. But just like you have crazy, over the top parents, you have crazy, over the top pet owners. Those that dress up their animals for the holidays, take them to visit Santa, and love to show you the pictures. Still, I'd much rather that than the alternative. My patients are all loved by their owners. That's the perk of owning your own clinic. You only deal with people who love their animals; otherwise, they wouldn't be paying the crazy fees to keep them taken care of. Pet insurance, now that's a racket I should've gotten into.

In vet school, we did a lot of volunteer hours, so I saw the other side—the neglected, the abused. I don't know how social workers do it. Seeing a dog beaten is bad enough; I can't imagine seeing a child that way.

Exiting exam room one, I pull out my phone, pulling up Ainsley's text—a picture of her blowing a kiss. The day seems a lot longer when you've got a woman and the promise of sex waiting for you at home.

"Are we working or sexting?" Brody asks, attempting to swipe my phone.

I pull it back just in time. "I can multi-task."

"Well, multi-task your ass into exam room two," he says. "Hey, how was Ainsley when you drove her home? Did you see her yesterday at all?"

"Didn't see her yesterday," I lie. "She seemed fine to me."

"Good," he says. "I asked her to meet me for lunch today. You in?"

"I'll let you know," I say.

He walks off, and I pull up Ainsley's number, texting her the story I just told Brody. Lies only work if everyone tells the same ones.

Then it's back to work. An angry turtle who refuses to come out of his shell, and a lazy spaniel who hikes his leg off the side of the sofa to pee on the floor instead of going outside—that's what rounds out my morning. Sometimes this job feels more like therapy than medicine.

Passing by reception, I hear my name. Brenda has worked for me and Brody since we opened the clinic. She's old enough to be our mother. She's the lifeblood of the office. Nothing here happens without Brenda. "Ainsley's outside," she says. "I'm assuming she's waiting on her brother."

I look though the picture window, seeing Ainsley pacing back and forth. Her strawberry blonde hair is pulled up in a ponytail, and she's dressed in shorts and t-shirt. God, she's beautiful. I wonder how long she's been out there.

"He's finishing up with a patient. I'll tell her to come wait inside," I say to Brenda.

Walking through reception, I open the door. Ainsley's eyes dart to me. She looks like she's about to vomit all over the sidewalk. I know she's worried about Brody finding out, probably thinking he'll kill me.

"This is by far the most selfish thing I've ever done," she whispers. "I've been so hellbent and determined not to let Brody run my life, I've forgotten I could be destroying his relationship with the most important person in his life besides me and Skye."

"Come inside," I say, wanting to take her hand.

"I'm not sure I can act like I haven't screwed you seven ways to Sunday."

I can't help but laugh. I really wish I could read her mind. The things she comes up with.

"Stop laughing," she says, grinning. "Illicit affairs are not for the faint of heart, I tell you."

The door opens, and a woman walks out carrying a small white poodle. It's hard to pay attention to the dog because the woman is dressed like she is going to a nightclub in a tight black spandex dress with killer high heels. Ainsley raises an eyebrow, walking inside. The entire waiting area is women, all dressed very sexy. Some don't even have pets with them. Some have goldfish. I think I even see one with a hermit crab.

"Ainsley Rose!" a friendly voice says. Brenda comes out from behind the desk to hug Ainsley. It's a welcome sight among the sea of silicone.

"Hi, Brenda," Ainsley says, glancing over her shoulder. "What's with all the cleavage and short skirts?"

She rolls her eyes. "There was an article on Charleston's most successful men. Rhett and Brody made the list. Ever since then, these harlots have been coming in by the droves. I make them all wait until our 'real' patients have been seen. Some of these floozies don't even have pets. They say they are considering getting this or that and want to discuss breeds."

"Or *breeding?*" Ainsley giggles.

Shaking my head, I lead Ainsley back to the office Brody and I share. It's set up so our desks face each other in the middle of the room with a few file cabinets surrounding them and a plaid dog bed in the corner for Sadie, our not-so-silent partner. Most days, I bring her to work with me. I hate the idea of her cooped up in the condo, and here she gets all kinds of attention from the staff.

Ainsley bends down to pat Sadie. I bend down next to her, my fingers gently grazing hers. "Can you do this?" I ask. "With Brody?"

"I'll be okay," she says, but it's anything but convincing.

I ask softly, "Are you having second thoughts? We can stop this right now."

Her eyes fall to her feet. Fuck, that sounded like I could just dump her without a second thought. I tilt her chin up. "I don't want to. I haven't stopped thinking about you all morning."

"Hey," Brody says, and we both pop to our feet. He wraps his arms around her tightly. "You alright?"

"I'm fine. You're making a big deal out of nothing," she says.

"Big brother rules say it's my job to protect you," Brody says, tapping her nose.

"I think you're the one who needs protecting," she says, a twinge of mischief in her voice. "Maybe I should kick the butts of all those bimbos in the waiting room."

Brody and I both laugh. "I'm engaged, but Rhett might need a little protection. He's gotten friendly with patients before."

Her head whips around like she's in *The Exorcist*. "Damn, Brody, that was one time," I say, looking away.

"I'll never let you live that down," he says, laughing. "I still can't use exam room two. Your naked ass is burned into my skull."

Damn it! Thanks for that visual, Brody! That was a while ago, but it doesn't matter if it was last year or last week, Ainsley didn't need to know. I try to catch her eyes, but they're on the floor again. Not sure what she finds so interesting about dog hair. We really need to sweep in here. Sadie gets up and nuzzles her leg, and I wish it was me who was comforting her.

"You seem busy, so I'll just go," Ainsley says quietly.

"Those women can wait. I'm taking my sister to lunch. But let's be quick. How about the hamburger place across the street?" Brody asks.

"Sure," she says, trying to sound happy.

"You coming?" Brody asks, turning to me. Without thinking, I look at Ainsley, her eyes willing me to say no.

"Oh, thought it was brother-sister time," I say.

"Well, you're her default brother, so come on," Brody says.

Ouch! I'm not her brother, and I've never thought of myself that way. Brody starts for the door, and Ainsley glances at me. I give her a little wink, indicating that everything will be fine, but she doesn't look like she believes me. As we head out, Brody immediately starts in on her. How's she feeling? What are her plans? He makes any helicopter parent look like they're on a pleasure cruise.

The place isn't far, and thank fuck, it's not crowded. It's one of those places where you order at the counter, and then they bring the food out to you. Ainsley orders first before going to grab a table. Looking back at her over my shoulder, I see her studying the chairs, trying to decide the best seating arrangement.

I hate seeing her stressed. I hate that I didn't buy her lunch. I hate that I didn't pull out her chair, so I'll be damned if I don't sit next to her. It's a four-top, so technically I could leave an empty seat between us. But I don't, not even when she puts her purse on it, a not-so-subtle hint for me to park my ass elsewhere.

Instead, I pick it up, move it out of the way, and sit down before Brody walks over. "Did you stay in bed all day yesterday?" he asks.

"What?" she cries.

"Since you weren't feeling well," he says. "Did you stay in bed and rest?"

"I stayed in bed," she says, trying to keep from smiling, both of us knowing how little rest we actually got.

We make small talk until the server comes over with the food, and I slip my hand to her thigh, using the tablecloth to hide our contact.

It's only meant to reassure her, but her cheeks blush just the same. I'd bet her panties are soaked, too. Still, this isn't a romantic comedy where the leads give one other hand jobs at the dinner table. I'm not willing to risk her feelings or her brother's with that kind of behavior, no matter how much fun it would be.

Brody said this would be a quick lunch, but he's suddenly droning on and on about her career plans, picking the right guy, local self-defense courses, and date rape drugs. He seems to have forgotten that we do have a waiting room full of patients, even if they are just looking for dates. Usually, Ainsley would be giving it right back to him, but she seems fascinated by the tiny seeds on her hamburger bun, picking them off one at a time, not having actually taken a bite.

Ladies, forget Paleo, Keto, Whole Thirty! Screw your brother's best friend if you want to lose weight. This may just be the diet trend of the year. Not that Ainsley needs to lose any weight, of course. Her curves are the stuff men dream of. I give her knee a little squeeze to try to get her attention.

"You have got to stop!" she barks.

Brody's mouth closes, and my hand flies off her leg, not sure who that outburst was meant for.

"What did I say?" Brody asks, looking at me.

I can only shrug. I stopped paying attention to Brody's lectures like five years ago. Maybe ten.

"I knew I shouldn't have agreed to move back here. It's only been a few weeks, and you are driving me crazy," she cries.

"Charleston is your home," Brody says. "You belong here with your family. Me, Skye, and Rhett."

"Back off, Brody," she snaps, getting to her feet and throwing down her napkin. "My love life is none of your business. I'm not fifteen anymore."

She turns on her heel and walks out. Brody looks at me, both confused and mortified. "Love life? What love life?"

SADIE BY MY side, I open the door to Ainsley's place, not sure what to expect from her. She could be pissed about a number of things—the women in the waiting room, Brody's revelation about my adventures in exam room two, or the fact that I had my hand on her thigh at lunch. So I'm relieved when she smiles at me like I've just given her the best orgasm of her life.

"Nice outburst today," I say, running my fingers through her hair. "Was that meant for me or for Brody?"

"Mostly Brody," she says, leaning up to kiss me gently, and giving Sadie a quick pat. "What did you two talk about after I left?"

"He asked me to keep an eye on you," I say, the corner of my mouth turning up in a mischievous smile.

"What did you say?"

"That he should give you some space, and I would watch out for you."

"You lied that easily?"

"I didn't lie." I squeeze her ass. "I plan on watching you . . ." I lower my mouth to her neck, my voice low and hungry. "Watching you come while I slide my dick inside you."

"Rhett," she says in a needy moan.

"Watching you scream my name while I fuck you with my mouth." I feel her tremble and chuckle low in my throat. Slipping my hands between her legs, I cup her, rubbing her through her shorts. "You're soaking wet. Did you get wet for me at lunch?" I ask, increasing the pressure, her hips pushing against my hand. "Tell me."

"Yes," she whispers.

I slide to my knees, taking her shorts and panties with me, and bury myself between her legs. Her nails dig into my shoulder as I grip her ass, pulling her tighter.

"Fuck, baby," I groan, my mouth moving all over her, inside, outside—sucking, licking, nibbling. I can't get enough. I lift one of her legs to my shoulder, pushing my tongue deeper inside. "That's it, baby," I growl, pushing her ass, encouraging her.

Her hands in my hair, she moans my name. Her voice is breathy and needy, and makes my dick twitch. Gripping her hips, I pull her tighter. I'm on my knees, which is fitting because she completely controls me. Everything I want, I crave, begins and ends with her. I want my days to begin buried deep inside her. I want my nights to end with her in my arms. I've never considered myself a greedy man, but Ainsley has changed me, and she's what I long for the most.

Giving her ass a smack, she cries out in pleasure. All I want is to make her feel good. My sole purpose is to give her pleasure. My hands slip to her ass. There's something about a woman's hips, the curve of her ass that make a man weak. Women don't exist for a man's amusement. They are a luxury. What we desire most. We could live without them, but we don't want to. I've lived without Ainsley, but now I know I never want to do that again.

Enjoying the taste of her, I don't realize she's on the verge until her head flies back, and she screams, "Oh my God!"

Her whole body quivers, but I don't stop. I can't. I'm too greedy. Sticking my tongue deep inside again, she thrusts against me. I pull her to the sofa and lay down underneath her so she's straddling my face. But she stops moving. I don't need to see her face to know she's embarrassed. Softly, I plant feather light kisses around her folds, feeling her muscles clench.

"You're so beautiful," I say, my tongue outlining her. "And you taste fucking amazing."

"Rhett."

She tries to move, but I hold her hips firm.

"I know you want this. You're open so wide."

"Oh my God!" she cries.

"Please," I beg, pushing on her ass, encouraging her again. "That's it, baby." Her hips start to move faster, and I groan, the vibration causing her to tremble. Her second orgasm rips through her, her legs give way, and she collapses on top of me.

Gently, I kiss her, and she practically jumps, but I catch her by her hips. She looks down at me and says, "I'm sorry, you can't breathe." I bust out laughing, and she grins. "I can only imagine telling Brody I killed his best friend by suffocating him with my vagina!"

My dick pulses against her. What can I say? Her crazy mind does it for me. Truthfully, there's not anything about her that doesn't get to me. She starts to slide down my body, hopefully to return the favor, but she stops, her head turned to the side.

I see we have an audience. Sadie's sitting straight up, her tongue hanging out.

"Sadie's watching us," she says.

I motion to Sadie to go away, shooing my hand at her, only she comes over to us, resting her head next to us.

"The little cock blocker is jealous," I say.

"Sorry, Sadie," she says, kissing her way down my chest and abs. "He needs my attention right now."

"I REALLY NEED to finish unpacking these last few boxes," she says, cuddling into my side on the sofa, making no attempt to get up. I'm sure she would've been unpacked days ago, but I've had her a little preoccupied.

Planting a kiss on top of her head, I say, "Why don't I help you?"

"That doesn't sound like fun," she says, raising an eyebrow at me.

"It will be if we do it naked."

She laughs, and I help her to her feet, pulling her into my chest, her tits pushing against me. I run my fingers through her long strawberry hair, leaning into her neck. "Rhett?" She means to scold me into action, but her voice is too soft and sweet.

"Payment up front," I tease.

She giggles, planting a sweet kiss on my cheek, then points to a large box in the corner. Usually when someone moves, boxes are labeled—kitchen, bathroom, etc., but this one is full of all kinds of odds and end. I pull out an old photo of the four of us taken on Ainsley's sixteenth birthday.

"Wow, look at us. We had no idea what we were doing raising you," I say.

"*You* didn't raise me. Brody raised me. You were just the hot friend."

I start laughing, having no idea she thought of me that way when she was a teenager.

"It's not funny," she says. "All my friends drooled over you and Brody. It was terrible."

Raising my eyebrow, I lean against the sofa. "What about you? Did you drool over me?" I see the heat rise to her cheeks and catch her in my arms. "It's okay. I drooled over you, too. Not then, of course. But later, when you were in college, I had very, very bad thoughts about you and me." She slaps my shoulder as I reach down into the box, pulling out an old, ratty sketchpad I bought her long ago. "You kept this?" I ask, flipping it open.

She nods and smiles. I don't have to read what I inscribed to her. She knows it by heart even after all this time and recites it for me word for word: *A. Rose, dream big! Sketch what makes you happy. Your dreams are still alive, find them.*

She softly strokes my cheek. "When I found this on my nightstand a few months after my parents died, I thought it was from Brody until I opened the cover. I never could figure out why *you* bought it for me."

"You were so sad for so long back then," I say. "When I would catch you sketching, your eyes would light up. I was cleaning up one day and saw all these sketches on napkins of this one particular wedding dress."

She flips a few pages in the sketchpad to show me, and I nod. "I used to draw my mom's dress over and over again. I always thought I'd wear her dress when I got married." She looks away. "But it was lost in the fire, too."

"I didn't know that part. I just bought the pad because it seemed like it was the only time you were happy. I can't believe you kept it."

"It was the best gift anyone ever gave me."

# CHAPTER TEN
## PRESENT DAY

### AINSLEY

I'M A HORRIBLE liar, nothing ever comes to me in the right moment. I hate that. And I'm totally the person that thinks of the witty comeback five minutes after the conversation ends. My mom used to say it's because I don't have a mean bone in my body. That was my mom. She believed the best about people.

She probably would've liked my date, Dr. Hottie, and thought his advice was sound. He said to remember Rhett, to think about him. I didn't have much of a comeback for that. No lie could take away my tears or save that wretched first date.

I figure I've got exactly two hours before my phone rings, Skye wondering how it all went down. Tearing off my dress, I unhook my false advertising bra, tossing it in the hamper. Yes, I know you should wash them separately and hang them to dry, but seriously, who does that? I reach for my bathrobe, my eyes landing on a box in the top of the closet. Does everyone keep a breakup box? Imagine if you kept a box for every ex-boyfriend you had. Good Lord, some women would need an extra storage unit. But I only have the one.

Rhett.

The breakup box.

I put the lid on it and haven't opened it since. I'm not sure what's closed up tighter, that box or my heart. Do I need to open that box to open my heart?

Do I want to open my heart again?

Gently, I carry it over to my bed, setting it down. Tucking my feet under me, I place my hands on top, trying to remember the last thing I stuck in there, so I'll have some idea what's facing me. Our relationship was mostly secret, so there's not a lot of the typical stuff. No concert stubs or dried out flowers from our first date. You won't find a heart balloon or a mixed tape (not that people actually do those anymore), but you get the idea.

I take a deep breath and open the lid to my past. My first sketchpad is on top, the one he gave me not long after I moved in with my brother and him. I wonder if he knew how much that meant to me. How much that influenced my life. I doubt I would be a wedding dress designer if he hadn't given me that pad, believed in me. I never told him that. Flipping open the cover, I run my fingers across his handwriting. It's a small piece of him. One of the few I still have.

Placing it aside, I look down and find his pale blue eyes, and I swear he's staring right at me. Pulling out a picture of Skye, Rhett, and Brody from the box, I remember the day exactly—my sixteenth birthday. They were all standing around me in front of my first car. Even Sadie's in the picture. They'd all taken turns teaching me how to drive. Skye had taken me for just the right sunglasses, while Brody insisted I learn on a stick and automatic. It was Rhett who got him to back off and let up a little.

I look at the girl in the photo, remembering loving Rhett even then. In my eyes, he was the ultimate guy, the measure to which every other guy had to live up to—hot, smart, funny, and sweet. Of course, he was clueless, insisting on calling me A. Rose, just to drive me nuts. Things were so much simpler then. When he didn't know how I felt. Before "just fun" led to the most consuming love of my life.

If only I could've separated sex and love, then none of this would've happened. We'd all still be friends. Rhett would still be in my life. He'd still be . . .

I slam the lid back on the box, my head shaking, not wanting to remember anymore how it all went so very wrong.

THE VET CLINIC is one of the sponsors for the Charleston shelter. Today's event at a local park brings out the most devoted animal lovers. There's a walk, a bakery with dog friendly treats, even a photographer so you can have a photo session with your pet. Brody's busy doing his part to raise awareness and funds, and Skye's been scoping out men for me. She has this whole theory that you can pick a man based on his pet. She thinks men who own cats aren't ready to commit. Men with reptiles should be avoided at all costs. Horse loving men are grade A, but steer clear of guys who are into birds. I've tried to point out that, while Brody loves animals, he might be the only veterinarian on the planet who doesn't have a pet. She simply said that's because she's enough of an animal for him. I could've lived my whole life without that knowledge.

Of course, dog lovers make the best boyfriends, according to her theory, but the type of dog is important. Labs, retrievers, spaniels are all acceptable. Men who have "fussy" breeds, like those with long hair, can handle high maintenance women. Owners of German Shepherds, pit bulls and the like are alpha males to the extreme. The cream of the crop guys own mixed breeds.

"How about him?" Skye asks, nodding in the direction of a rather buff guy walking a standard poodle.

"My tears are barely dry from my last date," I say.

She rolls her eyes, pointing out another fella. "Him?"

"Two things," I say. "I don't date guys who have longer hair than me, or who weigh less than me."

"Picky, picky," she says, laughing.

"Hey," Brody says, kissing Skye and me both on top of our heads. "Sorry I've been so busy."

"Used to it," Skye says with an unmistakable tone. I know Brody works long hours, especially since Rhett is no longer his partner, and I can tell it's wearing on her.

"Let's not do this in front of my sister," he says.

"Hire someone," she says.

Brody mouths *sorry* to me. "You should get some help," I tell him. "Skye's right. Rhett's gone. Guess we both need to accept it."

He taps my nose. "You always were the smart one."

I dart my eyes to Skye. My stupid ass brother needs to fix this. We can't lose someone else we love. He bends down in front of her, but she doesn't look at him.

"Ten years to get married," Skye whimpers. "And our wedding was . . ."

She glances up at me, not able to say it. There's a lot we don't say. We all know what happened. No use reliving it.

"I'm not getting any younger, Brody," she says. "We said we'd have kids right away."

"Do we have to do this here?" he asks, trying to keep his voice soft.

Skye and my brother have been together over a decade, and I've never seen them like this. They had one brief breakup years ago, but I don't even know what caused it. All couples argue, but usually not in public, in front of family, so openly. I guess that's how you know when things are really bad. You don't care who sees, the mask has already fallen.

"No," she says, getting to her feet. "I'm sure you have more important things to do."

"Skye!" he begs, but she just walks off.

I shove his arm. "Chase her."

"She wants to be alone."

"No," I say, pushing him again. "She wants to feel like she's *first.*"

He stares at me for a second before realizing I'm a genius. He calls her name, hurrying through the crowd. Watching his pursuit, I smile when I see him wipe a tear from her cheek, praying he doesn't say or do anything else stupid. I see Skye nod and smile back. I'm not naive enough to believe that whatever is going on between them is now fixed, but nothing ever gets fixed if one person walks away. I should know that better than anyone.

Maybe I should get a dog. Looking around, all these pet owners seem happy. There are all kinds of studies about dog owners living longer. I wander here to there, searching the sea of fur. It's kind of like searching for the right man. Too tall, too short, too round, too loud, too hairy, bad breath, bad teeth. At least dogs are loyal and love unconditionally. Of course, some of them bite, but men have been known to do that, too. It's been forever since a man nibbled any part of me.

I feel a tap on my shoulder and turn around. Rhett's parents both smile at me. Panic sets in, and my eyes immediately search for pale blue ones.

"Is Rhett here?" I ask, my voice sounding more hopeful than it should.

"No," Diane says. "We thought you knew, he's living in . . ."

Cliff gently places his arm on his wife's shoulder, knowing an update on Rhett isn't what I need or what Rhett would want.

"We wanted to come out and support the clinic, the cause. It was a big part of our lives for so long," Cliff says. "We weren't sure you'd be here. I hope you don't mind."

My eyes fill, and I wrap my arms around them, feeling both their chests start shaking, their own emotions getting the better of them. No matter what happened between me and their son, it doesn't change what I feel for them. I love them. Even if Rhett and I aren't together, my feelings for them don't change. They had to side with Rhett. I know that. I also know they wished he'd acted differently. But as my dad used to say, you wish in one hand and shit in the other, and see which one fills up faster.

Basically, wishing is bullshit.

"How are you, honey?" Diane asks, pulling away and wiping her face. "I walked by your store the other day."

My store is in the historic district of Charleston, close to the vet clinic. I've only been open a few months, but I'm busier than I expected to be. Charleston is becoming popular for destination weddings, and I've gotten a lot of long-distance brides who are interested, as well as the locals.

I guess it's inevitable that I'd run into Rhett's parents at some point. I'm too unlucky for it to be any other way. Bumping into an ex, or their parents, is usually cringe-worthy, but not with these two.

"The dress in the window is exquisite."

I swallow hard. She's the only one that knows about that dress. "That's my remake of my mom's dress. You know, with my modern spin."

"Keep making dresses like that, and you might get your own wedding dress show like on TLC."

It's sweet she supports me. We stand there catching up, all three of us. It's amazing how we can fill the conversation without bringing up Rhett. But even though we don't speak his name, he's there, like a ghost over our shoulders. I wonder if they'll tell him they saw me. If so, I hope they say I look better than I do. Maybe I should tell them I went on a date. Do I want that to get back to Rhett? Truth is, part of me does and part of me doesn't. I decide to keep it to myself.

"Are Brody and Skye here?" Cliff asks. "We'd love to see them."

Pulling out my phone, I say, "I'll text them."

Looking around for a landmark, I text them to meet me by the jumbo yellow dog bowl sign, and within a couple minutes I spot them, waving them over. I see Brody and Skye are holding hands. Progress, I think.

When Brody sees my company, his eyes catch mine. He doesn't have to say a word for me to know that he's asking if I'm alright. I give him a little nod that I'm good. They all exchange hellos and hugs, and then I notice that Brody's hand goes right back to holding Skye's. He knows he's got his work cut out for him.

As soon as the pleasantries end, things feel different. It's glaringly obvious who's missing in this sudden little reunion. And the more all of us ignore it, the worse it gets. How can someone's absence make them more present than ever?

# CHAPTER ELEVEN
## SEVENTEEN MONTHS AGO

I wonder when you first loved me.
A. Rose

### RHETT

WITH SADIE BY my side, I lock up the vet clinic for the night. Sadie's ears perk up, and she tilts her head back and forth, making me realize I'm whistling. Apparently, I'm turning into one of those sappy guys who walks around whistling, but I can't help myself. There's a smoking hot woman waiting for me.

I've spent every night with Ainsley this past week. I wake up with her every morning and fuck her to sleep every night. That deserves a little whistle. We never go out, except to walk Sadie or visit the ice cream shop. We can't risk someone seeing us, and I can't trust myself to keep my hands off her much longer than it takes for a stroll with Sadie. But it's starting to feel unnatural not to be able to hold her hand or kiss her cheek even for those short periods of time.

My phone dings in my pocket.

*Thought you'd like to know, got my period. No worries, A. Rose*

I look at Sadie, wondering why I haven't been more worried about that. We've been careful since that first time on the patio, but I haven't given our slip up any thought. Perhaps I should have. Obviously, Ainsley worried enough that she thought to tell me. Even though I wasn't stressed about it, it's still a relief to know we're all good. I decide to stop by the store for a carton of ice cream for her, hoping her period doesn't mean moodiness, tears, or cramps. I don't want to get yelled at just because I exist, and I definitely don't want her in pain, or to see her cry.

After a quick stop, I walk into her condo with Sadie, finding Ainsley at her dress form, which is in the middle of the den. The rest of the room is covered in fabric, beading, and lace. She looks up at me with a needle in her mouth. My breath stops for a second. I should be used to it by now, but I'm not. She's so damn beautiful. Taking the needle out and sticking it in a pin cushion, she asks, "Didn't you get my text?"

"Yeah, I brought ice cream."

Her smile lights up the entire room. Good, no moodiness. I hand her the carton and kiss her on top of the head.

She studies her dress form. "I'm sorry for the mess. I didn't think you'd be coming over."

"Why not?" I ask. "I've been over every night."

She walks into the kitchen for a spoon and starts in on the ice cream. "I told you. I have my period."

A rush of heat comes over my skin. I don't remember ever being this irritated with her before. Not when she used my shaving cream in college. Not when she walked in on me making out with my girlfriend, or took my car without asking. "You think just because you're on your period, that I would just what? Go find someone else to fuck?"

Ainsley's whole body recoils at that word. "No," she whispers. "I just thought since I'm out of commission for a few days, you might want to do other *things*." She stiffens her spine. "Not other *women*."

"I'm perfectly capable of spending time with you without the sex part. I'm not using you." I know technically our "just fun" arrangement means we are, in fact, using each other, but there's more to it than that.

"I didn't say you were." She steps toward me. "I just thought you might want to go have guy time or something. I didn't mean to insinuate you were a bad guy."

Her blue eyes stare at me. It feels like she's looking right fucking through me. It wasn't until right now that I realize how deep I'm in this. How much I feel for her. Sadie rushes to her side and hides behind her legs.

"Traitor," I tell my dog.

"Hey, don't yell at the dog," she says. "If you're mad at me, then yell at me."

I want to be mad at her, but I'm really pissed at myself for becoming attached to her. I should want time alone, but I don't. I just want her, and it's pissing me off.

"I'm not mad at you."

She puts her hand on her hip. "Seems like you're mad at me. I'm sorry. I really didn't mean to imply you're only good for . . ." She waves her hand in the air, unable to use that word for what we've been doing together a lot lately.

I should go running for the hills. She can't even say we are fucking. I know what we are doing means more to her than that. I know I'm not an empty lay to her. And that just makes me want her even more. Truth is, she's more to me than that. I'm not mad at her. I'm mad I can't have more of her.

Giving her a halfway smile, I say, "I am good at that, though."

"The best," she says with a laugh and wraps her arms around my waist.

I pick her up so we're eye level. "If you want to be alone, have a night off. Just tell me."

"I don't." Her blue eyes lower to the floor, and it breaks my heart. "I don't want you to get sick of me."

"Don't worry about that," I say, trying to ignore my heart doing somersaults in my chest, screaming I will never tire of her.

"There are other ways we can have fun together," she says, raising an eyebrow at me.

Tickling her a little, I tease, "Do they involve you on your knees?"

TURNS OUT SEXLESS fun involves pigging out on junk food, binge watching television, and slow dancing in her living room. As soft music comes from one of the music stations on the television, she leans her head on my shoulder, her arms around my neck. We aren't winning any awards for our dancing, basically just swaying slowly back and forth.

Her living room is cluttered with lace, beads, and fabric. Sadie's curled up on her sofa, snoring, and we're in the middle of it all. She traded in clothes for pajamas a few hours ago, she doesn't have an ounce of makeup on, her hair is loose, and it's the best damn date I've ever been on, and we haven't left her place. No sex involved. Just her and me.

I remember my dad telling me once that he and my mom can have fun anywhere. That even doing something terrible like pulling weeds in the garden is better if she's by his side. At the time, I rolled my eyes, thinking my parents were such a sappy embarrassment, but now I'm starting to understand.

That's the way it's always been with Ainsley and me. I just never realized it. Maybe it's because we were friends first. Maybe it's because of the six-year age difference, but she and I always had simple fun together. I just never knew what it meant. I never knew that all those nights we laughed our asses off after we burned yet another dinner meant more than we were both bad cooks.

As a guy, my checklist for finding a woman never went far beyond her being sexy as hell and her having to like Sadie. Having fun in bed was the main criteria. It never occurred to me that the woman I should be looking for is the one that I can have fun with anywhere, not just between the sheets.

Now I've found her, but I'm not sure she's mine to keep.

PEOPLE LIKE ROUTINE. Even the most unconventional people have some routine in their lives. We prefer a certain side of the bed. We always brush our teeth at about the same time each morning and night. Much of life's routines involve our work schedule. Relationships, no matter how serious or casual, tend to be the same way. Who makes the coffee? Who makes the bed? Who uses the shower first?

Ainsley and I fell right into a pattern with each other in the mornings. I make the coffee, she makes the bed, and we always shower together before I leave for work. Strangely, nothing about our routine feels stale or boring, so I'm more than surprised one morning when I wake up to find her soaking in the bathtub, bubbles up to her neck.

"Join me," she says, holding her hand out.

I'm definitely a shower guy. In fact, I don't know that I've ever used my bathtub, but hers is an invitation I'm not going to miss.

"It will be our first bath together," she says. I smile, wondering why women give so much importance to things like that.

"We shower together almost every day," I say, stripping off my boxers.

"That's different," Ainsley says. "Bathing together feels more relationshipy." She leans forward to give me space to squeeze in behind her, but instead I sit opposite her, feeling a heavy conversation coming on.

"*Relationshipy* isn't a word." She lets her body sink in a little deeper, studying me. What's she thinking? Is she looking for more out of our arrangement? Maybe it's not what she's thinking that's important. It's what I think. What I want. That's what she's fishing for. She needs to know how I feel about her.

Sadie comes walking in, gives us a look, then lays down on the bath mat. I shake my head and say, "I swear, I'm going to develop a line of dog chews designed to keep them busy long enough for even the longest fuck session."

"Sex chews for dogs. Vet approved," she says, laughing.

Grinning, I splash some water up at her. "For doggy style or . . ."

A sexy look on her face, she leans forward, filling her hands with bubbles. I raise an eyebrow, daring her. She simply smiles, placing the bubbles on my head. I must look like I'm topped with whipped cream. I try to return the favor, but she gets more bubbles, this time placing them on my nose.

A tight-lipped grin on my face, I'm trying not to laugh or else I'm going to get a mouthful of bubbles. Pulling her forward, I kiss her, making sure to get bubbles all over her face and hair.

Laughing and kissing.

Kissing and laughing.

This is how it happens. This is how "just fun" becomes more. I know she feels it, too. Glancing over at her, we stop laughing. Her blue eyes study me, and while her mouth doesn't move, she sure is saying a whole heck of a lot. I can see it—all the things she doesn't want to say, all the feelings flying around between us. It's all right there—love, lust, fear, denial.

She's doing her best to camouflage her emotions, but they are written all over her face. She moves to get up, the water sliding down her curves, but I take hold of her hand. One of us has to be brave, acknowledge what's happening between us. She needs to know how I feel.

In an instant, I get out, standing in front of her, wrapping a towel around us both. Avoiding looking at me, she says, "That was fun."

"Not just fun," I whisper, tilting her chin up. "It's just love."

# CHAPTER TWELVE
## FIFTEEN MONTHS AGO

I'm yours and always will be.
A. Rose

### RHETT

"LET'S GO OUT," I whisper softly.

Three months of sneaking around and hiding our relationship from everyone wears on one's nerves. We've binged watched every show on every streaming channel. We've ordered food delivery from all the major apps. We've had sex on every possible surface in every conceivable position, but not once have we gone to a nice dinner, a show, a movie. Not once have I stopped in the middle of the street just to kiss her. No other person on the planet has heard me say how much I love her.

She looks up at me from our cuddled-up position in my bed. "Brody."

That one word from her reminds me of the reason for all the secrecy. Not that I've forgotten, but I'm not willing to go down without a fight.

I say, "What if we drive to Kiawah Island? It's only about forty-five minutes. Just far enough we won't run into anyone."

She gives me that smile—the one I love, asking, "Can Sadie come, too?"

KIAWAH ISLAND IS a well-kept secret among a plethora of beach towns, but not as commercialized as other places. Since Ainsley and I are also a well-kept secret, it's fitting that she and I make the island our escape. Being here is about slowing down, and remembering what's important, and it has nothing to do with the world class golf or tennis amenities.

"I feel like I'm drunk," Ainsley says, laughing and smiling as we walk the beach together, Sadie on her leash beside us. "I'm so happy."

"Me, too," I say with a chuckle.

Ainsley is the happiest drunk person you'd ever meet. She's also the cheapest date in that regard. One drink, and she's usually laughing her ass off.

Freedom feels so good. We spend the entire day with Sadie on the beach and eat lunch at an outdoor bistro that allows pets. We lounge around and make out every ten seconds without regard for time or place. Being able to walk down the beach holding her hand? Well, I didn't even know how much it would mean to me.

Placing a blanket on the sand, I pull Ainsley down, wrapping my arms around her from behind. She leans back into my chest, snuggling closer, watching the gentle roll of the waves. The warm sun is like a blanket over us, the wind like a tender kiss, and everywhere I look, we are surrounded by couples in love, children playing, families.

She glances up at me. Everything she wants in life surrounds us. Having lost her parents so young, she wants it even more than most people. And damn if I don't want to give it to her. My fingers lightly stroke her skin. "You aren't getting burned, are you?"

She shakes her head, snuggling closer. "This is my favorite time at the beach. When the sun is starting to set." Glancing up at me, she whispers, "This has been the best day."

"Let's stay the night," I say, kissing her. "We can rent a hotel room or a little beach cottage."

Sitting up straighter, she asks, "Are you serious?"

I scoop her up, carrying her down the beach. "New plan," I tell her. "From now on, we spend the weekends here. During the week in Charleston, we still have to hide out, but on the weekends, we escape."

She kisses me in agreement. I know at some point we're going to have to face the firing squad, but neither one of us wants our perfect bubble burst right now. Besides, when I go to Brody, I can't come armed with, *Hey, dude, I like your sister.*

Ainsley and I are more than that anyway. I just have to wait for the perfect moment.

# CHAPTER THIRTEEN
## PRESENT DAY

I don't know how to do life without you.
A. Rose

### RHETT

WHEN I WAS a kid, I loved running outside to get the mail, always jealous that my parents got all the letters and packages. They tried to explain to me that it was mostly bills and junk, but I didn't care. Somehow, it felt important to get something addressed to you. Someone had spent the time and effort to send you something—that meant something.

So my dad started sending me letters. Every so often, he'd write me something on his law office letterhead and mail it, or if he had to take a business trip, he'd send me a postcard. He was usually back in town by the time I got it, but I didn't care.

Now I hate the mail. My parents were right. It's mostly bills and junk, but that's not the problem. The problem are the letters.

Brody's letters.

I get one from him at least once a week. When the emails stopped, the letters started. I'm not sure why he switched. Maybe he thought I blocked him. I didn't. I just never opened them, so I never responded. Maybe he thought letters were more personal, harder to ignore. I don't know what he's thinking, but they come faithfully each week.

Opening my desk drawer, I see the pile, dropping this week's on top. There are dozens and dozens and dozens stacked up.

I'll give it to the Rose siblings: Brody and Ainsley don't give up easily. Still, Ainsley hasn't called, emailed, or written in months. Frankly, I'm not sure I'd be able to leave any communication from her unopened or unanswered. I couldn't do to her what I do to Brody—ignore.

A man has his limits of strength.

She is my weakness. It took everything I had left to let her go. Correction, to force her to go. I'm not sure I could do it again.

Sadie starts barking, and I slam the drawer shut. Even if I wanted to read his new letter, or any of them, today's not the day.

No sooner than I get turned around, my parents are walking through my door, making an impromptu visit. They called me yesterday to warn me they were coming, but refused to tell me why. Making the five-hour drive from Charleston to Atlanta on that kind of short notice makes me think that whatever is going on isn't good.

I swear all parents are the same. Visits to their grown children always involve questions about whether we are eating enough, sleeping enough, taking care of ourselves. Mine take worrying to a whole new level these days, but the worry lines on both their faces look even deeper today. Normally, I'd ask about them, their work, how they are doing, but I don't get the sense from them that they want to do the small talk thing.

"So what gives?" I say, reaching down and patting Sadie.

They take a seat on my tiny sofa. My small place here isn't anything like my condo back in Charleston. It's more like a dormitory, but what more do I really need?

My dad looks to my mom, like they are drawing straws in their head. Apparently, my dad gets the short one because he starts. "You know Charleston can be a small place."

"Charleston is the second largest city in South Carolina," I say. "I don't think you came here to discuss urban expansion. What's going on?"

My mom pats my dad's leg, consoling him over his lame attempt. Then she looks straight into my eyes, the way only a mother can. "We ran into Ainsley."

"You drove all the way here to tell me that?"

"We saw Brody and Skye, too."

"Some kind of reunion?" I say snidely.

My dad's eyes narrow at me. "That's not important," he says. "We saw them and . . ."

"It doesn't matter," I say.

"You don't want to know how she looked?" my mom asks, her voice cracking. "Or if she was with another man? Or how Brody and Skye are doing? Or . . ."

She keeps listing things, but I'm stuck on Ainsley. I know how she looked—beautiful, like always. As for whether she was with someone, I've got enough to keep me up at night without that little bit of knowledge.

"Mom," I say, stopping her. "I'm sorry you felt like you had to come here and confess to me that you spoke to my ex, but . . ."

"Look at this, Rhett," she says, pulling out her phone and flashing a picture. "This is Ainsley's new shop. You missed this. You missed her opening up her own shop."

"Mom . . ."

"No," she cries, scrolling to another picture and holding it in front of my face. "You see that dress in the front window? That's the dress she was going to marry you in!"

It's never easy to see your mother break down in tears, my father wiping her cheeks with his fingertips. I reach out, taking the phone from her hand and slowly zoom in on the dress. Her hope of marrying me is the anchor of her shop, the dream of our marriage is what she uses to draw people in.

"How do you know this is Ainsley's dress?"

"I promised her I would never tell you," my mom whimpers.

Handing back her phone, I say, "I'm not sure what you want me to do."

"You're hurting that girl on purpose," she barks then gets to her feet, her eyes as hard as I've ever seen them. "Fix it."

# CHAPTER FOURTEEN
## FOURTEEN MONTHS AGO

No one makes me laugh like you do.
A. Rose

### RHETT

"PACK A BAG," I yell out as I walk through the door to her place. "We're leaving tonight for the beach."

She looks over at me from her dress form. "But it's only Thursday."

Brody and Skye have been so busy with their wedding plans that they haven't noticed our absence. It's been surprisingly easy to keep them in the dark, so sneaking an extra day in was not a big deal.

"Took tomorrow off," I say, wrapping my arms around her. "We'll make it an extra-long weekend."

Exhaling, she says, "But I still have to finish Skye's veil."

What the hell? The wedding is still a month away. Surely, she has time. "I thought you'd be excited."

"I am," she says, stabbing the pin cushion with her needle.

God, she really is a terrible liar.

Ainsley's not a high maintenance chick. She can be ready in five minutes flat. Seldom nags and enjoys the simple things in life more than most, but even she has her limits. I can tell our new arrangement of weekdays in the city and weekends at the beach has worn out its welcome. It's been a little over a month, and I can sense she's not happy. She doesn't say it, but every weekend it's taken her longer and longer to pack. She's no longer interested in where we stay or which restaurant we go out to. And now she's taking it out on the pin cushion.

Taking her hand, I lead her over to the sofa. Sadie joins us, like she's in on the conversation, resting her head on Ainsley's lap.

"You told me in the beginning—just fun," she says.

"Ainsley, you know that . . ."

She holds her hand up. "I'm wondering, is this still fun for you? Because it's not for me. I'm starting to feel like your mistress or the other woman, sneaking around all the time."

"Don't feel like that," I say. "I love you."

"You know how people use the phrase falling in love? *Falling* implies an accident, something you don't want to happen, like faceplanting on the sidewalk," she says, motioning between us. "Maybe that's what this is. An accident."

"You're missing the most important part of falling in love."

"What?"

"I fall, and you catch me. You fall, and I catch you."

"You totally read that on a bumper sticker."

"Actually, it was Pinterest," I tease her.

"I love you. I do," she whispers.

I notice we do that a lot. Whisper our I love yous. It's a secret, like our relationship. Shouldn't we be shouting it from the rooftops?

"Something has to change," I say, raising an eyebrow at her. "I think I need to talk to Brody."

The look on her face is priceless. I can tell she's been waiting for me to suggest this for a long time. "He might take it better if I talk to him," she says.

Shaking my head, I say, "This needs to come from me."

"What will you say?" she asks. "Will you tell him we've been seeing each other already or . . ."

I move next to her, getting down on one knee. "I'm going to tell him I want to marry you."

She laughs, shaking her head at me. Not at all the reaction I thought I'd get, but I'll take it over a rejection.

"You totally ruined my proposal plan," I say, smirking at her. "That's why I wanted to leave today."

Her head shakes a little bit. "What? You're serious?"

Reaching into my pocket, I pull out a little black box. "Had a private sunset dinner on the beach planned. Candles, flowers, and your favorite ice cream for dessert, but it looks like I've got to do this here instead."

"Oh my God," she says. "You aren't?"

"Can you be quiet for two seconds?" I tease her.

She laughs, holding her left hand out and wiggling her fingers, a certain sign I'm going to get the answer I want. "Ainsley . . ."

"Yes!" she cries, flying into my arms and knocking me backwards onto the floor, her on top of me.

"You haven't seen the ring. I haven't said the words," I say, pushing her hair back from her face.

She sits up, tilting her head at me. "You're so busted. This is why you were on Pinterest!"

I laugh. She caught me. So I may have searched romantic proposal ideas. My man card is still very much intact. Sitting up, I hold out the box in front of her, opening it. The proposal ideas may have come from the internet, but the ring I handled all on my own. As a wedding dress designer, she's seen thousands of rings.

Hers had to be special. It had to be her.

"A rose," she says softly, the sweetest smile on her lips. I slip the two-carat rose cut diamond with a platinum band on her finger. "It's perfect."

A man's life is funny. For so long, his dick runs the show. Chasing tail and thinking about how to score are his main objectives with the opposite sex. At some point, his brain jumps in the game, and career and success start to share the spotlight with tits and ass. Then without warning, his heart becomes the CEO, ordering the brain to put his woman first, commanding his dick to focus only on her.

Cupping her face in my hands, I say, "I promise . . ." My voice starts to break, and I stop. Her hand lands softly on my chest. "I promise you everything," I say. "All the things I know you really want. Family, kids."

Her lips find mine, her hands slipping under my shirt. This is one thing Pinterest didn't account for in the perfect proposal. Public proposals don't get you laid after. Want to propose in front of a big crowd? Or have a photographer hiding in the bushes? Then you don't get this moment right here. Suddenly, I'm very grateful she busted my beach proposal plan to hell.

Slowly, I start to unbutton her shirt and say, "I need you to promise me something, too."

"Anything," she whispers.

"Promise me that in fifty years, you'll still let me undress you. Promise me we won't turn into one of those couples who just takes off their clothes and gets to business."

Smiling, she says, "In fifty years, you won't want to undress me. My boobs will be at my waist, and my ass will . . ."

"Yes, I will," I say, pushing her shirt off her shoulders, revealing her light pink bra. "Promise me."

I find the hook on her bra, unlatching it. "In fifty years, you'll probably have arthritis and not be able to do that," she teases me.

Tossing her bra aside, I know I'm grinning like a fool. "Guess I'll have to take my dentures out when I do this then," I say, taking her to the floor and circling her nipple with my tongue.

She laughs. It's the most incredible sound—happy mixed with hope and the promise of a lifetime.

WEARING NOTHING BUT the new sparkle on her hand, Ainsley rests her head on my chest. Forget making it to the beach, we haven't even made it to the bedroom, still twisted up together on the living room floor.

Sadie walks over, plops down, then places her head on my shoulder. "Shoo," I say, swatting at the air in her direction.

Ainsley giggles, giving her a scratch behind the ear. "Is it too early to talk dates?"

Honestly, I've given no thought to the date or ceremony or any of it, figuring that would be Ainsley and my mom's domain. "Well, as long as it's not a double wedding with Brody and Skye in a month, I think we're good."

She wrinkles her nose up at the terrible thought. "I'd like to do it on my parents' anniversary. They were so happy together, and I think it would be nice to remember them that way. It's about seven months from now. That would give me plenty of time, I think."

"Perfect," I say. "I'm going to talk to Brody tomorrow."

"Tomorrow?" she asks, her eyes wide.

"Yep," I say. "I don't want you having to take your ring off and hide it. We're done with all that. Plus, if I wait, it could be a distraction for his own wedding, and I don't want that."

"Can I tell you something silly?" she asks. I sit up a little, preparing myself. Sometimes when I woman says something is silly, it's code for something much bigger. "I've been dying to change my online status to *in a relationship*, and tomorrow I can! It's silly how happy that makes me."

See, much bigger than silliness. This isn't about online status or trolls on the internet knowing. It's about her being mine and me being hers.

# CHAPTER FIFTEEN
## FOURTEEN MONTHS AGO

Ainsley Rose Bennett sounds like that should've always been my name.

A. Rose

### RHETT

I WAS SUPPOSED to be off today, thinking I'd be at the beach with Ainsley celebrating our engagement. Instead, I've worked a full day, just finishing up my last case of the day. I left Sadie with Ainsley today, thinking she could use the company. She's a nervous wreck. Brody wondered why I decided to work today, but a simple shrug and a "my plans changed" was enough of an explanation for him. Once he hears the real reason for my change of plans, he may not be so accepting.

In some ways, talking to Brody is like going to a girl's father before asking for her hand in marriage. After all, Brody is the only male family member in Ainsley's life, but he's not her father. I'm not here to ask his permission or for forgiveness for loving his little sister. This is happening, and everyone else will just have to deal with it.

I'm not quite sure how Brody's going to react. He could punch my face. He could laugh and think I'm joking. He could go stone cold silent. I've known Brody almost fifteen years, but I've got no idea how this is going to go.

"You're still here?" Brody asks, walking into our shared office and dropping some files on his desk. "I've got to meet Skye, some sort of seating arrangement emergency."

"Fun!"

"Dude, I'm so ready for the wedding to be over. You have no idea. It's all we talk about, and if we aren't talking about the wedding, we're talking about kids. She won't be happy unless she comes back from the honeymoon pregnant."

"You wouldn't have it any other way," I say, ragging him a bit.

"You know, you should try it sometime," he says.

"Actually, I'm seeing someone," I say.

"For more than one night?" he says, getting his own dig in.

"It's serious," I say. "I'm in love with her."

"Fuck me," he says, leaning back on his desk slightly. "Never thought I'd see the day. I'm happy for you."

"Thanks, neither one of us expected to fall in love with each other. It just happened." His forehead wrinkles up a little, not understanding why I feel the need to confess. "She's brilliant, funny, and I'd do anything for her. Anything."

"Man, I've never heard you like this. Guess Skye and I will have to meet this woman."

Time to drop the bomb.

"That's the thing. You both already know her."

His eyes dart up. "Please tell me it's not an employee, because . . ."

"It's Ainsley," I say. "I'm in love with Ainsley."

He doesn't laugh in disbelief. Not a trace of shock comes over his face, and I wonder if deep down somewhere he knew how I felt about his sister. Drawing a deep breath, it feels so good to have the truth out. The word *secret* has a negative connotation to it, so I'm relieved that Ainsley and I don't have that surrounding us anymore, no matter Brody's reaction, which at the moment is stoic.

"It started not long after she moved back to Charleston. I should've told you sooner."

"Told me sooner," he repeats, his voice louder than before. "How about you don't touch my sister in the first place?"

"It's serious between me and her."

"She's my little sister!" he barks. "I can't believe this! I trusted you. You're a shit friend, Rhett."

I don't mind him yelling and cursing at me. There's codes between friends, and I broke one. The cardinal rule—you don't mess with your friend's sister—ever.

He steps closer to me. "The night of the engagement party. I asked you to drive Ainsley home."

"Brody," I say, trying to stop him from making those connections in his mind. Every time he caught me smiling into my phone, the day he and Skye showed up and he teased me I was up all night with some girl, he doesn't need to know it was all about his sister.

"You lying bastard," he yells.

"I hope you can get on board with this," I say. "Because I've asked Ainsley to marry me." He throws his hands up. The shock that wasn't there before is definitely there now.

"Jesus Christ," he barks. "Marriage? You do know that's forever, right?"

Feeling the heat rise to the back of my neck, I'm doing everything I can not to lose it with him. That won't serve my purpose here. Just because he and Skye have dated forever doesn't make him the moral authority on relationships. He forgets I knew him before Skye. I could knock him down off his high horse, but I won't.

"Have you ever heard me say I love a woman?" I ask him. We both know the answer to that question. The stiffness in his body relaxes just a tad. "I've said it at least twice now. I'll say it again. I love Ainsley. I love your sister. You know I don't say that lightly."

"You lied to me. You made her lie to me," he says.

"We both know no one makes Ainsley *do* anything," I say. "We're happy, Brody. She makes me so fucking happy."

"It's not your happiness I'm worried about," he says. "It's hers."
That's a little below the belt, but I know he's mad. Shaking his head,
he walks toward the door. "I need to get the fuck out of here."

TWO NIGHTS IN a row, Ainsley cried herself to sleep in my arms
because her stubborn ass brother has yet to return one of her phone
calls. I think she'd handle it better if he just yelled at her. It's the fact
that he's cut off contact that's killing her. Thank God, Skye is still
speaking to her.

I wouldn't exactly say that Skye was happy for me and Ainsley,
but she didn't freak out, either. I guess it's hard for her to be too
supportive when her fiancé isn't onboard. Still, I think if Brody ever
comes around, she'll be happy for us.

Ainsley hasn't asked Skye to intervene on our behalf. She
wouldn't take advantage of their relationship that way. She really
wants her brother to come around on his own. But all this is wearing
on her. We really need someone to be on our side, and I know just
the people.

My parents.

Pulling in front of their house, I groan. God bless my mother,
but why on Earth is she waiting outside? She hasn't waited outside
for me to come home since I was in grade school. When I called and
told her about Ainsley and me, and asked if we could stop by, I didn't
expect a welcome home reception in the driveway, and they don't
even know about the engagement yet.

"Mom," I say when I get out of the car. "What are you doing out
here waiting for us?"

"Oh, I wasn't waiting for you," she says. "I was simply checking
the mail when I saw you pulling up."

"It's Sunday," I say, thinking I've caught her red-handed since the
mail isn't delivered on Sundays.

She simply shrugs her shoulders. "Forgot to get it yesterday."

No matter how old I get, I'll never get an upper hand on her. I walk around to get Ainsley's door, taking her hand. The sunlight hits her ring, and the sparkle can't be missed.

"You're engaged!" my mom screams out, pulling us both into her arms. I look over at Ainsley, a huge smile on her face. She really needed this. Needed someone to be happy for us.

Without warning, my mom pulls back sharply, her eyes right on me. "Wait, are you engaged because you *have* to be?"

Leave it to my mom to not beat around the bush. "No," I say, shaking my head. "We're engaged because we want to be."

"Well, darn," she says. "I wouldn't mind being a grandma in nine months."

Ainsley's eyes turn to me. We haven't even talked about children, other than making sure we don't have any right now. "Where's Dad?" I ask, hoping for a change in subject.

She turns toward the house, walking up the steps to the front door. Wrapping an arm around Ainsley, I lean over and whisper, "I'm surprised she didn't make a request for how many grandchildren she wants."

Ainsley holds up two fingers to me. Guess that's her request. I actually like being an only child, but I can understand why she'd want two. If she'd been an only child, she wouldn't have had anyone when her parents died. At least she and Brody had each other. I hope things smooth over with him soon. She relies on him even if she doesn't like to admit it.

"They're engaged!" my mom yells right as she gets into the house. "Cliff! Did you hear me? They're getting married!"

Before my dad can respond or even appear, my mom turns around, saying, "You should have the ceremony here! We could tent the back yard. It would be so pretty with the water. Oh, at sunset!"

She's unstoppable today. "Mom!"

"No," Ainsley says, taking my hand. "Diane, I'm hoping you'll plan the whole thing with me. My mom's not here, and I . . ."

"Oh honey," my mom says, hugging Ainsley tightly.

My chest tightens a little, knowing my parents think of Ainsley as a daughter already. I know it doesn't replace her own parents, but I can tell how much it means to Ainsley to have them.

"Married, huh?" my dad says, stepping into the den.

My mom holds up Ainsley's hand, showing off her ring. He hugs Ainsley then me. "Did I hear something about a tent in my backyard?"

Mom and Ainsley both laugh. "Don't you think that would be pretty?" my mom asks. My dad looks at me. We both know that tone in her voice. She's about to get what she wants.

My dad simply smiles at her, reading her mind. "We wouldn't want to step on anyone's toes, but your mom and I would very much like to pay for the wedding."

"What?" Ainsley cries.

"Dad, you don't have to do that," I say. "I've . . ."

"I know," he says, "but you're our only child. And with Ainsley's parents gone, we'd like to step into that role." Ainsley and I both thank them a couple times. "Do you think Brody would be okay with that?" my dad asks.

"I don't know," Ainsley says softly.

My parents exchange a glance. I haven't filled them in on all that drama. "Ainsley, why don't you and Mom go look at the yard and see what you think?"

She gives me a little nod, walking out to the backyard with my mom. My dad takes a seat in his chair, the one he always sits in to watch television, and I sit on the sofa. Angling his body toward me, he says, "Guess Brody doesn't approve."

"It's a mess," I say.

"Love always is," he says, grinning at me. "Feels good to be right, though."

"Right about what?"

"You and Ainsley," he smirks. "Called that one."

Laughing, I say, "Yeah, that's what's important here, Dad."

"What's important is that you and Ainsley are happy," he says.

I glance out the back windows, seeing my mom's arms in the air, her grand scheme coming to life. Ainsley's soft profile comes into view, the curves of her body—happiness doesn't seem big enough of a word.

"We are."

"Give Brody some time," he says. "It's nearly impossible to stay mad at happiness, and even harder to despise love. He'll come around."

# CHAPTER SIXTEEN
## FOURTEEN MONTHS AGO

I promise to kiss you every day.
A. Rose

### RHETT

MY DAD'S PREDICTION that Brody would come around has yet to happen. Of course, I never asked how long he thought it would take. The past couple weeks have been total hell. He's managed to give me all the crap cases, literally! I've had every anal expression, all the intestinal parasites, and even an extremely bad case of doggy colitis. If I wasn't trying to smooth things over, I'd take Sadie to his yard to shit all over it.

He avoids the office when I'm in there. We haven't had lunch together or swapped stories beyond what he absolutely has to say to me. By now, everyone at the office and all our friends know about Ainsley and me, so everyone knows why Brody is in a perpetually bad mood. The office staff will definitely get bigger bonuses for having to put up with all this drama.

It sucks, but I can handle it. It's Ainsley I'm worried about. Ainsley's gotten the same silent treatment from him, and she's not handling it well. She's used to him being up in her business, and he's cut that out cold turkey.

She says she's fine, wanting to proceed with our wedding plans, but her tossing and turning all night long tells a different story. Brody and I both love Ainsley, that's our common ground. We just have to find a way back to that.

Walking into Ainsley's condo after another shit day at work, I find her on the sofa with Skye. Sadie's right there with them, looking like the three of them are having girl talk. I barely land a kiss on Ainsley's forehead before she ropes me into their conversation.

"Tell me again what Brody said," Ainsley says.

Not sure what new information she thinks I'll have. We've been over it at least six times a day, every day since I told him about Ainsley and me.

"You haven't told Skye," she says.

Both women stare up at me. There's really not much to tell, but I recount the events for them just the same.

"I keep telling Rhett he should go to the bachelor party tonight," Ainsley says to Skye.

"Ainsley," I say. "I don't want to push anything with Brody, especially on what should be his night."

"No," Skye says. "I think you should go. It would be wrong for you not to be there. Besides, Ainsley will be partying it up with me." Sitting down beside Ainsley, I wrap my arm around her, seeing her ring catch the light. Skye gives us a small smile. "It should feel weird to see you guys together, but it really doesn't."

Skye's right about at least one thing. It would be strange not to celebrate that night with Brody. I helped plan most of it, for fuck's sake. I'm not sure it's the best move, but I'll do anything for Ainsley. Besides, I know I've got no chance up against these two. "All right, I'll go."

"You can blame me if it all goes to crap," Ainsley says.

"Oh, I will," I say, planting a sweet kiss on her lips.

THE ELEVATOR OPENS to the hotel rooftop, overlooking historic Charleston. The hotel is only five stories high, but it's enough to make Brody feel like a king for the night. One of his last nights as a bachelor. The thought of that used to hold no appeal for me, but Ainsley has changed all that. I'm counting down my nights as a single guy, and I won't need a party like this to say goodbye to them. I'll be happy to have them all behind me.

The electricity in the air stops me for a second. The place is lit up like a night club. Music is blaring, and every guy we know is here. Not to mention the women in the tiniest bikinis you've ever seen, hanging by the rooftop pool, serving the drinks. Skye made Brody swear on his penis that there'd be no strippers.

Technically, we aren't breaking her rule, but I'm not sure Skye is going to see it that way. She doesn't have anything to worry about with Brody. He's not a cheater.

Well, he currently is taking a shot out of some very nice cleavage, so maybe this would be a good time to talk to him, before he does something really stupid, something that could alter the course of his life.

Walking over, I place my hand on his shoulder, smile at his bartender, then lead him away.

He looks up at me, saying, "Don't tell Skye I did that." He gives me a look. "I know you're good at keeping secrets."

Guess he's still not over it. "She won't hear it from me."

"I wasn't sure you'd show," he says, blinking his eyes hard one time, the alcohol hitting him.

"Maybe now's not the best time to have this conversation," I say.

"How's my sister?"

I grin. I don't mean to, but she makes me so damn happy. "She's good, but missing you."

He looks off into the distance, looking like he could probably see the ocean from here. I hope the glow of the city below is like a lighthouse leading him back to his family. "Of all the women in the world."

"If I could've stopped it, I would've," I say. "But I love her."

His eyes turn back to me. "I know you do." His head shakes. "I've seen it for years. You're always there for her. I know you'd do anything for her. I just never thought it was more than friendship. It blows my fucking mind. I mean, we talk about women all the time."

"You don't talk about Skye. I think that's what happens when you really love the girl. You don't go spilling shit to your buddies because she's too special, and what you have is too important. At least that's how I feel about Ainsley," I say, feeling like we just might be getting somewhere.

"She lied to me. You lied to me. For months," he says.

"For that, I'm sorry," I say.

"For that?" he asks, his voice losing some of its friendly tone.

"I'm not sorry for loving your sister. I could never be sorry for that," I say. "If you want to stay pissed at me, that's fine, but I need you to talk to her, Brody. She's putting on a brave face, but I know she's hurting. Neither one of us wants that."

He nods.

Thank God, finally some progress. "I appreciate it," I say, extending my hand.

When he takes it, he pulls me close. "Don't hurt her, Rhett. I swear to God, if you hurt her . . ."

"I won't," I promise quickly.

He takes a deep breath. "I've been thinking about this whole thing. It's all I can think about. And honestly, I can't think of someone who'd love her more than you would."

He grins and for the first time in weeks, I feel like I'm going to be lucky enough to keep my best friend *and* marry his sister.

He slaps my back then grabs two shots off the tray of a passing waitress. "Time to celebrate. You need to catch up!"

Maybe it was the shot he took that paved this path. Alcohol does tend to make all things look better. Even the ugliest people look hot with beer googles on. Bad ideas seem great, and dating your best friend's sister doesn't matter anymore. Alcohol made Brody forgiving.

Problem is, it makes me stupid.

# CHAPTER SEVENTEEN
## FOURTEEN MONTHS AGO

### AINSLEY

THE PENIS IS not a pretty organ. Wait, is it even an organ? A gland? What the hell is it? Okay, the penis is not a pretty body part. So why Skye's friends decorated the private room at the wine bar in penis paraphernalia, I'll never know. There have to be classier bachelorette party decorations. There's a big banner that reads "Same Penis Forever" in neon pink, penis shaped shot glasses, penis straws in our ice water. There's even a gigantic penis piñata in the middle of the table. I have it on good authority that it's filled with flavored condoms. Gross!

And I'm sorry, but I am not eating that cake. Penis shaped with chocolate icing for the pubic hair. Um, not so much. But Skye's having a blast, laughing and carrying on. All her friends are here and her fellow nurses. I know most of them. It's a good group, even if their party decorating taste is questionable. At least the wine bar is nice. We started the evening with a private tasting of a half dozen different wines, which turned into a couple dozen bottles. That coupled with very little food, and let's just say the local car service companies are going to love us tonight.

Actually, I've barely had anything beyond the few sips at the tasting. Most people drink when they're nervous, but I'm too anxious to even swallow. Rhett's at Brody's bachelor party just a mile or so from here. He didn't go there with the intention of having some big discussion with Brody, but I don't think either one of them would be able to ignore the situation, especially if they are drinking. Alcohol makes for very loose lips. I just hope it doesn't make for tempers, too.

Glancing down at my phone, I discreetly hit the home button, making sure I didn't miss any calls or texts in the cock loving craziness. Nothing. I really thought I would've heard from Rhett by now about how things went with my overprotective brother. I've had my phone next to me on the table since we arrived.

I jump when I hear a ring, only it's not mine, but Skye's.

"It's Brody," she says, her eyes flying to me. "I swear if he got arrested, I'm going to kill him."

Not taking my eyes off her, I imagine that he's calling her pissed off about Rhett and me. She gets to her feet, her hand going through her hair. She looked completely wasted five seconds ago, but whatever Brody just said sobered her right up.

A few other phones start to vibrate and ring. Something bad must have happened. I really hope Brody and Rhett didn't come to blows. I stare down at my phone, willing it to ring. Why isn't it? Why hasn't Rhett called me?

Skye's hand lands on my shoulder. Every eye at the table suddenly lands on me.

"There's been an accident. Rhett's hurt."

"AINSLEY, DID YOU hear me?" Skye says, now both her hands on my shoulder.

The laughter and fun that filled the air five seconds ago is now replaced by a buzz, a white noise. I can't think. I can't focus.

I see Skye's mouth moving. I hear what she's saying.

Buzz, buzz, buzz.

It's wrong. How much did I drink?

"Rhett's fine," I say, reaching for my purse and digging inside. "He's fine. He's with Brody . . ."

"Honey," she says. "Brody called me. We need to get to the hospital."

"No," I say, emptying the contents of my purse on the table. "He's fine. I'll call him. You'll see. This is some mistake. I just need to find my phone."

Slowly, too slowly, her arm slides in front of me, reaching toward the table. "Here's your phone."

I take it, holding it in my hand, and I stare down at it, like I've forgotten how to use it.

Buzz, buzz, buzz.

"Is he dead?" I hear one of Skye's friends ask in a whisper.

My head whips around, and suddenly I'm on my feet. "He's not dead!"

Skye's squeezing my shoulders now. "We need to get to the hospital."

"He's not dead," I say and look at Skye for confirmation. Her eyes leave mine. "I love him. He can't be. I love him. Skye, tell me," I cry, begging now.

"I don't know," she whispers, tears rushing down her face. "We need to get there."

I hear someone say they've called a car service for us. Turning around, I knock my chair to the floor. Instinctively, I start to bend down, but someone else says, "I've got it. You go." Another person hands me my purse, stuffing the contents back inside. I should thank them, but all their voices and faces are blurring together.

Buzz, buzz, buzz.

My legs start to move. Where's the door? Skye takes me by my elbow, saying, "This way."

High heels aren't made for hurrying, and I wobble. Skye looks at me, and I step out of my shoes, leaving them behind. I'm aware that everyone is staring at me, like they know something I don't know.

"He's not dead," I say to Skye when we reach the sidewalk. "I would know. I would feel it."

She just nods. Goose bumps cover my arms, and I start to shiver.

I've had this feeling before. When the fire came. When my parents died. It was like the flames were burning me, too.

But Rhett is not dead. He can't be. I love him. But I know better than anyone that love doesn't stop bad things from happening. Love didn't stop my parents from dying, and love can't . . .

Buzz, buzz, buzz.

Skye frantically rubs my arms, looking up and down the street. "Where is the damn car?"

Red lights come around the corner, the sound of the siren blaring through the street, drowning out the buzzing in my head. An ambulance speeds past us. "Rhett!" I scream, taking off down the sidewalk, bare feet, chasing it. The cement pounds against my heels, sending a shooting pain up the back of my legs. My heart thunders against my chest, and I can hear my own blood rushing through my veins. "Rhett!"

Doing my best to dodge pedestrians on the street, I struggle to keep up, the sound of the siren fading more and more. I can't lose it. I know he may not be inside, but feel like as long as I can hear the sirens and see the lights, he's okay.

Pushing harder, the ambulance gets to the corner, only briefly slowing down to make a wide turn. The sound of the siren dulls, the lights growing dimmer until they're gone.

# CHAPTER EIGHTEEN

## PRESENT DAY

You are my best friend.
A. Rose

### RHETT

ASS IN CHAIR, staring at my phone, the same routine as yesterday, the day before, and the day before that. My fingers tap my leg, but I don't feel it. The last time I felt my legs was when I jumped into the shallow end of that hotel pool. My butt has been stuck in this chair since.

Paralyzed.

Wheelchair.

Life as I knew it—over.

The life I planned with Ainsley ended before it started. That was my call, not hers. God knows, she fought me on it. In the end, I won. I was a complete bastard to her, but I got what I wanted.

Her freedom.

Not consumed with my bowel management, bladder function, or if or when I'd ever be able to get it up again. I didn't want that for her. I love her too much for that. I'm not going to be one of those miracle stories where the person learns to walk again.

The irony is, I can't feel a thing below the waist. Yet . . .

My hand lands on my chest.

I feel everything.

How much I miss her. How much I love her. How bad I want to see her, touch her, taste her, feel her.

I was just going about my life and boom. Everything changed.

Everything I had planned. Everything I wanted was gone with one splash in the water. I don't remember the first few weeks after the accident, but I remember exactly the moment I realized my fate. It's not the doctors' words that I recall or my parents' sobbing. Those have faded with time. No, that's not what haunts me.

Ainsley's smile.

We just heard I'd never walk again, and she smiled at me. I'm sure she meant it to be reassuring. I know she was just thankful I was alive, but it broke my heart worse than my back could ever be.

In the months after I was released from the hospital, I stayed with my parents, not returning to work, not seeing my friends, not living. It was more than feeling sorry for myself. It was the anger than did me in. Anger paralyzed me more than my accident. For a long time, I couldn't see my way out of it.

Her engagement ring dangles from a chain around my neck, as a reminder of what anger cost me. When I think of the things I said and did to her . . . Of how poorly I treated her . . . It makes my stomach churn, and my chest ache. It was only after I totally crushed Ainsley that I came here, to an inpatient rehab in Atlanta. My parents basically forced me, no longer able to take the hell I was putting myself through.

It's helped. Only about five hours from Charleston, my parents make the trip in to see me a lot. I'll be leaving here soon, ready to live independently. What holds me back now isn't my legs. It's the people I've hurt.

I want to say I'm sorry to Ainsley. I need her to know that. It's been over a year since I've seen her, held her, touched her. A year since I broke her heart, made her cry. It's past time I apologize.

I pick up my phone, punching the first number. I've gotten this far before.

The second number.

My mom and I are close, but I wouldn't say I always do what she tells me. That was never the case, but when's she's right, she's right. Her words echo in my head. *You're hurting her on purpose.* As shitty as I was to Ainsley, even I know you aren't supposed to intentionally hurt the ones you love.

Third number.

Sadie sits up, her tongue hanging out, her tail starting to wag across the floor like a broom, encouraging me.

Fourth number.

Maybe I should leave her alone. From what my parents told me, she has her own store. Her online status tells me that she's trying to move on. It's not fair for me to risk that. I pushed her out of my life.

Fifth number.

This is the farthest I've ever gotten. Fuck, I hate the new calling requirements, that you have to use the area code before all calls. It makes the process even longer and harder. Instead of seven little numbers, I have to do eleven. The damn one plus the area code.

Sixth, seventh, eighth, and ninth numbers come quickly. Before I lose my nerve, I dial the tenth number. Just one more to go.

My finger hovers over the keys. Should I press it? Would she even answer?

I hang up the phone, and Sadie slumps back down.

# CHAPTER NINETEEN

## PRESENT DAY

### AINSLEY

I WANT TO hate him. I've tried to hate him, but I can't, and seeing his parents the other day brought everything back. All the love, all the hope, all the loss, all the pain.

At this point, I doubt I'll ever get over what happened with Rhett. I tried. I really did. I believe in the marriage vows, in sickness and in health. I know we weren't married yet, but we were engaged to be.

Will I ever be done crying over that man?

I cried almost continuously after he was paralyzed. He was out of it for weeks between surgeries and the trauma, so I let myself cry basically all the time. Once I knew he'd live, the tears slowly subsided. Yes, I wanted to be strong for him, but it was more than that. I won't say I was grateful he was paralyzed because that would be sick and twisted, but there was definitely gratitude in my heart. Life without Rhett was so unimaginable to me at the time that I focused on him being alive more than his injury.

I'll never forget that night—the bachelor party—how badly I wanted Rhett to go, hoping it would help the Brody situation. I teased Rhett he could blame me if it all when to shit. Little did I know how that night would turn out. I'll never forget the look on Skye's face as she answered her phone at the wine bar—panic, utter fear.

My phone never rang that night. In fact, I never got another call from Rhett. I stayed at the hospital, never left his side except when the doctors forced me to. God knows, Rhett is as stubborn as they come. Once he broke my heart and banned me from his hospital room, he never called me again.

All this time, not one call.

I never even considered he'd break up with me. That was the furthest thing from my mind. I knew he was depressed. I knew how bad things were, but I thought we'd face it together. Isn't that what love is?

He banned me from visiting, but that didn't stop me from sitting in the hospital waiting room day after day. After he was released and went to his parents' house, I still tried to see him. I tried every day until what should have been our wedding day. That was the deadline I gave myself—a little over six months from the date of his accident. After that, I never tried again—no calls, no emails, no letters. I didn't keep in contact with his parents. I had to make a clean break. If anyone around me has updates on Rhett, they keep it to themselves, and for that I'm thankful. It simply hurts too much.

Tears roll off my cheeks. I have to stop this.

Brody and Skye are on their way over to my condo, and I need to put on a cheery face. They are having some problems of their own. They don't need mine. I invited them over, thinking it might be good for all of us. We don't hang out as a group much anymore. Going from the four of us to the three of us seemed wrong. So when I see them now, it's usually separately.

Holding a washcloth under some cold water, I stare at myself in the bathroom mirror. I avoid mirrors a lot these days. They always say when you're in love, you glow, but no one ever talks about what you look like when you lose love, when it punches you in the gut. Love has done some serious damage. The glow is replaced by a dullness. I'm barely a shadow of the woman I was—a dark figure moving through the sunlight.

Smiling and laughing don't come as easily to me.

Loss has replaced love.

Everything from my skin, to my eyes, to my hair has lost its shine. Taking the washcloth, I apply it to my eyes. Eye creams, cucumbers, cold compresses, I know the dark circles under my eyes are beyond help, but I try anyway.

That's me. I try. I try more than most. I try longer than I should. I try so hard it hurts. Other women would've given up on Rhett the day he tossed them aside, but not me. Some women might have dumped him when he was injured. I never even considered it. I try. I try until my heart will no longer let me.

The phone rings, but I keep the cloth on my eyes as I pick up.

"Ainsley?"

The cloth drops to the floor with my heart.

NOTHING CAN PREPARE you for your ex calling. Nothing. Why today? Why now?

"Rhett?"

He clears his throat, like that's going to erase the awkwardness of this moment. "Hey, how are you? How's Charleston? Brody and Skye?"

"Everything's good. I'm good," I say, still frozen to my spot. Guess I'm a better liar than I used to be, because I'm bawling like a baby. "How are you?"

"I'm doing a lot better," he says.

"That's great. I'm happy for you," I say, and I am. No matter how badly he hurt me. I don't want him to suffer any more than he has.

"I'm at a rehab facility in Atlanta. It's helping."

I had no idea. I didn't know he wasn't in Charleston. I've cut myself off from him, and the people around me have respected my need for a complete blackout on Rhett information.

"I know I have no right to ask, but I was wondering if you could come visit me." I hear his voice crack. Hot tears flow down my cheeks, and there's no hiding my sobs any longer. "Oh, Ainsley, baby, please don't cry. Please, baby."

All it takes is that little term of endearment for me to break the rest of the way. Collapsing to my bathroom floor, I cry, "I waited so long for you to ask for me. You never did."

"I know I shouldn't ask now, but . . ."

"I'm on my way," I say, wiping my tears.

I hang up, grab a duffel bag, fling some clothes and toiletries inside, and am out the door within fifteen minutes. I've waited for this moment for so long, and I'm not about to waste a second. I open the front door and smack right into Brody and Skye.

"Hey, where are you going?" Brody asks.

"Atlanta," I say, closing the door and locking it. "Rhett called. He needs to see me. He's at a facility there."

"I know," he says.

Skye and I both stare at him. He shuffles his feet a little. "I've been writing to him."

"You never told me that," Skye says. He never told me, either.

"Have you talked to Rhett?" I ask.

"I try every week, but he never answers." Brody places his hands on my shoulders. "I'm not sure why he's reaching out to you now, but you shouldn't go alone. Skye or I will go with you."

"I'm leaving now," I say, pushing the button to the elevator. "So I can see him first thing in the morning."

"Ainsley," Skye starts. "Brody's right. Stop and think for a minute."

I don't want to stop and think. I don't want to think about what this means. I don't want to think about what we will say, how we will act, what he wants. I just want to see him, at least one more time. To know that he's really all right. To say the things to him that I never got to say. I want him to see my tears. I want him to hear me scream. I want him to feel what he did to me. But mostly, I want him to see what he lost. For the first time since all this started, I feel a tiny flame in my chest.

They say the second step in grieving is anger. Guess I just got there.

I step inside the elevator. "I'm leaving now. I'll call you."

# CHAPTER TWENTY
## THIRTEEN MONTHS AGO

### AINSLEY

I DON'T KNOW how many days it's been. It all seems like one big nightmare. The days and nights run together; time moves so slowly in the hospital. Every second seems like an hour. He's been unconscious for a lot of it—the trauma, surgery, and different procedures.

I'm thankful he was out for a lot of it. Maybe he won't remember, because I will. Every long second. There's not a detail I don't remember—the color of the hair scrunchy the admit nurse wore, every item in the vending machine, the smell of Rhett's hair when they wheeled him out of surgery. I live and breathe it all. It's as if I'm acutely aware that each minute could be my last, so my senses pick up on everything, but the constant drumbeat in my head is: *It will be okay.*

It's a constant prayer, as if saying it enough can will it to be true. They are the words I whisper in his ear when I'm not sure if he can even hear me. Over and over again, more times than I can remember. *It will be okay.*

A promise. My promise to him. And I always seal it with a little kiss on his lips.

It's truly amazing what we are capable of as human beings. Things you think you could never get through, somehow you do. I never thought I could sit and wait through hours and hours of surgery, never eating, never going to the bathroom, but I did. I never thought I could sleep in a chair for nights and nights on end, but I have. I never thought I could hold in my tears when the doctor told us Rhett wouldn't walk again. But I had to.

The doctors had been vague as to his prognosis, hoping once the swelling went down and the rods were in place, something might change. But yesterday, they finally delivered the final blow.

The paralysis is permanent. He won't walk again.

When something like this happens, there's a lot of stages you go through.

There's the initial shock.

Is this really happening?

Why Rhett?

Then there's the deal making.

Please God, I'll do anything if you make Rhett okay.

Now comes the anger—at least for Rhett. Alert and fully aware of what's happened, he jumped straight to the anger stage, often distant, short-tempered, and in pain.

"Rhett, you have to eat something," I beg. "You need your strength."

"Why?" he snaps at me. "Doesn't take much energy to lay here every fucking day."

"So your body can heal and . . ."

"Did you fucking hear what the doctor said!" he shouts. "I'm not getting better."

"I heard him say you won't be able to walk," I say. "But you will get better. We will learn how to get around in a wheelchair and . . ."

"We?" He uses his arms to pull himself up a little in his hospital bed. "Did you get your back broken, too? There is no *we*!"

I hold my left hand in front of his face, the diamond ring bright as hell under the hospital lights. "We!"

He grabs my hands hard, much stronger than I expected from a man who's been through what he has, pinning them to his bed, pulling me close to him. We're in a hospital. He's been seriously hurt, but the muscles between my legs still clench together. He has to know he still gets to me.

"Remember the patio?" he asks.

The first time we had sex. He knows I remember. He pinned me to the wall and fucked me . . .

Standing up! My eyes start to water.

He releases me, saying, "That's right. We're never doing that again."

"Rhett," I say softly. "It doesn't matter . . ."

"It matters to me!" he shouts. "Don't you get it? I'll never be able to make love to you again."

"No, the doctor said . . ."

A bouquet of flowers flies past my head, slamming against the wall behind me. I look at Rhett, breathing heavy from the throw. "I'll never be able to make love to you the way I want to. We'll never be able to have children."

I know these things aren't true. I've spent my nights Googling and reading everything I can about paralysis. Most patients go on to have full and satisfying sex lives, but Rhett's not going to listen to that right now. He doesn't want to hear that even though most men with paralysis have a problem ejaculating, there are things doctors can do to help. It's not going to matter to him right now. All he's thinking about is what he can't have, not what he can.

"You can't want this. You wouldn't want half a man."

"I just want a life with you Rhett. Any life," I say, sobbing.

"I promised you everything, and now I can't give it to you."

"You *are* everything!" I cry out.

A nurse rushes in, seeing the mess on the floor. I wipe my face, bending down to clean up. There's no reason why the nurse should have to do it. It's not her job to clean up our mess.

"Everything okay in here?" the nurse asks.

"We're okay," I tell her, looking over at Rhett.

The flowers weren't in a vase, so there's no broken glass, but the petals are everywhere, the stems shattered—roses. Picking up the petals, some still look fresh, others starting to wilt. The rose is a symbol of love. Maybe Rhett and I are like the rose. Beautiful, but not destined to last.

Holding my eyes, his voice colder than ever, he tells the nurse, "Get her out of here, and don't let her back in."

# CHAPTER TWENTY-ONE

## PRESENT DAY

### AINSLEY

I WALK INTO a vast workout room, gripping the strap of my purse and scanning the room for Rhett. I made it to Atlanta in record time, spent the night in a hotel close to the facility, didn't sleep at all, second and third-guessed what the hell I was doing. I dropped my life with one phone call from him. I didn't make any arrangements at the store. He called, and I came. Does that make me crazy? Weak? The last time I saw him, he was yelling and throwing things at me. Maybe this is a mistake?

"Can I help you?" a deep voice asks. Turning around, I'm greeted by a warm smile coming from a man in scrubs. "I'm Jay, one of the PT assistants."

"I'm Ainsley Rose. I'm looking . . ."

"Rhett," he says, smiling, and I nod. "He's being stretched out in the back. Come on, I'll show you."

I follow him through the room, trying not to stare at all the men and women with no limbs or those confined to wheelchairs. Before Rhett was paralyzed, I don't think I ever gave thanks for my legs, but I do now. Being here brings it all back.

I hear one man crying, another cursing, others cheering and laughing. I stop "not" looking. This is their reality. They live it every day. The least I can do is not treat them differently. I wouldn't want Rhett to be ignored or deliberately overlooked.

Jay looks back at me, giving me a grin. "How did you know who

I am?" I ask.

"Rhett talks about you a lot."

My legs stop working. Jay turns and looks at me, placing his hand on my shoulder. "It's good you came. He needs to see you." I give a little nod indicating that I'm all right, even though I'm more nervous than I've ever been.

I follow him to a set of double doors. "Ready?" he asks, placing his hand on the door. When I don't respond, he removes his hand. "Take your time."

I know Rhett is just beyond those doors. I've waited for this moment for months. It's finally here. Why am I hesitating? "Thank you," I say. "It's been a really long time since I've seen him."

"You don't have to explain a thing to me," he says, lifting the cuff of his pants slightly, showing me his prosthetic leg.

"I had no idea," I say.

"That's how I know you'll be okay. You see me, not this," he says, motioning to his leg.

"You met me two minutes ago," I say, smiling.

"It's been a meaningful two minutes, wouldn't you say?" he asks with a laugh.

"The thing is, I'm angry at him. Hurt and so many other emotions, and I don't want to lose it."

He shrugs. "Lose it? From what Rhett's told me, he deserves for you to yell at him. Would you have yelled at him before the accident?"

"Yeah. I might have kneed him in the balls."

"Maybe don't do that," he chuckles. "But treat him the same way. He's the same man."

"I know that," I say. "But does *he* know that? That he's the same man."

"I think he's getting there," Jay says.

He places his hand back on the door. After I take a deep breath, he pushes it open, and my eyes immediately land on Rhett sitting on a table in a t-shirt and athletic shorts while a young man stretches out his legs. Rhett's tan and still has the same muscular build. I'd almost forgotten how handsome he is. And he looks so good—strong. Sitting there, no one would ever know he doesn't have use of his legs.

Rhett looks up, his pale blue eyes shooting right at me. I can tell his instinct is to leap off the table and come to me, but he can't. I'll have to go to him, but my legs aren't working, either.

Before I know it, Sadie's running at me, jumping up, her tail moving at lightning speed. She's grayer around the face than she was last time I saw her. I guess this has been rough on her, too. I pat her, but my focus is on her owner.

"A. Rose?" His voice catches. "I didn't think you'd really come. Especially not the next day."

"I told you I was on my way," I say in a whisper then take a few steps toward him, not trusting the kindness in his face.

The last time I saw him, he was so cold, cruel, and angry. But this is the face of my Rhett. This is the man I know. All the hurt, anger, and sadness get pushed aside, replaced with thankfulness. He holds open his arms, and I fly to him, tears flowing down my cheeks, burying my head in his neck.

"You look so much better," I cry. "Like you."

Rhett runs his fingers through my hair as Jay and the therapist excuse themselves. I'm not sure how long we stay like that, but I don't care. I haven't hugged him in so long, and neither one of us seems able to let go. The muscles of his back feel so familiar to me, the way he smells, everything about him. It's like no time has passed at all. Every part of me remembers him.

My phone interrupts our moment, forcing us to release each other. I look down, seeing it's Brody and hit decline. I don't return to my place in his arms.

"Brody," I say.

"Some things never change," Rhett says, taking my hand and stroking my knuckles gently.

He's right, but I slip my hand away. "Some things do," I say.

Using his arms, he pushes himself up and over into his wheelchair. It surprises me how easy it looks for him now. "How about I show you around?"

Nodding, I move toward the back of his chair. He pushes the wheels before I can get my hands on the bars, his subtle hint that I don't need to help him.

I spend the next hour getting a tour of the facility, with Sadie following along. He moves around in his wheelchair without any assistance from me. I find myself forgetting he's even in the chair at all unless I'm looking directly at him. Everything about his demeanor is exactly the way it was before the accident—happy and fun.

The place isn't at all what I expected. Even though it's for rehabilitation, there's nothing "hospital-like" about it. It looks more like a luxury apartment complex, just with very specialized amenities. He shows me the basketball court, tennis court, the various therapy rooms, and counseling centers. Everywhere we go, someone greets me by name. It's as if everyone knows who I am. It's a little unnerving.

Most importantly, Rhett seems happy, adjusted. It's great to see him back to his old self. Still, I wonder why he called in the first place. What am I doing here? Why did he finally want to see me? It can't be to give me a tour.

"The indoor pool's through there," Rhett says, pointing toward some double doors. "I haven't been able to go in there yet."

"I haven't been able to go swimming since, either," I say. "How about we go in there together?"

He gives me a little nod, and I open the door, holding it for him. He slowly rolls in, Sadie beside him. I watch him staring at the water and know he's replaying those fateful seconds in his mind. God knows, I've replayed those hours he was in surgery over and over in mine.

Tears start down my face. "I'm sorry," I manage to say. "You didn't want to go that night. I made you."

He grabs my wrist, gently pulling me to him. "Is that what you think?"

I cling to his shirt, sobbing, unable to catch my breath. "If I . . ." My chest starts to heave, and I can't get out any words.

He takes my face in his hands and whispers, "Stop."

"But . . ."

"Ainsley, stop this right now. This is not your fault. I was drunk and did something stupid."

"It's my fault," I sob.

"Jesus Christ, all this time, that's what you've thought?" he asks, stroking my hair. I nod. "No, baby. We were partying and having a good time. This isn't your fault."

"I thought maybe that's why you didn't want me anymore."

"I promise you," he says, his eyes tender, taking both my hands in his. "You are the reason I lived."

His words make the shattered pieces of my heart break even more. "But after you heard you wouldn't walk again, you refused to see me. I loved you so much, and you just blocked me out."

"I was so angry at the world. I wanted you to have a life. A chance at a normal life with a man who could give you the world, not be a nurse to me."

"I just wanted you, Rhett."

"I'm sorry," he says, his words so honest. Gently, he wipes my tears with his fingers. "I thought I was doing the right thing, letting you go."

If only he could wipe away the hurt as easily as he wipes away my tears. "I loved you," I cry. "I loved you so much."

# CHAPTER TWENTY-TWO
## SEVEN MONTHS AGO

### AINSLEY

I WAITED SIX months, one week, and two days—until what was supposed to be our wedding day. I came to see him every day, sitting in the hospital waiting room, or on his parents' front porch after he was discharged and came to stay with them. Sometimes, like tonight, I sit on the porch swing of his parents' house—other times, on the front steps. The white railings of the porch have been my prison while I wait. Unlike inmates, I have no idea how long my sentence will last, and I don't get any Sunday visits from the love of my life. He's in a prison himself, a self-imposed solitary confinement.

I've been waiting so long the seasons have changed. I've watched the trees and bushes die, the cold wind replacing the Charleston heat that invades most of the year. Even in the rain, I waited.

Every day, I sat and hoped he'd want me.

It's nearly midnight on what should be the happiest day of my life. In five minutes, I'll keep the promise I made to myself. If he doesn't see me, I won't come back. I won't call or write anymore. I'll give him what he wants—a life without me.

Taking out my sewing needle, I place the last fabric rose on the bottom of the dress. This has been my saving grace, my hope—making my wedding dress, the modern version of my mother's dress. Rhett's mother, Diane, has seen me sewing it every day. She comes out to sit with me most days. Many months ago I stopped hoping she was coming to tell me that Rhett was asking for me.

I made her swear she wouldn't tell Rhett about the dress. I wanted it to be a surprise when he changed his mind. And I truly did believe he'd change his mind. He had to. I loved him too much for him not to. There were no other options in my mind. Today of all days, I thought he'd want to see me, but the day is almost over. Does he even know what today is—or would have been? I don't usually stay this late, but I have to see this to the bitter end.

It's so much easier to measure fabric than to measure love. With fabric, you can cut the exact size you need. Love isn't so easy to measure. Sometimes it's too little, you feel neglected. Sometimes it's too much, you feel smothered.

How do you know if a person's love is the right fit for you? How can you measure it? Is it the number of times they say it? The number of times you make love? The number of days you wake up in their arms? You can't measure it. It would be so much easier if you could.

Love is immeasurable.

But when it's the right fit, you just know. I thought that was Rhett and me. I was sure of it.

I hear the door open behind me. I can tell by the slow creak that it's Diane, and she's not bringing me good news.

Without looking up, I ask, "How is he?"

She takes a seat beside me on the porch swing and says, "Same."

Even though he's been out of the hospital for months, he hasn't accepted his new life, choosing instead to sit and stare at the television all day. He does the minimum he has to for self-care, believing his life is over. He's in a dark place. I know he doesn't want me there with him. I know that's what this exile is about.

Diane runs her fingers over the fabric of my dress. She had this whole shindig planned for her son and me. A big wedding here at their house, in the backyard. She talked of tents, dance floors, bands, flowers. Rhett and I weren't engaged for long before his accident, so none of the plans were firm, no deposits set, but in her mind and mine, the wedding was a dream about to become a reality. Of course, it's all lost now.

"You know what I pray for at night?" she asks.

"I'm sure it's the same thing I pray for," I say.

"Yes, for Rhett to get better," she says. "But beyond that, what I want for him most isn't that he goes back to work, or learns to drive a car. My biggest dream for him is the same one I've always had. The one I think most parents want for their children. I want him to find someone. I want someone to love him. Someone who can see beyond his injury." She grabs my hand. "That's you. I know it in my heart, and it tears me apart to see him treating you this way."

All I can do is nod. Holding in my tears takes too much energy for anything else.

"Enough," she says. "Come inside the house. I'm going to make him see you."

In all these months, she's never invited me inside, respecting her son's wishes. There were times I wished she would've, but I realize that's not really what I want. I want Rhett to ask for me, to want me, not to force myself back into his life.

"No," I say. Releasing her hand, I slip my engagement ring off my finger, sliding it into the palm of her hand. "Please make sure Rhett gets this back."

I hear her whimper next to me, but I can't look at her. I need to be brave.

Tying off the last piece of thread, I hold the dress up in the moonlight, the pale pink color of the roses that adorn the bottom of the dress shining under the stars. It's done. And so is my heart. All this time, I could accept his injury, but I couldn't accept life without him.

As midnight comes, I know I have to.

# CHAPTER TWENTY-THREE

## PRESENT DAY

### AINSLEY

RHETT OPENS THE door to the one place I haven't seen on my visit—his room. My heart races as I follow him inside. It's a nice setup—a desk, small sofa, a great view of the green space outside, the bed anchoring the room. Sadie walks in and lays down on her dog bed in the corner. It's silly for me to be so nervous. We practically lived together before his accident, but there's a sudden awkwardness—alone in a bedroom after all this time apart.

"You can relax. It's not like I can jump you or anything," Rhett laughs.

I smile. He always did have a way of putting me at ease. "I can't believe you're making sex jokes."

He rolls his chair closer to me and takes my hand. "I wanted to hold your hand all day, but can't roll and hold hands at the same time." He looks away. "It's the small things that bother me the most." I look down at our joined hands. Rhett's thumb lightly strokes my knuckles. "It's just me and you. You don't have to be nervous."

I slip my hand away from him. "It's been a long time."

"I know," he says softly.

Stepping away, I glance at some books and pictures on a shelf. One of me blowing him a kiss, in front of all the others. "So tell me what you do here. What's a regular day like?" I ask.

"Several hours of different therapies each day to maintain muscle tone. We have classes on simple things like how to get dressed, bathe.

How to play different sports and learning to drive a specially equipped car. Then there's all the talking. We each have individual counseling sessions three times a week. Then there's groups for spouses and children. We have group sessions, too, where we meet with people out in the real world who talk to us about everything from discrimination, to how to travel on a plane, to . . ." He looks into my eyes. "To how to be intimate."

Be intimate? That's not a phrase I've ever heard Rhett use before. Fucking was his word of choice. My stomach clenches, remembering Rhett throwing a bouquet of roses at me, screaming that he'd never be able to make love to me again, that we'd never have children, yelling for me to get out, that I wouldn't want half a man. That was the last time I saw him. All those nights outside on the porch, I was so close to him, but he never would see me. I never went inside. I close my eyes tightly, trying to exorcise the last image of him burned into my brain.

"I'm sorry about that day. About all the terrible things I said," Rhett says.

"I know you were hurting," I say, not wanting to relive it, not wanting to get upset or angry.

"Come here," he says, trying to pull me into his lap in his chair, but I tense. "It's okay. This is a perk of being in a chair. No one thinks twice about your fiancé sitting in your lap."

"Won't I hurt you?" I ask, letting the fiancé comment slide. He can't possibly still think of me that way.

"I won't feel it if you do." He laughs again, encouraging me onto his lap. "How long are you staying?"

"I didn't think about it. Tomorrow, I guess."

"I'm glad you're here now," he whispers. "Will you dance with me? I can't step on your feet now."

He reaches out and turns on some music on his phone, whirling me around in his chair. I giggle, and he smiles at me, slowly swaying me with the chair. Somehow, it feels just the same. I lean my head on his shoulder, and he wraps his arms around me as the music plays. I lift my head, and he cups my face in his hands, rubbing his thumb on my cheek.

He whispers, "I love you. I never stopped. I was just so angry."

I give him a little nod that I understand. I always have. He slides his hand to my neck and pulls me to his lips.

"I've missed you," he groans as his tongue finds mine.

Feeling like my world has just turned upside down, I stop. Before I have time to process what just happened, I feel it.

I pull back, my eyes darting down. A raging hard-on stares up at me. Do I still do that to him? Is this simply a reflex? Surprised, my eyes dart to Rhett's, a devilish grin on his face.

"Still works," he says.

It's stupid, but I start to cry. I'm crying happy tears over my ex's erection. This is one for the record book. I'm unsure what to say. Congratulations doesn't seem appropriate. "Rhett, I'm so happy for you."

"Happy for us," he says, searching my eyes. Confusion sets in, and he senses it. "It won't be like before," he says sadly.

"Rhett, I . . ."

He cups my cheek. "Please, baby, I want to try to make love to you. It's all I think about."

I've never had a panic attack, but now seems as good a time as any—my head starting to spin, my heart pounding, my legs going weak. Will I have to be on top? What if I hurt him? Will he be able to orgasm? Will I?

"It's okay to be nervous," he says. "I'm scared to death, but I need my paraplegic virginity to be lost to you." I can't help but giggle. "You're the only person I trust to do this with. Make love with me, Ainsley," he whispers as his lips land on mine.

Suddenly, I realize this is why I'm here. This is why he called me, what he wants from me. The tiny flicker of anger erupts into a fire storm.

Giving him a hard shove on his chest, I leap off his lap. "Looking for a little fun?" I bark. "That's all I'm good for?"

"You know . . ."

"You know what I know? I *know* I waited for you every day for months, telling myself you'd change your mind, want me. I told myself I'd wait until our wedding day. I was sure you'd see me." I open the door, and Sadie follows me, clearly taking my side.

"I thought I was doing the right thing, letting you go," he says.

I turn back to him, reaching down to pat Sadie one last time. "I would've loved you the rest of my life."

"I didn't want that for you."

"So you threw me away," I say, fighting back tears. "Guess what? I will *still* love you the rest of my life." He rolls toward me, but I step away, motioning between us. "But this? What you just did? I can finally let you go."

# CHAPTER TWENTY-FOUR

## PRESENT DAY

Your name means advice—wish you'd take some.
A. Rose

### RHETT

IF I STILL had use of my legs, I'd kick my own ass. I moved too fast. Clearly, I'm out of practice with the opposite sex. My legs aren't the only thing paralyzed, my game is now non-existent. Shit!

"Ainsley!" I call out to her, following her out of my room and down the hallway.

I'm prepared to roll behind her car all the way back to Charleston if I have to. A hand lands on my shoulder, stopping me.

"Let her go," Jay says.

"It's not like I can run after her," I say, hitting the tires of my chair.

"Wheels are faster than legs."

No one could replace the friendship I have with Brody, but Jay has come pretty close. He's one of the physical therapy assistants here, but he's way more than that. He was the first person I met when I came here. I didn't like him much at first. He told me all the things I didn't want to hear—beginning with, stop feeling sorry for myself. He told me point blank I was being a dick. It took a little bit for it to sink in, but slowly it did. Before I knew it, we were friends.

I look at the door Ainsley disappeared through, wanting to chase after her, but knowing she's gone. I only have myself to blame.

"Let's take Sadie for a walk," Jay says.

Sadie knows the "w" word better than she knows her own name and brings me her leash, just like she has since she was a puppy. I bend down to attach it. Even walking Sadie has changed since my injury. She has to be on a shorter leash now. We've tried all kinds of attachments and different gadgets, but in the end, she wanted me holding her leash, or else she wouldn't go anywhere.

I've gotten the hang of it now, but it took some time. Sadie's gotten used to the tires of the chair now, and knows a safe distance to keep so she doesn't get hurt. It helps that she's older. She doesn't really dart after every squirrel or cat that crosses our path anymore, or get excited at every smell.

I'm not the only patient here who has a dog. Most are service animals, though, trained to do everything from pick up dropped stuff, to turning on the lights, and even pulling a wheelchair if need be. They tried to put Sadie in some classes by herself, to see if she could be an actual service dog, but she flunked out. I guess you can't teach an old dog new tricks. She refused to do anything unless I was with her, so we've basically just figured it out on our own.

The door opens to the outside, and I immediately look for Ainsley. I know she left, but my heart still searches for her. It won't ever stop looking for her. I've been a total ass to her. I know that, but being an asshole doesn't mean you don't love someone.

"What did you think would happen?" Jay asks as we make our way down a little sidewalk.

"I don't know."

"What did you want to happen?" he asks.

My mind flashes to Ainsley naked in my bed. I've got no idea how sex will be now. We have couples come talk to us. It was awkward as hell to listen. We even watched a video one time. You haven't lived until you've watched handicap porn. Yeah, I know I'm not supposed to use that word, but I'm not sensitive about it. Call me whatever you want. God knows, I've called myself worse.

"Seriously, man," he says, shoving my shoulder. "Tell me you didn't go there with her."

"I didn't plan it," I say, trying to defend myself, but knowing there is no defense.

Jay sits down on a bench, rubbing his leg a little. We have different injuries, but we have the same fucking phantom pain. It's a bitch.

"You want to get laid," he says. "I can sneak a woman in here for you tonight."

I know it happens. Apparently, there's a whole network of women and men that see it as their calling to offer themselves to the newly disabled. They consider themselves some sort of saints. Then there are those that have certain fetishes, and actually get off on fucking an amputee or paraplegic.

Those options don't appeal to me. Truth is, I want Ainsley. She's the only woman I've wanted since that night on the patio. I love her. I always have. I just haven't done much of anything to show her I love her recently. She doesn't know that when I lie in bed at night, visions of her carry me to sleep. She doesn't know that she's the first thing I think of when I wake up. She has no clue that I wear her engagement ring around my neck, or that when things get really hard, I whisper her name for strength.

"No, thanks," I say.

"Can I ask you something?"

"You just offered to hand deliver me a piece of ass. I'm pretty sure you can ask me anything," I say with a grin.

"Why'd you finally call her?"

I don't really have an answer for that question. I know it wasn't just my mother chastising me. "It was time."

"Time for what?" he asks. "Fucking? Or something else."

"Time for . . ." The word that pops into my head is *everything*. Time to give her everything. I didn't call her to get her into bed, although that would be a bonus. I didn't call her to simply apologize, although I know I need to—many times. I called for one reason only. "I want her back."

Jay grins. "You're not worried about all the things you can't give her anymore?"

"No, I still worry about that," I admit. "About what she'd be giving up to be with me."

He reaches for his wrist, unbuckling the band of his watch. "I know that feeling," he says, holding out his arm, the jagged scar on his wrist a telltale sign of a suicide attempt. "It doesn't lead to anywhere worth going."

All this time I've known him, I had no idea. Jay's the one that seems to have all his shit together.

I would've never thought his struggle was so bad, he'd try something like that. I'm not sure what the suicide rate is for people like Jay, who have lost a limb. But the suicide rate for those with spinal cord injuries is significantly higher than the general population. For those of us that still have use of our upper body, poison and slashing of wrists are the methods of choice. Others choose to slowly kill themselves by refusing to take care of themselves.

I'm not going to lie. I thought about taking myself out, mostly because I thought it would be easier on everyone else if I'd just died that day. Ainsley could mourn me and move on. My parents wouldn't be spending their retirement on my care. It just seemed like the easier choice. At one point, I even convinced myself that I would be doing it out of love.

Why didn't I take a gun to my head?

Every day, there seemed to be a reason not to. Sometimes they were silly, like who would rub Sadie behind the ear as she likes, or wanting to live long enough to see who won the Super Bowl. Not exactly inspiring reasons to live, but they'd get me through the next hour, and in those early dark days, that was all I could hope for.

I give Jay a nod, and he puts his watch back on. I get the feeling there aren't many people he's ever showed that scar to.

"Ainsley seems like a good woman," he says. "But you better be sure about what you do next. Don't try to win her back only to change your mind again."

"I'm sure I love her."

"You have to be sure you can let her love you," he says.

WHAT DOES IT mean to *let someone love you*?

Since when did Jay become a fucking shrink? God knows we have enough of those in this place. I let Ainsley love me. She loved me on the patio, in bed, on the sofa, the floor, the shower. Basically, she loved me everywhere.

And I loved her. The difference is, when I think about the ways I loved her, they aren't the same ways I let her love me. Sure, I fucked her. But that's just one way I loved her. The ice cream during her time of the month was me loving her. Helping her with homework when she was a teenager was me loving her. Holding her when she cried was me loving her. The nights she laid in my arms, and I listened to her sleep was me loving her. That terrible drawing of a rose I left her—that was love.

I didn't let her love me in those ways. I'm the man. That's the way it is. We don't cry. We don't ask for directions. We provide. We are doers, problem solvers. We want to take care of our woman, our family. Be the man, that's what we are supposed to do. Damn it, I still want to do all those things.

She's let me see her at her worst and at her best.

That's letting me love her.

At my worst, I pushed her away.

That's not letting her love me.

She trusts me to help when she needs it.

That's me loving her.

I didn't let her help me when I needed it.

Denied her love again.

And she's not the only one. When Brody needed my help when his parents died, I was there. But he's been reaching out to me for months now, and I haven't opened one single letter.

Opening my desk drawer, I pull out the stack, knowing they are basically in order from the latest to the oldest. I start at the bottom, pulling out the first letter he ever sent.

*Rhett,*

*There are things I need to say to you, but things I'm not going to write in a letter. They need to be said to your face. I owe you that. I'm not going to stop writing until I hear from you, so your stubborn ass better get used to trying to read my doctor's handwriting.*

*Your desk is right where it's always been. I'm not looking for a new partner. I'm waiting for my partner to come back. I don't care how many hours I have to work to keep the place going. It will be here when you come back. Until then, I'm going to give you weekly updates on all the patients, so when you do come back, you'll be ready.*

The letter goes on to describe Mr. Burgess' crazy cat, a new Macaw patient that swallowed a whole cotton ball, and a myriad of other tales.

Each letter reads like a summary of the patients charts for the week. Occasionally, he throws in some anecdote about Skye, but rarely is it anything personal, keeping his word to only say some things face-to-face.

Flipping the page, I give Sadie a scratch, realizing how much I've missed it, working with Brody, helping sick animals. My life is waiting for me.

This whole time, I've blamed the chair for holding me back, but it's such bullshit. People in wheelchairs work, have families. I could've gone back a long time ago. Only I got stuck looking at all the things I couldn't have anymore, instead of looking at all the things that were right in front of me.

My parents, Brody, and Skye, they've all been waiting for me. I wonder if that's true for Ainsley. From the sound of things, Brody will wait forever, but will his sister?

I made a terrible mistake with her earlier. We started off our relationship with sex last time. This time has to be different. This time, I have to let her love me in other ways. This time, I have to let her love the broken parts.

# CHAPTER TWENTY-FIVE

## THIRTEEN MONTHS AGO

I was prepared to love you my whole life.
A. Rose

### RHETT

I HATE THE door. Yes, the God damn door. I hate it. I hate the door to my hospital room as much as I hate this wheelchair.

That's the door Ainsley walked out of. Granted, I kicked her out, but I still hate that door. Staring at it, day after fucking day, knowing she'll never walk through it again. I could change that, but I won't. I had to let her go. It was the right thing for her.

But the worst pain I've ever felt is what I'm left with, and it has nothing to do with my injury.

Pissed or self-pity—those are my only two moods these days. I'm either pissed at the world, or am too busy feeling sorry for myself to care about much of anything.

Why?

Why the hell did this happen to me?

I've never done anything to deserve this. I'm basically a good person. Work hard, contribute to society, pay my taxes—isn't there some psychopath terrorist this could have happened to?

Everyone acted like it was a major victory that I transferred myself into my wheelchair unassisted for the first time today. Big fucking deal. I didn't cure cancer. I'm literally sitting up. Guess this is how my parents reacted when I was a baby and sat up for the first time, clapping and carrying on. That's when I asked them to leave.

I need a minute alone.

I need a minute when someone's not asking how I am, or if they can get me anything. How the hell do they think I am? And unless someone can bring me legs that work, there's nothing anyone can do for me.

Turning away from the door, my eyes land on another door, the bathroom door, complete with a full-length mirror attached. It hits me. I will never stand in front of a mirror again. I will never see my whole body upright again. Never walk. I will never stand under my own power again.

I will spend the rest of my life looking up at everyone.

The door I hate so much flies open. Brody's got the nurses yelling at him, threatening to call security. I wave the nurses away.

Brody and Skye are on my list of banned visitors, too, although I never told them that to their face. I simply told the nurses and my parents that I didn't want to see anyone. It's been a couple days since I threw his sister out. I'm surprised it took him this long to storm into my room.

Brody and Skye have come to the hospital every day to check on me. They'd come all happy to see me, smiling, trying to encourage me, bringing me a stupid trinket or something. I really hate seeing people smile these days. I don't have the energy to smile back, and frankly, there's nothing to be happy about anymore.

"You promised me you wouldn't hurt her," he says, his voice straining to stay calm when he obviously wants to kick my ass. "Ainsley's sitting in the waiting room, crying. She's been there for days and days. I'm not sure she's left or eaten anything."

"Take her home," I say. "Take care of her."

"You need to see her," he says.

"No."

He shakes his head at me in disbelief. "So that's it? You're just going to continue to refuse to see me, Skye, all your friends, our employees, everyone that cares about you? You're going to break my sister's heart?"

"Don't stand there now and act like you ever wanted me to be with her!"

He releases a deep breath. "On the roof that night, you asked me to talk to Ainsley. You told me she was hurting and wanted me to talk to her. I'm standing here now, telling you the same thing, and asking you to talk to her. Ainsley doesn't deserve this."

I wave my arms over my broken body. "I don't deserve *this*!"

Brody winces and runs his fingers through his hair. "Rhett, I know you're going through hell, and this is terrible, unfair . . ."

He continues for another minute or so, saying the same kind of thing with different adjectives. I can tell Brody is uncomfortable. Most people are uncomfortable around someone in a wheelchair. They don't know what to do or say. There really is nothing *to* say. Wish Sadie was here. She'd give me a lick instead of a lecture . . .

Shit. I'll never walk my dog again.

I interrupt his monologue, saying, "I did what I thought was right. It's better to break her heart now. Look at me, Brody," I demand. "You want this for her? Does it get any worse than your sister marrying a . . ."

"It could be a *lot* worse," he says.

"That's not possible."

"You could be dead."

"Better than a life like this," I snap back.

"You can't mean that."

"I do," I say, looking him straight in the eyes.

A shocked breath of air leaves his chest. Maybe now he's finally getting it. Maybe at last he has some sense of understanding of how I feel. I push myself towards him. "I won't be able to stand at the altar and marry Ainsley. I won't dance with her at our reception. I won't carry her over the threshold. Don't you get it? I won't be able to . . ."

"You need to learn the difference between *won't* and *can't*," he says, looking down at me. "Because you *can* still marry her. You *can* still dance with her. You *can* still carry her. You *can* still love her. You're *choosing* not to."

Here we go: Focus on the positive. Mind over body. Everyone from my parents, to the doctors, nurses, and shrinks all spouting the same crap at me. I don't need to hear it now from Brody. Fuck all that. Go peddle that shit somewhere else.

"Look, I feel so bad this happened to you. I really do," Brody says. "Everyone does. I just think . . ."

"You said all this before."

"I'm just trying to help," Brody pleads.

"I don't need your pity."

"Of course not," Brody bites out, "because you're doing a damn good job of feeling sorry for yourself."

In all the years we've known each other and lived together, through all the horrible things we've been through, we've never spoken to each other like this before. These are the last words we will ever say to each other.

"Get the fuck out of here."

# PART TWO

PRESENT DAY

# CHAPTER TWENTY-SIX

## AINSLEY

MY CHEEKS ARE hot, but this time it's not from tears. I'm pissed. I drove five hours to see him. Five hours for him to make a pass at me. What the hell did he think? I'd just straddle him in his wheelchair, and we'd go at it? A new song starts playing through my radio. Fittingly, it's Kurt Cobain singing, "Where Did You Sleep Last Night?"

It's funny how songs do that. How you can hear a song at the exact moment you need to hear it. Kurt is taunting me, and I remember a quote of his, "Nobody dies a virgin. Life fucks us all."

Dude might have had his demons, but he hit the nail on the head with that one. I crank up the song.

We want to believe that people change. Maybe some can. But movies, romance books, love songs all depict the hero changing for the "right" woman. Maybe women need to take that as it is—Fiction.

I mean, if I had a daughter, and she brought home a guy like Rhett, would I want her to marry him? Or would I tell her to run screaming for the hills? And my advice would have nothing to do with his broken back, but everything to do with the fact that he's a big ass jerk deep down.

I'm sick of men and their moods. Women get a bad rap for being moody, but men can give us a run for our money in that department. I read a whole article on it. It even has a name: Irritable Male Syndrome. IMS is the male version of PMS. And Rhett seems to have an extreme case at the moment.

Damn him! All the times I imagined what it would be like to see him again, I never imagined him asking me to take his *paraplegic virginity*. I mean, is that even a real thing? Or did he just make that shit up?

Honestly, up until that point, things had been going well. I guess they were going well enough that he expected a little nookie to top things off.

Does he really think that's what I need from him?

He's really bad at the whole feelings thing. I was never a big science person in school, preferring literature and history, but if I recall correctly, the heart is a muscle. And muscles need to be used or they atrophy. Rhett may have been doing tons of physical therapy at the rehab center to get his body back in shape, but he's probably been snoozing through whatever therapy programs they offer, or skipping altogether. His heart needs to pump some serious iron.

I left, got in my car, and started driving. The open road hasn't been good for my mind. Nothing ahead of me but stretches of highway, too much space and time to think. Distracted by my anger and grief, I smell the ocean air before I realize that I haven't driven back to Charleston, but to Kiawah Island—our secret escape.

I haven't been back here since the last time I came with Rhett. I'm not sure what led me here now. Maybe this is the final step for me to let him go, to finally accept that what we had is over.

Parking my car, I don't open the door or roll down my window. I don't want to smell the ocean any more than I have, or be kissed by its breeze. It's dark out, making it impossible for me to see the water. There's only a vast void of darkness. Perhaps that's fitting.

In the morning, it will give way to a majestic blue. The promise of a new day is ever-present. I haven't lived with that promise in a very long time. The life I wanted was shattered. Truth is, I may have stopped sitting on his parents' porch, but I've still been waiting. Yes, I opened my shop and business has been good, but personally, I've been in a holding pattern.

I used to want to fall in love, get married, raise a family more than I wanted anything in life. I wanted what was stolen from me as a child. The thought of having those things again used to make me so happy, but now I can't even imagine them.

Maybe Rhett was right after all. Maybe we should've stuck to his original plan for us. Maybe it's time I just have fun. There has to be a bar and a hot single man around here. Turning around, I look for neon lights, the telltale sign of some mischief. I don't see any, but find I'm parked right next to a hotel. They must have a bar.

Checking my reflection in the rearview mirror, the lip-gloss and mascara I put on before I saw Rhett has all washed away. My strawberry blonde hair isn't brushed, and my bloodshot eyes look like I've already tossed back a few. Let's hope there's dim lighting.

Hopping out of my car, I head into the lobby. The smell of fresh cut flowers fills the air. In that instant, I realize I've been here before. My body freezes as memories flood back, like Rhett kissing me right outside the elevator door, the king size, four post bed he playfully tied me to.

I have to stop doing this to myself. It's time to make new memories, erase Rhett from my psyche, permanently.

Taking a deep breath, I stop at the doorway of the bar. There are no neon lights to be found. Instead, the barstools are covered in leather, the tables and chairs a deep, rich wood, and the staff all attractive. Time to make some new memories. I've never had sex with a bartender. I hear Rhett's voice in my head . . .

*And you never will.*

"Fuck you, Rhett!" I say under my breath.

Making my way to the bar, I glance at the bartender's hand, a gold band on his finger. All right, I guess Rhett wins that one, but there are plenty of other men in here. Glancing around, I have no idea how to do this. Sadly, I've never picked up a man in my life. Two serious boyfriends, that's my number. I'm not even sure how to give off the *I'm available* vibe.

I'm in jeans, so I can't hike up my skirt higher, and my shirt doesn't have buttons, so I can't even show cleavage, not that I have much. Potentially, I could sit here all night alone. It's up to me to make a move.

Suddenly, a drink slides in front of me. The bartender grins, motioning to a man at the end of the bar, who raises his glass to me. I guess a woman alone at a bar is enough to give off the available vibe. My next bedfellow isn't bad looking, either. Probably early thirties, he's wearing a dress shirt, the top few buttons undone. A man's version of cleavage. His sleeves are rolled up, and most importantly, there's no ring on his finger.

There's no point in wasting time or pretending this is something it isn't. I push the glass back toward the bartender. "Ask him if he has a room."

The bartender doesn't seem fazed at all. He's probably heard and seen it all. I watch as he walks to the other end of the bar and leans in to relay my message. Smirking, the guy raises one eyebrow at me. He hands some bills to the bartender then gets to his feet, grabs his jacket from the back of his chair, and makes his way toward me. He's broad shouldered and tall.

My heart starts to pound. This isn't like anything I've ever done in my life.

"The answer to your question is yes," he says, looking down at me. His eyes are a deep brown, his voice rough.

"Good," I say.

He reaches into his pocket and lays down a twenty-dollar bill for the bartender, like he's paying for my drink, only I didn't have it. Guess he's paying him for relaying my message. Then he casually takes my hand, intertwining our fingers like he's known me forever.

His hands are smooth, so he must not do manual labor for a living. I hope he's not one of those guys that gets manicures. That's just too weird. Leading us over to the elevator, he pushes the button. "What's your name?" he asks.

It takes me longer to answer than it should. "Skye." Sorry, Skye, I'm using your name as my one-night stand alias.

"You didn't have to lie," he says as the elevator door opens, and we step inside.

"I'm a terrible liar," I admit.

"I see that," he says, grinning.

"I don't usually do this type of thing," I say.

Good Lord, why do I feel the need to explain myself to this stranger? The plan is to fuck him without apology.

"I can tell," he says, leading us out of the elevator and down the hallway.

"How?"

"You're not exactly dressed like you're on the hunt for a man."

"So when you sent that drink over?" I ask. "This isn't what you wanted?"

"You're not stupid," he says. "Make sure to thank him for me."

"Thank who?"

"Whoever the bastard was that hurt you enough that you came to the bar tonight, alone."

My legs stop moving. He's figured me out in less than three minutes. Am I that transparent? This isn't going to help me get over Rhett. I could fuck the entire eastern seaboard and not forget Rhett.

What am I thinking? Having a fling isn't going to heal my broken heart. I'm not doing this *for* me. I'm doing this *to* Rhett. That's the opposite of what I want to do. I don't want to do anything for him anymore, give him any more of my time. I'm doing this to hurt Rhett, and that's just not good enough.

As soon as I release his hand, he knows I've changed my mind. He simply gives me a nod, understanding.

Who knew a one-night stand could be such a gentleman?

# CHAPTER TWENTY-SEVEN

## AINSLEY

"I LOVE THE dress in the window," my new client says. She's getting married in two months, and is hoping I can design and sew a dress for her. She's delusional. Custom made dresses usually require at least six months lead time, but her husband-to-be is in the military and being deployed. They want to get married before he leaves, and I want to help them. "Would you consider selling it?"

"It was my mother's dress," I say quickly. "So I'm afraid not."

I leave out the rest of the story. I like each dress I design to have a story, but that dress, the story of my dress, isn't a fairytale. My mother is gone, the original dress is ashes, and the man I was supposed to marry in that dress was seriously injured. I couldn't sell it in good conscience, even if I wanted to. The dress is obviously cursed. I should probably have an exorcism preformed on it.

"Besides, you want something unique to you."

My store is more a design studio than an actual store. I don't have dresses on racks. Because my designs are one of a kind, there aren't samples to try on. I do have an extensive portfolio, and shelves and shelves of different examples of crystals, beads, and laces. The whole point of what I do is that no one will have the same dress. Each of my dresses is unique and special, like the women who wear them.

"Can you do it?" she asks. "Is there enough time?"

The door to my shop opens. Skye and Brody both walk in. My store stays open later than both the vet and fertility clinics, but the last time they were in my shop together was when they helped me move in. Now they are showing up unannounced. It doesn't take a rocket scientist to figure out something's up.

I refocus on my client. "No beading?"

"Lace," she says, her face hopeful. "I love lace. And I have this from my grandmother that I plan on wearing for you to draw inspiration from."

She reaches into a box, revealing a cathedral length veil. It looks like something a princess would wear. Inspiration strikes, my head starts spinning with ideas. Taking it from her, I hold it up. "I see a simple dress. Maybe a sheath. Something classic, timeless." I place the veil on her head. "Low cut back."

"Oh my goodness, he'll love that," the bride-to-be says. "So you'll fit me in?"

I nod, and she nearly leaps into my arms, hugging me. Brody gives me that proud brother smile of his. I'm glad he's proud, but I have no idea how I'm going to pull this off. Two months isn't enough time, not with my current client list. Oh well, sleep is overrated. I finish up with my new bride then turn the store sign to closed.

Turning back around, I feel like I'm about to face the firing squad. "Okay, what's up?"

"Nothing," Brody says. "We're just on our way to dinner and thought we'd see if you'd like to join us."

I don't believe that for a second. "As you just heard, I've got less than two months to make her dress, so . . ."

"Just tell her," Skye says to Brody.

I've never seen him look at her the way he is, full of annoyance. "Brody, what's this about?"

"Rhett," he says, placing his hands on my shoulders.

It's been two weeks since my visit to see Rhett. Two weeks of him calling and texting. Two weeks of me ignoring and deleting all his messages. I never told Skye or Brody about what happened at his facility. They asked, but I don't have the energy to get into it all. My silence on the subject was enough for them to gather it didn't go well. But from the look on Brody's face, they know something I don't. "Is he hurt? Or . . ."

I feel my body start to tremble, and Brody hugs me. "No, nothing like that. He's fine. He's really good, in fact."

He encourages me to sit. Can it be good news? No one ever says *I think you should sit down* before they give you good news. But this little sofa is where I usually reveal my designs to my brides. Only happy things happen in this spot.

Skye doesn't sit. I wonder if that's because the news is bad or if she's simply letting Brody and me have a sibling moment. "So I guess you talked to him," I say.

Brody looks up at Skye, who simply raises a disapproving eyebrow. "Actually, I went to see him," he says.

"You what?" I nearly fall off the sofa in shock, as Skye gives Brody an *I told you so* look.

"Why? When? Why didn't you tell me?"

"Remember, he was my friend first, before he was anything to you."

"What the hell is that supposed to mean? How can you say something like that to me?" I snap, getting to my feet.

"Wait, sis," Brody says, shaking his head. "That came out wrong. Of course, I know what you had with him was more . . . I know you're hurting more. But he is my best friend."

*Is.* That little word holds a lot of meaning.

"I told Brody to tell you before he went," Skye says.

"I wanted to see what he had to say first," Brody says.

"And?"

"He's coming back to Charleston. To the clinic. The condo. He's coming home."

"No!" My whole body shakes, rejecting the very idea that Rhett will be living in the same building as me again, working just down the street, with my brother. "No," I say again and continue to repeat the word. No part of me is ready for this. No part of me is ready to see him again. I can't be hurt by him again—not daily, not in person, not anymore. I can't.

"Ainsley, he's coming back for you," Skye says.

That stops me cold.

"He didn't say that," Brody says, glaring at his wife.

"It's obvious," Skye says sarcastically.

"Skye," he snarls, "Ainsley doesn't need your theories right now."

"Shut up, both of you!" I cry. "What the hell is wrong with you? I lost the love of my life. You two still have each other. Grow up."

They look at each other, both of them knowing I'm right. I really don't have the energy or patience to deal with their stuff right now. Apparently, my stuff is on the verge of coming back to town and bringing a heaping pile of emotional shit with him.

"I feel like when Rhett got hurt, we just fell apart," Skye says quietly.

"It's my fault," Brody says. "We should've gone ahead with the wedding like you planned."

"No," Skye says. "Cancelling the big wedding was the right thing to do."

Skye and Brody's wedding was set for just two weeks after the accident. When Rhett got hurt, they cancelled. Instead, they ended up having a simple service, just the two of them and Skye's parents. I wasn't even there. She didn't wear the dress I made. I wonder if Rhett knows any of that.

"We should have it now," Brody tells her. "Like you wanted."

My brother can be very sweet when he tries, but I can tell Skye's not convinced, shaking her head and saying, "Maybe."

He pulls her into his arms. "I've been working so hard because I wanted to keep business healthy for when Rhett came back. I needed to believe he'd find his way back."

My eyes catch his. All these months, he's been waiting on his friend like I waited. He taps my nose.

"I don't want you to feel like I'm picking sides," he tells me. "I made it very clear to Rhett how I feel about the way he treated you."

I nod. "It's not like you can force him out of the business. I know that."

"That's not it. Rhett offered to back out of our partnership. It was me who insisted he come back."

Turning my back to him, I cover my mouth. It's stupid. He knows I'm crying. So what if he hears it.

"He was coming back to Charleston no matter what."

All the pain in my chest explodes. "I'm really glad you're getting your friend back, Brody."

"Ainsley, don't be that way."

"It's too much, Brody. It's just too fucking much. Please go."

My brother steps toward me, but Skye stops him. "Rhett wasn't supposed to be done with his program there for another couple weeks," she says. "But he's leaving early. He'll be back in Charleston the day after tomorrow."

"Of course," I say, holding everything inside. I can't let it out. The anger, the pain, the hurt, the sadness—it's all in a box inside my heart like the breakup box in my closet, only if I take off the lid of this box, I'll never get it back on.

"He won't start back to work for a little bit," Brody says. "Some of the doorways are just standard size, and . . ."

"It's a tight fit for his chair," I say, looking at the front door to my shop, remembering how I insisted on double doors. The idea that Rhett would come through my door still a hope in my heart all those months later. "I know."

"So we're going to widen a few. Make a few of the exam rooms more accessible for him," Brody says.

"That's great," I snap, knowing I'm being bitchy, but unable to stop myself.

Skye takes Brody's hand. "This is a lot on her. We should go."

He moves toward me, but I step away. "Skye's right. You should go."

It's not in Brody's nature to leave me when he knows I'm upset, but he also knows when he's not going to get anywhere with me. Tonight is one of those times. I need some time to digest all of this, figure out how to handle it. I follow them to the door, letting them both kiss me on the cheek before they go. When the door closes behind them, I turn the lock.

But the lock on my heart opens, and I sink to the floor and cry.

# CHAPTER TWENTY-EIGHT

You will never be alone.
A. Rose

## RHETT

FROM THE SIDEWALK, I look up at the building. The last time I was inside my place was the day of my accident. I went from the hospital, to my parents' house, to the rehab center. I've never been back. My condo has been empty a long time. I left a lot of things empty.

I wonder if Ainsley's inside at her place. Is she at her dress form working up her latest design? Is she taking a Sunday afternoon nap? Does she know today's the day I'm moving back? Does she care?

I've tried and tried to call her, text her, but she won't respond. Serves me right after the silent treatment I've given her and hitting on her the way I did.

"Ready?" my dad asks.

He came to Atlanta to help me move back to Charleston. I didn't have much at the rehab center outside of some clothes and a few pictures, but he still made the trip. He brought my new car with him, equipped with hand controls for the brake and gas. I tried to tell my parents that I didn't need a car. The vet clinic is close to my condo, and most grocery stores deliver now. I thought I could do without one for a little while, but they surprised me with it. Honestly, I thought the last car my parents would ever buy me was when I turned sixteen, but they want me to be as independent as possible, and consider transportation as part of that deal.

So I drove the whole way back from Atlanta myself. It's about five hours, and we only had to stop once. My dad looked just as nervous as he did when I was sixteen, but we made it without incident. I think he hoped that my lead foot would have disappeared with my inability to actually feel my feet, but nope. I still love to drive fast.

I'm grateful to my parents but hate that they've had to do so much for me. They foot the bill for my rehabilitation program and hospital bills that my insurance didn't cover. They've been paying the mortgage on the condo as well, refusing to touch my savings, even though I insisted they sell it. They wouldn't, never losing hope that I'd one day return to my old life.

Today is the first step of that.

Normally when I drive, I transfer into the driver's seat, remove the wheels of my chair, lift it to the passenger seat, and I'm ready to go, but since my dad was in the passenger's seat today, we stored it in the backseat.

My dad carries a bag, reaching for the front door to the building. I can't help but smile. He's been with me through this whole process—he should realize that I can open my own door. Things like that used to piss me off, but now I realize he just wants to make my life easier. So if opening my door makes him feel like he's helping, I let him. No use in getting mad at someone who has the best of intentions.

Rolling inside the foyer of the building, I take a deep breath. Ainsley is so much a part of this place. The walks with Sadie, the rides up the elevator—she's everywhere. I guess if she wants to avoid me, she'll just take the stairs. No chance of running into me there.

The elevator door opens—empty. Guess it's too much to hope for to run into her my first day back. Still, I find myself holding my breath, praying the elevator will stop on her floor, but no such luck.

We reach my floor, and using my arm, I hold the elevator door open for my dad to exit first. You don't lose your manners when you lose control of your legs.

"Promise me there's not some big surprise party in there waiting for me," I say.

"Just Sadie," he says. "And your mother. That should be enough for us to handle."

Apparently, my mother's been in high gear since I announced that I was checking out of my program early. My dad says he's barely seen her. She's been in full-on renovation mode, making sure there's enough space for me to maneuver my chair, making sure all kitchen essentials are in lower cabinets, remodeling my closet so all my clothes hang on the lower racks, hiring people to install a shower hose and chair. I hear she's even had an ADA toilet and grab bars put in. Yes, my mother is even concerned about the comfort of my ass.

I appreciate it all. I really do, but if you can't have a good laugh about your mother talking to you about the cushioning on your toilet seat, then what can you laugh about?

My dad opens the door to my place, walking inside. For a second, I just sit, peering inside. I know at some point I'll probably build my own house, something designed for my new life, but right now this feels perfect. It feels like I'm right where I'm supposed to be.

Sadie barks, running toward me, jumping up, her front paws in my lap. My parents brought her back to Charleston a week or so ago. It's the longest we've been apart since I was in the hospital. Obviously, she missed me.

"Hey, girl," I say, rubbing her ear. I watch my parents out of the corner of my eye, seeing them holding each other tightly.

This has aged them. Since my accident, my mother hasn't had her nails done. She's let herself go gray, no longer keeping her hair color appointments every six weeks. But at least she has her hair. My dad lost more than he cares to admit. I've been in Atlanta for a while, but they didn't pick up with their old routines. I'm not sure if it's because money is tight for them now, or if they just don't find those things important anymore. Either way, they are reaching the age where I should be the one taking care of them. That's what I plan on doing. This chair will not stop that.

"I did as I promised and kept everyone away," my mom says, kissing my cheek.

The one person I did want here, I couldn't have my mother invite. I have to fix things with Ainsley on my own. I roll around, seeing all the work my mom has had done, and thank her for each and every detail. She truly did try to think of everything, down to the easiest place for Sadie's dog food.

"We do have one little surprise," she says.

"You guys have done enough," I say.

She walks toward my spare bedroom. I hardly ever used that room. I had it set up as my home office, but rarely needed it. She opens the door, stepping inside.

"What did you do?" I ask in disbelief. My home office is now my home gym. I know these specialized machines cost a shit ton of money.

"Jay recommended free weights and the FES bike," my dad says, holding up one of the electric stimulators that will attach to my legs to help pedal the machine.

When I first was hurt, all I could think about was all the things I could no longer do. The more time that has passed, the more things I've discovered I can still do. They had a ton of activities at the rehab center, like wheelchair tennis, which I completely sucked at. I wasn't much of a tennis player when I had use of my legs, not sure why I thought it would be different now, but I play a mean game of wheelchair basketball, and plan to find a local team to join.

I have a binder full of exercises I can do from my chair to keep in shape. You'd be surprised how hard a sitting ab routine can be. I still have my six pack to prove it. I can't believe my parents did all this, although I don't know why I'm surprised. They've been with me every step of the way.

"I'll pay you guys back for all . . ."

They both wave me off. My mom says, "We're really proud of you, honey."

I reach out and take her hand, sensing she's about to cry on me again. I swear, I've seen her cry more since I said I was coming home than when I was first hurt. I guess she'd rather I see her cry happy tears than sad ones.

"We should let him get settled," my dad says.

My mom promptly looks at him like he's insane. "I thought we should stay a few days just in case . . ."

"It's my freshman dorm room all over again," I say, chuckling. "Remember Mom booked the campus hotel for the first two weeks?"

"I managed to get her out of there in four days," my dad says proudly.

"Hey," my mom says, smacking both our shoulders. "Remember, you didn't pack your underwear, and I had to go buy you all new pairs, Rhett. You were glad I was there then."

"Mom, I'm not eighteen," I say softly. "I'll be all right."

"I still think it would be best if we stayed. Just tonight."

"Honey, we aren't that far away. Rhett will call if he needs us," my dad says, giving me a look that I better or else.

I hate that we are back to this, back to them worrying about me like this. I know they mean well, but I feel a certain anger bubbling up inside, and I reach for what rests against my chest.

The memory of the day my mother handed me Ainsley's engagement ring is still fresh. It was just after midnight on what should've been my wedding night. I expected my mother to pour some tough love on me, but she simply placed the ring in my hand and walked out of my room. She didn't need to say anything else. I knew what Ainsley returning the ring meant. She wasn't coming back. Even though it's what I thought was best for her, even though it's been months since that night, the pain of knowing she was truly gone still makes my heart feel like it's being stabbed with a hot welding iron.

Holding onto the ring, I take a deep breath. It's not fair what happened, but I don't have to let it consume me.

"I will," I promise. "And you can call and check on me."

She looks toward my dad, unconvinced. "It would make me feel better if Ainsley could . . ."

"No," I say, sharper than I should.

Ainsley's not talking to me right now, and I don't want her to start out of obligation. I know she wouldn't be able to deny my parents if they asked her to look in on me. Hell no, that's not happening.

"We'll see you soon," my dad says, giving my mom a nod. I know she doesn't want to go. But she knows what I really need is for them to do just that, to allow me to start my life again on my own. So they both kiss and hug me, promising again to see me soon, then leave. The door closes behind them, and I turn to look at Sadie.

Sadie and I spent a lot of time alone in this place. I realize it's been a long time since I've been alone, really alone. In the hospital, a nurse or doctor was always close by. At my parents' house, they hovered like a Black Hawk helicopter always on a mission. In the rehab center, I had my own room, but I was surrounded by other patients, staff. This is the first time in a long time that it's just me.

It's up to me to take care of myself.

If I ever want to take care of someone else, I have to be able to take care of myself. And I want that. I want to be able to take care of my parents as they age. I owe it to them. It's what I'm supposed to do. And more than that, I want to be able to take care of Ainsley. I may not be able to walk beside her, but I can still carry her.

I'm ready.

# CHAPTER TWENTY-NINE

I'm still here, waiting.
A. Rose

### RHETT

MY FIRST DAY back at home went well enough. My mom only called three times. Add that to the three texts she sent, and it's less than I expected. I'm trying to be patient with them. If this chair has taught me anything, it's patience. Everything seems to take longer than it used to. Maybe that's by design, life forcing me to slow down and take a good, hard look at myself, at the pain I've caused, the people I've hurt.

Brody's on that list, but he seems to be over it. Have to say, it surprised the hell out of me when he knocked on my door at the rehab center, suspecting he was there to kick my ass after how I treated Ainsley. There was definitely some cursing, a brief lecture, but that wasn't the main purpose of his visit. To put it simply, he just needed his buddy back.

Running the vet clinic alone is exhausting. Things with Skye have been tense, and he just needed to get some of it off his chest. If I wasn't already set to go back to Charleston for Ainsley, his visit would've sealed the deal. I'd have gone back for him. I'll see him tomorrow at the clinic. I'm not working yet, but he wanted to go over the renovation stuff with me and make sure everything is covered. I'll be going over around lunch time. Apparently, he has an hour window in the middle of the day where he doesn't see patients. That was never the case when there was two of us, but I guess for his sanity, he had to do something.

My plan tonight is to take Sadie out for a walk then try to crash early, yesterday's drive and moving back now finally catching up with me. Holding Sadie's leash, I wheel my chair through the sidewalks of Charleston. No longer can I walk her through the park. It's not because my chair can't go through grass. It can. I have to do a series of little wheelies, and managing those with Sadie isn't the easiest thing in the world, so now we stick to sidewalks and search for little patches of grass.

Gone are the poop bags that attach to her collar. I smile, remembering Ainsley concerned that Sadie was embarrassed carrying them. Since bending down isn't an option, I carry a special scooper for our walks now. Guess I'm the one that gets to be embarrassed now.

It's pretty late out, so the streets aren't crowded. It makes it easier to get around, but also, I'm still not quite used to the stares. You'd think in this day and age that people would know better than to stare, but they still do. I used to love catching a woman glancing my way. Now the look is usually sympathetic, not horny.

Sadie sits down on the sidewalk. Good God, old age has made her lazy. More than once, I've had to put her on my lap and wheel her home. That's always good for some stares, too.

"Come on, girl," I urge. She whimpers a little. "What's wrong?"

She just continues to sit, staring across the street. I look up to see what has her attention. *A Rose Wedding Dress Designs.* Now I know Sadie can't read, but she's starting to freak me out with how intuitive she is. I knew Ainsley opened a place, but I didn't know exactly how close it was.

I moved back knowing that I want her in my life, but having no plan on how to make that happen. It's late and dark except for the streetlights, so I don't expect that Ainsley's inside. But I'm too curious not to take a peek. Plus, I don't think I could get Sadie to go in any other direction.

Crossing the street, my eyes fix on the dress in the front window. My mom showed me a picture of it, but seeing it behind the glass, my heart stops. They say it's bad luck for the groom to see the wedding dress before the bride is walking down the aisle. I don't think Ainsley's and my luck could get any worse than it has.

I stop, staring at the dress. I've seen her sketch her mother's dress a thousand times, but never, never did it look like this. Strapless, it looks like the top is almost see-through lace, but it's the bottom that captures my attention. It looks like a rose, the faintest pink color. So pale, you almost don't notice it. Each flower looks as if it's been lightly painted, etched ever so carefully with some words, but I can't make it all out.

A. Rose.

My rose.

It's perfect, safe behind the glass. If only Ainsley were as untouched as that dress. If only I hadn't ripped her to shreds the way I did. My throat starts to tighten up on me, the angry words I said to her, all the hurt I caused, still burn in my throat, deep in my soul. The guilt sits in my belly like a rock. I hurt her so deeply. I hurt her more than I'm hurt.

The worst part—it was all lies. I hurt her to get her to leave. I yelled and cursed and threw things to force her out. I *wanted* her to give up on me. It took months and months for her to finally let go. Each day was torture. Every day, I wanted to tell her I loved her. I wanted to hold her close, but I believed she'd have a better life without me.

Deep down, there's still a part of me that believes that. I'm not sure I'll ever be able to shake it, but I'm determined to use that part of me to make me love her that much more. That's the only way I'll ever get her back.

Love her more.

Let her love me.

Love is the answer.

"SURPRISE! WELCOME BACK!" the entire office staff screams out in unison as I roll through the front door of the vet clinic.

I should've known Brody was up to something when he suggested I leave Sadie at the condo. He knows she hates loud noises, always hiding during thunderstorms. I made my parents swear they wouldn't make a big party out of my return, but I never made Brody make the same promise. I've never been hugged by so many people in my life. Everyone from the vet tech to the guy who delivers our mail is here.

The crowd parts when Brenda heads toward me. Her eyes ripple with tears, and it's all I can do not to let mine do the same. She's the lifeblood of our office, the heart. She doesn't say a word as her arms go around my neck. After that, I swear there's not a dry eye in the house. I even see Brody wipe away a tear. Life is funny. Often, we move through it without realizing just how much we're loved. Sucks that it takes something like this for us to realize that.

"Enough of this," Brenda says. "I ordered cake!"

Everyone's tears are washed away by the promise of a little sugar. Without realizing it, my eyes search the crowd.

"Ainsley's not here," I hear a familiar female voice say.

Turning my head, I find Skye walking toward me. Her face doesn't look nearly as welcoming as everyone else's. Brody warned me that things between them were rocky. He told me Skye was different now, and I guess I just assumed that was him blaming her instead of taking his share of the responsibility for their problems. But seeing her in person, I know exactly what he means.

"I didn't expect she would be," I say, reaching out for her. "It's good to see you."

She doesn't hug me. In fact, she doesn't move one inch closer to me. "I'm glad you're doing better," she says with a politeness that's more *go fuck yourself* than sincere.

"I'm sorry I missed your wedding," I say then shake my head. "Ruined your wedding."

She laughs sarcastically. "That's what you apologize for? You're sorry I didn't get to wear a fancy dress and toast with champagne?"

"That was just my warmup apology," I say, grinning, trying to make her ease up.

"Whatever," she snaps, turning away, then smacks right into Brody, who takes one look at us and knows something is wrong. Holding my eyes, he places his hand on her shoulders, whispering something in her ear.

I see her shoulders tremble a little, and Brody pulls her into his arms. He flashes me a small smile to let me know she's okay. I'm beginning to realize the people closest to me each handled my accident in different ways. Some cried a lot. Some worked a lot. Some disappeared. Some soldiered on. And some, like Skye, just got pissed.

Some people wrap themselves in their sadness, wearing it like a blanket. Skye wears her anger like an armor. She didn't want to hurt. Maybe she *couldn't* hurt, too busy dealing with everyone else's pain to deal with her own.

"Skye's mad at you," Brody says, grinning at me.

"Think I got that," I say.

"She's been taking it out on me for a long time," he jokes, and she playfully smacks his shoulder, pulling slightly away from him. He looks down at her, tucking her hair behind her ear.

"Skye," I say, "why don't we go talk alone somewhere?"

"The office?" Brody suggests.

When she takes a step in that direction, I follow her. She doesn't hold the doors open for me. She doesn't look back to make sure I'm all right. It's kind of refreshing. We make our way to the office, and I'm amazed at how much cleaning up and clearing out Brody has done. There was no way I could've moved my chair around in here before, but now there's plenty of room.

Skye leans up against his desk, her arms across her chest. "I'm on

Ainsley's side."

"There are sides now?"

Her eyes narrow. "Yes, and Brody may think everything can go back to the way it was, but . . ."

"It can't."

"No, it cannot," she says, articulating every syllable. "You crushed them. You crushed the two people I love the most in this world besides my parents."

"I know."

"No, you don't," she barks. "You weren't here. You wouldn't see us. Brody has done nothing but work, trying to keep things exactly the same for when you came back. And Ainsley . . ."

"What about A. Rose?"

"I'm just barely starting to be able to recognize her again," she says. "She's been a shell of herself. So don't tell me you *know*. Because you have no fucking idea."

I know what I did. I know how bad I hurt them all, but knowing it and having it staring you down are two different things. "A wedding should be one the happiest times in your life. Instead, you and Brody got married under this umbrella of tragedy. I can't imagine what that must've been like."

"Hell! How could we be happy? While you were in such pain! It's impossible." She unfolds her arms, glaring at me. "You will never understand."

"Skye, I wish I knew what to say to you. I was in bad shape after the accident. I didn't want Ainsley to see me like that. I didn't want her to spend her life taking care of me. I'm sure you know it was a really bad time for me. I was in a dark place. I can't explain it."

"It was a bad time for all of us," she says.

I realize in that moment that Skye doesn't need me to apologize. She needs something very different from me.

"Thank you, Skye."

The angry shell she wears so proudly cracks, and she sinks down into Brody's chair.

"You've been taking care of both of them for me," I say.

She starts to cry softly. "We were supposed to be a team. Me, you. Remember? All those years ago, Brody thought we were helping him with Ainsley, but you and I, we both knew we were holding them both together when their parents died. Me and you! We got them through that together."

Inching closer to her, I nod and understand. She's been doing this all on her own, keeping Brody and Ainsley okay. In that moment, I realize Skye is another person I left. I abandoned her.

"Didn't realize I meant so much to you," I joke.

She breaks into a full-on smile then points her finger at me. "I'm still on Ainsley's side."

"I know, I know," I say, placing my hand on top of hers. She takes my other hand. "I am sorry for leaving you alone with this. I'm here now. I'm staying." She nods, a little forgiveness settling into her soul. Grinning at her, I say, "So I hear you want to have a baby?"

# CHAPTER THIRTY

## AINSLEY

MY EYES FLUTTER open, a vision of white greeting me. My head shoots up from my makeshift pillow.

I fell asleep sewing a wedding dress. Dear God, I hope I didn't drool on it or get makeup on it. A tiny rap on my door turns my attention that way. I see Skye shaking her head at me through the window. Oh crap, we were supposed to meet for a movie night.

I get up, unlocking the store door for her. "Sorry, I'm being buried alive in organza."

She looks around, her eyes holding a judgment I'm not used to seeing from her. "When's the last time you left the store?"

I guess the takeout cartons in the garbage can are a dead giveaway. "What do you mean?"

"I mean, those clothes look like you slept in them."

"Well, you did just catch me napping."

"Ainsley," she says. "Are you avoiding going home?"

"Now why would I be doing that?" I ask.

Playing stupid does not agree with me. We both know why I'm avoiding the condo.

"I saw Rhett the other day," she says. "Brody had a welcome back party for him at the office. I went on my lunch break."

"I know. Brody left me some message about it."

"Which I guess you didn't respond to."

"Nope."

She exhales. "I told Rhett I'm on your side."

"You don't need to do that," I say. "I don't expect you and Brody to not be friends with Rhett. I just can't."

"Good," she says. "Because Rhett and Brody are having a guy's night."

"It's been a while," I say, as my gut violently jerks, like I've got the worst food poisoning in the world. The last time they hung out together, Rhett got hurt. "Let's hope they're not drinking this time."

Skye steps back slightly. "Do you blame Brody for that night? For what happened?"

Shaking my head, I say, "No, of course not."

"I know you aren't happy about his return, but I think it's going to be good for Brody. Rhett's going to be taking over some afternoons at the clinic so Brody can have some time off. It will be good for Brody to have his friend and partner back."

"I hope so, for Brody's sake."

Letting out another deep breath, she says, "I think we need some ground rules now that Rhett's back."

"I don't need rules."

"Well, as your best friend, I do," she says. "Do you want me not to even mention his name? Or is it okay for me to talk about him?"

"I think denying his existence is best," I say.

"Okay, Rhett Bennett is officially removed from our topics of conversation."

"Perfect," I say.

"Good," she says, a big smile on her face. "Because I have news! Brody and I have decided to go ahead . . ."

"And get married again!"

"Not exactly," she says. "We're going to have a big party, more like the reception would have been."

"I think that's great. Will you wear the dress I made for you?"

She nods. "I'd like to have some wedding pictures. Everything was so crazy when we actually got married, we didn't bother. So this time, I'll wear the dress. He'll wear the tux, and we'll get to celebrate with everyone we love."

I'm sure that includes Rhett, but I'm not about to rain on her parade. "When?"

"Hopefully, in a month or so," she says. "Now let's get you out of here and grab some snacks for movie night."

"Is snacks code for wine?"

"Not tonight," she says.

I've never known Skye to turn down wine. Beer, sure, but not wine. Taking her by the elbow, I ask, "What have you done with Skye?" She simply smiles. "Oh my God, are you pregnant?"

"Shh!"

"So you are pregnant?"

She shakes her head. "I don't know. I was supposed to start today, and I haven't. It's probably stress."

"Well, let's get a test and find out!"

"I'm like twelve hours late," she says. "I don't want to get my hopes up."

My whole body starts wiggling with excitement. "A baby! I'm going to be an aunt. You're going to be a mommy!"

Her face breaks into a full smile. "Maybe I could take a test."

"Yes," I say. "As long as you don't want to do that with Brody?"

She shakes her head. "I don't want him to know if it's negative. I only want to give him good news."

"Well, come on," I say. "Let's go buy a test."

She points to her purse. "Swiped one from the office today."

We both squeal a little bit. Suddenly, I can't wait to get out of the store. We head to my place because Skye thinks Brody and Rhett might be at theirs. Plus, my place is closer, and Skye doesn't want any evidence at her house, not even hidden in the trash can.

I wonder how this must feel for Skye. This is what she does. She sees couples get happy news and disappointing news every day. I've never had a pregnancy scare, never taken a test.

"Have you ever taken one of these before?" I ask.

She stops dead in her tracks. "Why would you ask me that?"

"I haven't, and I was just curious if you have."

"It doesn't matter," she says.

I take her by the elbow. "Skye?"

Her eyes well up. "Brody doesn't know."

SKYE QUIETLY CRIES on my sofa. I hand her a glass of water, wondering what the hell is going on with her. She takes a sip then says, "Remember all those times you made me promise not to tell your brother something?"

"Yeah."

"I need you to promise me now," Skye says. "Promise me that you won't tell Brody what I'm about to tell you."

I look down, knowing Skye has always kept her word to me, but feeling guilty I can't give her the same promise. If she did something to hurt my brother, I'd have to tell him. Still, I know Skye, the kind of person she is. She wouldn't do anything to intentionally hurt Brody, so I go ahead and say, "Promise."

"Remember when Brody and I broke up for those few weeks back when he was in vet school?"

"Yeah, he was crushed."

"I was pregnant," she whispers.

I remember things being really tense, but I didn't have a clue what was going on. "Brody didn't want the baby?" I ask.

"No!" Skye cries. "I never told him. He doesn't know."

"I don't understand. Why wouldn't you tell him?"

"I was really scared. I mean, you were living with him. Your parents hadn't been gone long. He had a lot of responsibility on his shoulders. I didn't want to add to that."

"So you . . ." My heart starts to pound in my chest. If she tells me she aborted my brother's baby, there is no way I can keep that from him. No way!

"He was with you somewhere. I can't remember. I was waiting for you guys to get back, so I could tell him. But I started having these sharp pains, really, really bad cramps. I ended up having a miscarriage."

"Oh Skye!" I say. "And you never told Brody?"

She shakes her head. "Rhett found me on the . . ."

"Rhett? He knows?"

She nods. "He took me to the hospital. Stayed with me. They had to do a D & C."

"I don't understand," I say. "Why the breakup?"

"I was a mess," she says. "Emotional. Bleeding for a few weeks. I needed to hide that from Brody. I just couldn't face him."

"Skye, he was heartbroken."

"I know," she says. "It was Rhett that finally got me to talk to Brody again, but I couldn't tell him. Your parents were gone. I didn't want to tell him our baby was, too."

"Rhett kept this a secret for you?"

Skye nods. "He took care of me those few weeks, checking on me, bringing me food, letting me cry, trying to convince me to tell Brody. I never did."

"Why does Brody think you broke up with him?"

"I told him I was overwhelmed by everything at work, his school, caring for you," she says. "I lied to him. Leaving him so suddenly for those couple weeks, I think that's why, once we got back together, it took him so long to propose. I think he always wondered if I would just up and leave him again."

"You're married now," I say. "You should tell him."

"What's the point?"

"Love shouldn't lie," I say. "If love should be anything, it should be honest."

I know that better than anyone. If you truly love someone, you should never lie in the name of love. Never lie to spare them pain. Love them enough to tell the truth. Then love them enough to sit in the pain with them. That's what love truly is.

She reaches for her phone. "I'm going to call Brody. Suddenly, I don't want to pee on this little stick without him."

Makes sense, I think. They should share this together. But before

I can suggest Skye skip movie night and go home, she's got the phone to her ear.

"Where are you?" I hear her ask. "Oh, I thought you were at our house."

Crap, I wonder if that means they're upstairs at Rhett's place.

"Can you come down to your sister's for a minute?" she asks him.

My suspicions were correct. They're both here. Suddenly, my stomach does a flip.

"Skye, you shouldn't do this here with me," I whisper. She says bye to Brody and hangs up. "This should be a private thing with you and Brody at your place."

"Ten minutes ago, you were all set to take the test with me," she says.

"Well, that was before you invited Brody. Shouldn't this be something the two of you do together? Not the three of us?"

"Just be honest," she says. "You're worried it's the four of us."

"Well, yeah."

"Brody wouldn't bring Rhett down here," she says. "He's not stupid."

As Skye utters those words, the door flies open, and we both turn to find Brody's stupidity on full display. Rhett is right behind him in the wheelchair, both of them rushing inside like my condo is on fire, like they are on a rescue mission.

Skye called Brody, not Rhett. How dare Rhett come down here, too? Barge inside? Not even knocking?

Rhett's pale blue eyes soften when they land on me. Obviously, he was worried something was wrong with me. I knew he was back in town, but it wasn't real until this moment, until I laid eyes on him. He's really here, in my place. He looks even stronger than he did a few weeks ago when I saw him. And God help me, he's still the sexiest man I've ever laid eyes on. It doesn't matter that he's in that chair. He still makes my whole body tingle. I hate that it does. I wish I could move on, forget him. He hurt me when he abandoned me.

He hurt me again in Atlanta. I can't be hurt by him a third time.

Brody's eyes go between Skye and me. "You're both fine?"

"Of course," Skye says.

Brody shakes his head, smiling. "When you asked me to come down, I thought something was wrong."

Byproduct of having multiple tragedies in your life, you start to think every phone call is the next disaster waiting to strike.

"No," Skye says, glancing at me. "I have to take a test, and I wanted you with me when I do."

"Huh?" Brody says, looking back at me and Rhett. "A test? You've been out of school for . . ." He stops, his forehead wrinkling up. A grin comes over his face. "Really?"

"Maybe," she says in a hopeful voice.

I watch him stroke her arms so delicately, like she's made of pure glass. I know they've had a rough few months, but the love between them was never lost. There's a disbelief in these moments, like you're out of your own body. I know the feeling. Only last time it happened to me, it was after I heard Rhett was hurt.

"Let me get you home," Brody says to Skye.

"Actually," Skye says, looking at the three of us. "I think it seems fitting for us to find out together. We've all been through so much."

Brody looks back at Rhett and me for our thoughts. We can't really say we don't want to share this moment with them, no matter how uncomfortable we are being in the same room together. Well, I'm not sure how uncomfortable Rhett actually is. We both just give little nods.

Skye reaches for her purse. "Ainsley, can I use your bathroom?"

"Sure," I say. "You know the way."

She takes Brody's hand. "I'm coming?" he asks.

Skye glances at Rhett then back to me. "Yeah, there's something I want to tell you while we wait for the results."

They disappear into my bedroom, closing the door behind them, leaving Rhett and I staring at each other. Last time we were here, I was convincing him to go to Brody's bachelor party. Rhett pushes the wheels of his chair, inching a little closer to the center of the room. The seconds tick by, each one seeming longer than the next. I used to love laying in his arms in the quiet stillness, but now the silence is torture.

"Do you think she's actually pregnant?" he asks.

I shrug. What a stupid question. How the hell am I supposed to know?

"She told you about what happened before?" he asks.

Assholes are always good at vague questions. Well, I can be as aloof as the next gal. I nod.

"You know, we're going to have to learn to be in the same room together," he says, earning another nod. "You're going to have to talk to me. I mean, we're probably going to end up being godparents to that baby."

"Then we'll have something to talk about. Right now, we don't."

"Ainsley, I want you to know how sorry I am about what happened last time I saw you."

"You mean, when you thought I'd just fuck you?"

His eyes close. "It was a mistake. I'm sorry. I know you're upset with me."

"Upset?" I snap. "I'm so *mad* at you. I don't know that I've ever been this mad in my whole life. And it's just not about that day. It's about all of it. All these months. My love wasn't enough. Do you know how that feels?"

"I'm sorry."

"Stop saying that!" I bark. "Apologizing is not the answer."

"Ainsley," he says gently.

Holding his gaze, I say, "I want you to hurt, like I hurt. I hate that I want that. I hate that I'm this person. But I want to do something to hurt you, like kiss another man right in front of you, just to get back at you. How terrible is that? I mean, you've been hurt more than one person should, so how horrible am I that I want to hurt you?"

He smiles at me. "For the first time, this chair might be an advantage."

Does he really think he can charm his way out of this one? That smile isn't going to work on me this time. I can't believe it. I won't let my heart believe it.

The bedroom door opens, Skye is tucked safely under Brody's arm, her eyes red. One firm shake of his head lets us know the results aren't what we all hoped. The room feels very heavy. I knew that she might not be pregnant, but I didn't realize how much I really wanted her to be. How much we all wanted her to be. How much we all need a win.

"Next time," I say, walking over and wrapping her in my arms.

Brody leaves her side, and I hear him whisper to Rhett, "Thank you."

I guess he is not holding Skye's secret against Rhett. I guess he's just too thankful that Rhett was there for her.

"Glad she finally told you," Rhett says to Brody.

"Brody, let's go home," Skye says softly, and he nods, placing his arm back around her.

I follow them as they head to the door, giving them both a hug. Rhett does the same, but doesn't follow them out into the hallway. Brody looks back at him.

"You guys are heading down. I'll catch the elevator on the way back up," Rhett says.

That makes sense, but I know there's more to it than that.

The elevator door opens, and Brody and Skye step inside. When the door closes behind them, Rhett says, "We spent our whole relationship making sure you didn't get pregnant." His head shakes as he looks down at his chair. "Seems stupid now."

He moves past me, pressing the elevator button. I stand in the doorway, confused by what he meant. Does he wish we had a child together? Or is this more of him worrying he won't ever have the chance to be a father?

Obviously, he's not over all the ghosts that haunt him.

# CHAPTER THIRTY-ONE

You promised me everything.
A. Rose

### RHETT

"FUCK!" I SAY through gritted teeth. It's God's cruel joke that I can't move my legs, yet I have phantom nerve pain. Sadie jumps up on the bed with me, whimpering like she feels it, too.

I have pills I can take, but I hate the way they make me feel. So much of my life is out of my control, I don't like to feel even more out of it. Looking over at the clock, I see it's late. Too late to call anyone to distract myself, but laying here staring up at the ceiling while it feels like my legs are on fire isn't going to work, either.

There's no telling what brought this on. Sometimes no matter what I do, it just happens. But I suspect the long drive home, the stress of the last couple of days hasn't helped. Sadie lays her head down on my legs, and the pressure actually takes the edge off a little. I reach down and pat her.

"One, two, three . . ."

Counting and breathing sometimes help. Why is this happening right now? I've got to get some sleep. Tomorrow, I planned on looking into a wheelchair basketball league or figuring out how to train for a half-marathon. Physical fitness is important for someone like me, and I can't be lax about it for one second. I rely on my upper body to keep me mobile, so I can transfer in and out of my chair, take a shower, that kind of thing. So I can't let up. I was so pissed and depressed after my accident that I lost some muscle definition. It's taken me a long time to build that back up, and I'm not going to lose it again.

The worst thing to do is lay here and think about the pain. I learned that the hard way. The more I obsess over myself, the worse things are. It's always better to think of others before myself. That helps with the pain. It actually helps with everything.

I pick up my phone and text Brody. I know it's late, but I doubt he's sleeping, either.

*How's Skye?*

They both looked so disappointed about the pregnancy, or non-pregnancy. I don't think they've been trying long. I missed their wedding, so I was really hoping they got good news. I don't want to miss any more big moments in their lives. My phone dings.

*I haven't talked to her.*

What? How do you avoid talking to your wife about a negative pregnancy test? Not to mention, the other thing she told him. Brody isn't the most sensitive guy, but still! I start typing a response, then I see what I've done. Oh shit.

I didn't message B. Rose. I messaged A. Rose!

My heart starts to pound in my chest. I hope I didn't wake her. I guess she's not sleeping, either. She responded to me. That's a good sign, right? And her response was quick, so she didn't agonize over what to say or anything. But it was kind of short, to the point. Does that mean something? Shit, I'm taking a long time to respond, although, her response doesn't exactly have to illicit a response from me. Damn, I'm really overthinking this. I have her attention. I can't let this opportunity pass.

*How are you?*

Burning a hole in my phone, I wait for the three little dots to appear. I wait and wait—trying to will a response from her, but there's nothing. I can't blame her. I've been an asshole. My phone screen goes black, and Sadie softly snores. I push out a little grin. My legs don't hurt as much anymore. Was it Sadie who made the pain bearable? Or something else?

Ainsley makes the pain bearable. Ainsley makes life bearable. No, that's not true. Ainsley makes life . . .

She makes my life. That's it. Just that.

Ainsley makes my life.

Then there's a light in the darkness, my phone screen coming to life, bearing one little message.

One little word.

*Goodnight.*

"HOW'S THE FIRST week home been?" Jay asks.

He's called a couple times to check on me. The only person that checks on me more is my mom. She still calls or texts at least three times every day. My dad has promised me that he's working on her, but I understand these things take time.

I fill Jay in on the basketball wheelchair league I joined, how they're going to let me play in the next game even though I just started. I'll probably ride the bench the whole time. I tell him about the changes at the office, explaining that I start working later today. Brody and I decided I'd start back half days a few days a week then work my way back up to full time. Frankly, I would've preferred to hit the ground running, but he insisted we take things slow. I think my parents must've gotten to him. I'll be working mostly in the afternoons so that Brody can cut out a little earlier. He has a wife to get home to. I think that's making Skye happy.

"The woman?" Jay asks.

"Sadie is fine," I laugh.

"Ainsley?" he clarifies, as if I didn't know who he meant.

"I've got to get my ass to work," I say.

"Rhett, your legs may not work, but your heart does."

"What the hell does that mean?" I ask.

"It means next time I talk to you, I want to hear that you've made some progress with that girl. I liked her."

I'm tempted to hang up on his fake philosopher ass, but I laugh instead. "I'm working on it," I say before hanging up.

Truth is, for the first time in my life, I'm not sure how to handle a woman. I used to be a master at making a woman smile, knowing just when to make my move, but now I'm lost. I don't know if it's best to give Ainsley space, or if I should be showering her in flowers and phone calls.

The only good thing is, I've got a lot of other things to keep my mind occupied: going back to work, living on my own for the first time since the accident, the new basketball league I found.

Because it's my first day, I decide to leave Sadie at the condo. She used to come to work with me, but I thought it might be best to leave her at home today. Besides, she's getting up there in years, and I think she enjoys a few hours of having the place to herself to just sleep.

"Wish me luck," I tell her.

She lifts her head at me but doesn't bother to remove herself from her place on my sofa. Clearly, she's not concerned about how today is going to go. The office isn't that far, so I won't be driving. I used to walk to work. Now I'll just wheel there. So that part of my day is basically the same as before.

It's a beautiful, sunny day in Charleston. Thank God I don't have to deal with any weather issues on my first day. Wheelchairs and the rain aren't the best combination, and I refuse to wear one of those stupid ponchos made for people in wheelchairs. Yes, I am that vain. The sidewalk is crowded with tourists, but it doesn't matter to me. When people see a wheelchair coming, it's like the sea parting for Christ himself. I stop at a crosswalk, waiting for the walk sign.

"Zoom, zoom," a little voice says beside me.

I look over at a toddler, holding his mother's hand. "Shh!" she whispers to him.

"Zoom, zoom," he says even louder, pointing at me.

His poor mother looks absolutely mortified. Unable to help myself, I bust out laughing. You've got to love kids. They are just as honest as animals. You know right away if they hate you or love you. And this little guy isn't scared by my chair or looking at me like I'm any different from him. In fact, I think he's jealous I've got wheels. I'd give him a ride, but his mom would probably freak out at a strange man offering to take her son for a lift, and rightfully so.

"I'm so sorry," his mom says, shaking her head. "Thank you for understanding."

The sign turns to walk, and I hold my hand up to the kid to give him a high five. "Zoom, zoom," I say, as I wheel away, hearing him giggle behind me.

I'm still grinning when I get to the office. Brenda's at the front desk as usual, but there aren't any more tarts waiting in the lobby. I guess they got word that Brody's married, and I've no longer got use of my legs. I won't miss them. Brenda greets me with a smile, giving me a brief rundown on the day's schedule.

I'm not sure how Brody kept this place going without me. Even when there were two of us, we were busy as hell. How he managed it solo, I'll never know. But I suspect that's a big reason why his relationship with Skye suffered the way it did. More than one relationship was hurt by my actions. I haven't made much headway with Ainsley, but I know taking some of the burden at work will help Brody and Skye.

Plus, it feels damn good to be in my scrubs again. When I was in the hospital, I hated seeing the nurses and doctors in their scrubs and lab coats. Jealous doesn't begin to describe how I felt. But now I'm back. There were a lot of times I never thought I'd see this day.

Brody did a good job renovating this place in such a short time. A few extra inches go a long way. I guess that's true for doorways and dicks. I'll have to remember that for when Ainsley is talking to me again. She always laughed at my sex humor.

Grinning, I wheel into the office. My smile turns into a huge laugh when I see the welcome back gift waiting for me on my desk. Motherfucker left me a Wheelchair Barbie. She's blonde with a purple and pink chair, and she's poised right in the middle of my desk.

"At least she's not a blowup," Brody says behind me.

I laugh, but there's a twisting in my gut. Brody still sees me as the same guy, the one who used to get a ton of women, never commit. It makes me happy he's not treating me any differently, but I'm not that guy anymore. And it doesn't have anything to do with my chair. Believe it or not, you can be a male whore without use of your legs.

It has nothing to do with my accident. It has everything to do with his sister.

Ainsley—not my accident—changed me forever and for good.

"Welcome back," he says, giving me a look then dropping a couple dozen files in front of me. "I saved you all the anal glands that need to be expressed, all the cysts that need to be popped, and every possible intestinal parasite."

"You couldn't save me one new puppy case?" I ask. There's absolutely nothing like seeing a little kid holding his new puppy.

He laughs, then his face turns serious. "If you need anything, or if it feels like too much . . ."

"Brody," I say, appreciating his concern, but this isn't us. We don't get all emotional and sappy with each other, and there's no reason to start now. "I'm good."

I grab the first patient file off my desk, and the day officially begins.

"KILLED THE FIRST day back at work," I tell Sadie, attaching her leash to her collar. I'm sure she's probably got to piss, but you wouldn't know it by her demeanor. She barely even acknowledged that I'm home. A tilt of her head, a wag of her tail, but she stayed on the sofa. Lazy thing!

I glance around my place. Ainsley's always on my mind, how she was always waiting for me when I got off work. I want to share my good news with her, tell her about my day. And I want to hear about hers. My first impulse is always to pick up the phone to call her and tell her when something exciting happens. Even after all this time, I can't shake that desire.

I want her to be here when I get home, for us to walk Sadie together, have dinner, make love to her until we both fall asleep. Instead, it's just Sadie and takeout. The life of a bachelor, I guess.

"Come on, girl," I say, shutting the door and pressing the elevator down button. Since she played hooky today, I have to go back out to walk her.

The elevator stops one floor below mine. My heart immediately jumps in my chest, hoping Ainsley is the one waiting to go down. The doors open, but no one is there. Damn it! I guess I'm not that lucky.

Sadie rests her head on my lap. Her eyes are still as bright as when she was a puppy. Stepping out of the elevator, my luck changes. I see Ainsley stepping inside the building. I only have a second before she spots me, just long enough for my heart to start to ache.

Our eyes meet, but before I can say a word, Sadie starts barking like a fool. Ainsley might hate my guts, but she still loves my dog, coming over to give Sadie some love.

"I miss you," Ainsley says to Sadie, giving her a hearty scratch.

There's so much I need to say to her. *I'm sorry. I love you. I want you back*, but none of those words seem sufficient, and I doubt Ainsley wants to hear any of it.

"Want to take a walk?" I ask before realizing how stupid that sounds, since I can't walk. "I mean, would you like to walk Sadie with me?"

She looks everywhere but at me. This is how she and I started in the first place, those innocent walks with Sadie that led to so much more, but her hesitation now is torture.

"I'm trying to throw you a line here, Ainsley," I say. "I hope you'll take it."

"What about all the times I threw a line to you?" she asks, pressing the elevator button. "I'm sorry, Rhett, but I don't want this. When I look at you, all I see is . . ."

"The chair," I say softly.

"No," she says. "All I see is the man that hurt me. You look at me and remember us falling in love, our friendship. I remember the pain, the pain of sitting and waiting for you, the pain of leaving my ring with your mother. All of it. If you came back to Charleston for me, it was a mistake. Your A. Rose isn't here anymore."

"Then I'll love the woman that is."

# CHAPTER THIRTY-TWO

## AINSLEY

HE'LL "LOVE" THE woman that's here? What the hell is that? He wouldn't know love if you beat him over the head with it. A woman knows her limits, and I just hit mine.

Picking up the phone, I dial my brother. Right when he answers, I say without hesitation, "I'm moving out of the condo."

"Why?" he asks, drawing out the word like he's afraid of my answer.

"It's time," I say. "Since you own it, I wanted to let you know. So you can decide if you want to sell it or rent it to someone. I'll be out by the end of the week."

"That's quick. Did something happen?"

"No," I say with more force than I intended.

"Where are you moving?"

Crap, in my emotional breakdown, I forgot to plan that far ahead. "I'm not sure yet. I may just crash at my shop for a little while."

"Is that smart?"

"I don't care."

"I'm just spit-balling here," he says. "But you saw Rhett, didn't you?"

"I'm moving."

"Okay," he says. "I'll talk to Skye and decide what we want to do with it."

"Thanks," I say, feeling like I'm starting to come down off some weird high, my hands trembling slightly, my skin clammy. There's a long silence and with each passing second, I feel worse and worse.

"I'm coming over," he says.

"No," I say, my voice cracking.

"You know, I never saw you break. That whole time in the hospital and after."

"You saw me cry plenty of times," I say.

"Cry, yes," he says. "But never break."

"Well," I say, sniffling. "Rhett finally broke me."

"I don't think so."

"You're going to defend him?"

"All I'm saying is, it's about time you lose it. You're blaming him for it, but maybe it's just time."

"Brody?"

"Think about it," he says. "Right when you know Rhett is better—almost to the second that you know he's going to be okay—that's when you finally get angry. You couldn't let yourself do that before. You were too worried about him. It's like you couldn't be broken at the same time. So you just held yourself together, and as soon as he healed, you broke."

Some place deep inside me, I know there's truth to what he's saying. I had no idea my brother was this enlightened. God knows, he acts like a Neanderthal most of the time. When the truth smacks you in the face, it hurts. I can't even argue with him. I can't even get a word out. All I do is sit on the phone with him and cry.

I've avoided this for a long time, afraid that if I allowed myself to truly feel all this shit, it would emotionally cripple me. Rhett is the one hurt. How could I give myself permission to break right along with him? I couldn't. I didn't.

"Did I ever tell you what I said to Rhett that night on the rooftop before the accident?" Brody asks.

"No," I whimper.

"I told him that I couldn't imagine any man loving you more than he does." He draws a deep breath. "I still think that's true."

"He just told me he loved me," I whisper.

"Hence the sudden desire to move."

"I never know when I'm going to run into him, and it's hard."

"He's playing in his first wheelchair basketball game this weekend. You should come."

"I just said I don't want to see him."

"No, you said it's hard not knowing when you will see him. This way you'll know. You'll have some control."

"I don't think that's a good idea."

"Skye and I are going. Cliff and Diane, too," he says. "It will be fun."

"It's not that I don't want to see everyone."

"You can't avoid Rhett forever. When you decided to date my best friend, you signed up for this," he teases. "Think about coming."

"Okay," I say. "I'll talk to you later."

"One more thing. Do I need to put the condo on the market?"

"Not yet," I say, hanging up.

Brody wants me to go to the game. Rhett wants me to walk Sadie with him. My customer wants me to make a dress in less than two months. But what do I want? That's what I need to think about. What do I want?

Do I want to hate Rhett forever? Never see him again?

I know I don't want to feel like this forever. I know I want the hurt and anger to stop. I also know that there is nothing that Rhett or anyone else can say or do to make that happen. Rhett can say he's sorry a million times, but apologies only work if you accept them, take them into your heart—that's where the forgiveness happens.

My heart may not be ready for that.

I told Rhett that when I look at him, I just feel pain. I told him I'm not the same woman, but what I didn't tell him is how much I still love him. I can't help it. I've wished I could fall out of love with that man, but for some reason my heart refuses to let go. Through all the hurt, all the pain, the love remains. No matter how hard I fight it, the love remains. What I didn't tell Rhett is that my love for him scares me more than anything else.

So what do I want?

The truth is, I don't know what I want. But I know I have to find out.

WHAT THE HELL am I doing here? I don't even like basketball. I don't get it. I know there are positions, but to me, it looks like a bunch of chickens running around with their heads cut off. Baseball, I get. Football is in my wheelhouse, but the only sport more confusing to me than basketball is curling. You know, the one that's basically shuffleboard but you also sweep the ice with a broom. And it's an Olympic sport!

Standing outside the gym, I hear balls dribbling, whistles being blown, the game about to start.

Am I giving Rhett the wrong idea by being here? Does he even know Brody invited me? Blowing out a deep breath, I pull my hair up into a ponytail with my hands, trying to calm down. I know my brother is right, eventually Rhett and I will have to learn to co-exist. We have the same friends, he works with my brother, we live in the same building—interaction is inevitable.

In a normal situation, I would never let a man treat me the way Rhett did and keep him in my life. But our situation isn't normal.

Peeking my head in, I see Brody, Skye, Cliff, and Diane in the stands. It's not as if there are a ton of people here, so it's not hard to spot them. And that means it isn't hard for Diane to spot me lurking in the wings. Can't really back out now. She gives me a little smile and waves me over. I step inside, doing my best not to look out onto the court. The team plays in a local recreation center gym, so it's not a big place. Not a lot of places to hide.

I make my way to the third row and join Rhett's cheering section. It's funny. I was his cheerleader when he didn't want one, and here I am again. Does he want me here this time?

Taking a seat in the bleachers between Skye and Diane, I get a few side hugs and pats on the back, like I've accomplished some great feat.

"Rhett doesn't even think he'll get any playing time today," Diane says. "Since he's new."

I spot him huddled up on the sideline. His brown hair is all messy, the way I used to love it. He's smiling. I remember all the days in the hospital when I would've given anything to see him smile again.

"Is that a new chair?" I ask her.

"Yes, it's made especially for basketball. Certain seat height, straps for his legs, and those strange looking tilted wheels."

I nod along, noticing each feature of the chair as she mentions it, when a pair of pale blue eyes find mine. I can tell he's surprised I'm here, but he flashes me a huge grin. I suddenly feel everyone staring at me, but I don't look away from Rhett. How can one look from him still make me feel all tingly inside? One of his teammates, an older looking guy with a beard, glances my way then leans over, saying something to Rhett, smacking his shoulder. The team takes the court, and suddenly I feel like I'm on display.

Skye pats my hand, whispering to me, "You're here to support a friend. That's all."

"I'm not sure I can . . ."

"Look," Cliff yells. "Rhett's going out there. He's playing. They have him at shooting guard!"

"What does that mean?" I ask, but no one answers because a whistle blows.

The players start vying for the ball, dribbling, passing, shooting—just like you see on TV, but there are wheelchairs. The rules and equipment for wheelchair basketball are pretty much the same as the regular sport. The guys dribble and push their chairs. The small crowd cheers, yells, and moans when something doesn't go the way they want it to. The pace of the game is fast, much faster than I was expecting.

My heart is the only thing faster right now, thundering in my chest. I feel like I'm the one on the court. Telling myself to take deep breaths, I can't get it to slow down. This is beyond nerves about being in the same space as Rhett. This runs much deeper than that. A wave of heat rushes over my body, and my legs suddenly feel weak.

Cliff, Diane, Skye, and Brody leap to their feet. "Three points!" Cliff yells, holding his hand up to Brody for a high five.

Brody leaves him hanging when he sees I'm still seated. "Ainsley, did you see that? Rhett just scored."

I give him a thumbs up, but I'm not watching the game, my eyes glued on my feet. Maybe the cute sandals I have on will calm me down! They all sit down, and I sense everyone staring at me again.

"Maybe she needs some air," Skye says. "She's very pale."

A loud clash of metal jars me, two players' chairs clanging against each other.

"I can't be here," I say, getting to my feet.

Rushing down the stands, I hear a whistle blow, but I don't turn back. I shouldn't have come. I have to get out of here. Telling myself I'll feel better when I get outside, I hurry to the door, pushing it open with such force that it slams against the wall.

The night air hits me, but it's not as refreshing as I was hoping. Twisting my hair, I hold it up off my neck, walking in a circle in the parking lot. Do women in their twenties have heart attacks? My whole chest is tight. Just breathe! Everything's fine. Just breathe.

"A. Rose." Rhett's voice stops me.

I look over, seeing him in the doorway, his hairline wet with sweat. "What are you doing?" I ask. "Aren't you supposed to be on the court?"

"I saw you walk out," he says. "You looked upset."

"So you left your team?"

"No one's more important than you." He moves a little closer. "Don't leave."

"I can't watch that," I say, pointing back toward the gym.

"Okay," he says. "My parents, Brody, and Skye, we're all supposed to go to dinner after. You should come, too."

"Bennett," someone yells from inside. "You can kiss and makeup later. We need your ass on the court!"

Rhett shakes his head, irritated. "Go," I say. "I'll see you later."

"For dinner? Or kissing and making up?" he asks, a big grin on his handsome face.

Even though I try not to, I smile. "Dinner!"

What the hell? I committed myself to sharing a meal with him. How did that happen?

He goes back inside, and I look up at the sky, the stars settling in. One minute with Rhett, and my heart settles, no longer beating hard and fast. Now it's soft and gentle, soothing, like a baby's lullaby. I wish he didn't still do that to me, but he does.

That's how you know you aren't over someone. If your emotions continue to be all over the place, you're still in their web. Even if the emotion is extreme anger, sorry to say, that means the person still has a hold on you. You're not free. You're probably still in love with them, too. Otherwise, you wouldn't give a damn.

I gently kick a few pebbles in the parking lot, knowing that's why I had to get out of the gym. As soon as the game started, all I could think about was him getting hurt, getting hit in the face, his chair being knocked over. I couldn't stand it. The thought of seeing him hurt or in pain again. It was too much.

I was witness to all his pain before. I was the punching bag for all his anger. I handled it all. I ended up with nothing but a broken heart. I'm not going to sit in those stands and cheer him on, hoping and praying that I don't see him get injured again. I know in my brain that he'll probably be just fine, but my heart is scared shitless.

Like an angel on my shoulder, I hear a voice in my head. *If he did get hurt, would you rather not be there?*

My heart knows the answer to that question.

I step back inside the gym. This time, I look straight out onto the court, finding Rhett on the sidelines. He flashes me a grin. Quickly, I look away. I know my heart still belongs to him, but that doesn't mean I have to let it win.

"I WANT YOU to meet the team," Rhett says.

His parents, Skye, Brody, and I hung around after the big win, waiting for Rhett and firming up dinner plans. He's still sweaty, but he looks happy, smiling wide. We all walk over to some of the other players, and Rhett makes introductions.

I hang back a little, letting his parents enjoy this moment with him. After all, he and I aren't together, and it's not my place to share his victories anymore.

"The girlfriend?" a rough voice says behind me. Quickly, I glance at Rhett and the others to make sure no one heard that, but they've all stepped away, still celebrating.

I turn around, finding a bearded, older gentleman looking up at me. I recognize him as the guy that Rhett was talking to in the huddle. Shaking my head, I say, "No."

"Well, damn," he says. "I let Rhett start in my position to impress you. All for nothing."

"I wouldn't say it was for nothing," I say. "You did win!"

He lets out a big, hearty laugh, raising his hand to me. "Elliott, T12 paralysis. Gunshot." My eyes go wide. He starts laughing again. "Just kidding. Car accident. Gunshot sounds cooler, though."

Smiling, I ask, "Do you always introduce yourself like this? With so much information?"

He laughs again then shrugs. "How I ended up in the chair is usually the first thing people want to know. So a few years ago, I just started introducing myself that way. That way, they don't have to feel bad about being curious."

"I'm curious, what else you do besides basketball?" I ask.

"Would you believe me if I told you I'm a Navy SEAL?" he teases.

Smiling, I shake my head. This man is quite a character.

"CPA." His head tilts, moving a little closer to me. "So, not the girlfriend?"

"The ex," I say softly.

"Ah, the accident destroyed more than his legs."

"It was his choice to end things, not mine."

He gives an understanding nod. "Five years," he says. "After this happened, I divorced my wife. Five years later, we remarried. I get it. Rhett's not the first man to let *the one* slip through his fingers."

"I'm not his one," I say. "But I'm glad it worked out for you and your wife."

"I'm a living, breathing cautionary tale," he says, tipping his head to me before rolling away.

OPENING THE DOOR to the restaurant, I walk to the hostess counter, knowing I'm later than everyone else. Why Brody picked this restaurant, I'll never know. It's just a couple blocks from the condo, which is convenient for me and Rhett, but not anyone else. I know Brody loves the spaghetti here, but there must've been a dozen other Italian places between here and the basketball game.

Finding street parking in historic Charleston is about as hard as finding a unicorn. So rather than fight traffic or pay for parking, I used my spot at the condo then walked over. I fully expect everyone else is already here. In fact, I texted Brody and told him to go ahead and order without me. I didn't want to keep everyone else waiting.

I tell the hostess I'm meeting a group, and the five of them should already be here. "I just started my shift, so I'm not sure," the hostess says, apologizing. "If you'd like, go ahead and take a look in the restaurant for your party."

Thanking her, I turn the corner, searching for my crew. The place isn't big. It's one of those classic mom and pop joints that always have the best food. The very best part is when they grate the parmesan cheese over your dish right in front of you. I love how they always tell you to say "when" for them to stop. Instead, I want to say *just leave the whole block of cheese*, thank you very much.

There's a six-top table in the center of the room, but I see only one man sitting there. Crap! Rhett looks up, smiling and giving me a little wave. This was the other reason I decided to take a little extra time getting here, not wanting to risk the possibility of being alone with him.

Walking towards the table, Rhett's hands go to the arms of his chair. The motion, the good manners are so familiar. It's his instinct to stand up before the woman sits down, but he can't. For that brief moment, he apparently forgot he was paralyzed. I see his eyes close for a second.

"I thought I was late," I say, reaching the table and pulling out my phone to check the time. "Where is everyone?"

"Two minutes before you got here, I got a text from my mom saying my dad was tired, and they were going to skip dinner."

"That's not like them," I say, looking down at my phone and finding Brody's response to my message. "Brody just texted that Skye isn't feeling well, and *they* are going home, too," I say, raising an eyebrow at Rhett.

"I swear," he says, holding his hands up. "I had nothing to do with this."

I'm inclined to believe him. He looks as surprised as I am.

"Brody!" I snark, saying his name like it's a curse word. Tossing my purse down, I take my seat. "Remember how we were so worried about what Brody would think of our relationship? Now he's playing matchmaker."

"I don't think it's Brody. This has my mother written all over it," Rhett says. We stare at each other across the table for a minute before Rhett gives me a little shrug. "I'm pretty hungry."

"Me, too," I say, devising ways to kill my brother for orchestrating this. I'm sure Skye was in on it, too. Even if it was Diane's suggestion, they all went along with it.

"Just dinner," he says with a smirk.

Everything is "just" something: just fun, just love, just dinner.

Like use of the word "just" makes things less significant. If I were a betting woman, I'd say before long, he's going to be using "just friends" on me.

The waitress comes over, pouring water into our glasses. "Looks like it's just the two of us," Rhett tells her. She briefly glances at him and nods. "Sorry we took up this big table."

"It's fine, no problem," she says. "Are you ready to order?"

Rhett motions for me to start. "This will be separate checks," I say, looking at the menu.

"No, it won't," Rhett says.

The waitress looks up from her little notepad, eyeing both of us, more than a bit puzzled. Holding his eyes, I offer my best smile, "Separate checks or I leave."

"You play dirty," he says with a mischievous look.

Satisfied I won, I place my order, then Rhett does the same. The waitress starts to leave, but before she gets too far, Rhett stops her, saying, "Separate checks is fine, but I'll be paying both."

My jaw on the floor, I'm not even sure how to respond to that. I guess I could call his bluff and leave, but I'm starving. Damn it, I forgot how charming he could be in a completely frustrating way. No matter, I'll just swipe my bill when she brings it. The waitress eagerly walks off, and we're left staring at each other across the table again.

"I saw you talking to Elliott after the game," Rhett says.

"He's an interesting guy," I say, not giving Rhett much to work with.

Why should I make this easy on him? It's not easy on me.

He studies me for a minute, but I don't look away. "You never told me why you left the gym the way you did."

"It doesn't matter."

"I'd like to know," he says.

"I really don't want to talk about it."

He releases a deep breath, his hand reaching for his chest. For the first time, I notice a chain around his neck, disappearing under his shirt. He never wore any type of necklace before. Must be some sort of medical alert thing or something.

"Are you dating someone? Or have you dated?" he asks, throwing me for a loop.

A five-minute date where I burst into tears, and a near one-night stand—does that constitute dating? Why am I even thinking about it? It's none of his damn business.

"Have you?" I ask.

His whole face changes, his forehead wrinkling up, his eyes narrow. "Yeah, I was getting it on with all the nurses."

"Well, you were just looking for someone to take your paraplegic virginity."

He releases a deep breath. "I'm sorry, okay? How many times do I have to say it? It was the hardest thing I've ever done, breaking things off with you."

"It didn't seem . . ."

"It was harder than hearing I'll never walk again," he says.

My eyes start to water, and I blink back my tears. "It was hard for me, too," I admit.

"I know," he says softly, reaching his hand across the table, but I don't take it. "Then you came to see me, and you were so beautiful and sweet. We kissed and . . . It was stupid of me to think we could just pick up where we left off."

"Is that what you wanted?" I ask. "To pick up where we left off? Or were you just looking to get laid?"

"You know the answer to that."

"I know I wasn't *enough*, Rhett. My love wasn't enough." Tears start to fall. "And nothing's changed." I get up, needing to escape to the restroom.

"Ainsley," he calls after me, but I don't turn back.

Thank God, the restroom is empty. And double thanks that it's a single bathroom, so no one has to witness my breakdown. I look like a complete mess, my face red and splotchy. I'm tired of crying. I'm tired of being sad. Grabbing some toilet paper, I wipe my eyes and blow my nose.

I seriously need to stop having breakdowns in public. This is it. This is the last one. From now on, I only lose my shit in the privacy of my own home. I take a deep breath, looking at myself in the mirror, sealing the promise I just made, gathering strength to go out there and face Rhett again, and all his damn questions. I don't remember him being so damn inquisitive. Maybe things have changed.

Love is a two-way street. Some people think that means that both people have to love equally for the relationship to work, but that's not it at all. Real love happens in both giving and receiving. You have to give to another person, and you have to let them give to you. Rhett wouldn't let me love him. He didn't want it. For him, love is a one-way street.

And let me tell you—it hurts like a mother to have someone reject your love. How could I ever trust him again? Trust that the next time things got hard, he wouldn't do the same thing to me all over again?

I can't risk it. He has to know that. It's not fair to let him believe there's a chance. It doesn't matter that I still love him. Sometimes love gets it wrong. I'm going to march out there and tell him there's no hope for us. That's the kind thing to do.

Emboldened by my plan of action, I open the bathroom door and head out. It only takes two steps before I stop in my tracks. The determination I had ten seconds ago must've gotten left in the bathroom. Damn it! That's another thing, I never used to curse as much as I do now.

"You totally got screwed on that six-top," another waitress say to ours. They're standing at a computer around the corner from me, so I can hear everything they say.

"Can't really complain," our waitress says. "Did you see the guy? Cripple."

My nails dig into the palm of my hand. I hate that word. I actually hate all the words—handicapped, differently abled, disabled. I mean, aren't we all disabled in some way? Why do we feel the need to label people? Aren't they just that? People?

"It's such a shame. He's so hot. What a waste," our waitress says.

"Think that's his girlfriend with him?" the other waitress asks.

"Probably not. Do you think he can even get it up anymore?"

I come out from my hiding place and yell, "Take that back!"

The entire restaurant is suddenly staring at me, but I don't care—not this time. I didn't want anyone to see me cry, but I'm more than happy to let them see me call this little girl out!

She stammers, "I don't know what you . . ."

"I heard everything you said," I bark.

She looks around, her manager joining us. "Is there a problem?"

"You employees are rude, selfish little . . ."

"A. Rose," Rhett says, coming over to us. "Everything okay?"

"She just started screaming at me for no reason," our waitress says, conjuring up some tears for her boss and the restaurant audience.

My finger flies in her face. "He is not a waste," I say through gritted teeth. "You have no idea what a real man is." Her eyes fall. "And because you're so curious about his dick, I can assure you . . ."

"Okay," Rhett says, taking me by the waist. Before I know what's happening, he has pulled me down onto his lap, wheeling us away. "That's enough," he says, continuing to roll.

"Wait!" I call out, causing him to stop. I grab my purse, and the basket of breadsticks off the table. "I'm taking these!"

"Dear God," he mumbles, rolling us out of the restaurant.

As soon as we make it to the sidewalk, I get off his lap. He busts out laughing. "Christ, Ainsley, you totally went rogue in there."

"You didn't hear what she said," I say, handing him a breadstick and starting down the street.

He takes the stick, bending it down like a limp noodle. "I can imagine."

Playfully, I smack his hand. "Stop that."

"Me?" he says. "I thought you were going to get in a fist fight."

"I could've totally kicked her ass."

"I have no doubt," he says. "But I don't need you to fight my battles."

"I guess not," I say, picking at my bread.

"I mean, I'm flattered that you did," he says, grinning at me.

"I hate that people are so ignorant and make assumptions. They have no idea what type of man you are."

I stop when I realize he's no longer rolling beside me. Looking back at him, he's got the goofiest smile on his face. "I thought you were going to come out of that bathroom and say you never wanted to see me again. Instead, I realize you still love me."

"Rhett," I say, gearing up to argue with him, but there's no argument to make since he's caught me red-handed. I do still love him, but I whisper, "I can't."

"Not yet," he says.

"Maybe not ever."

"I'll risk it," he says.

"Friends?" I ask, feeling stupid. I thought for sure he was going to play the "let's just be friends" card on me, and here I am laying it down.

"For now," he says, wheeling up beside me, and asks, "Ice cream?"

BY THE TIME we finish our ice cream, we've settled back into each other. How is that possible? How can he still feel so familiar? I almost forgot how cute and charming he is. Like so many walks before, he ends the night at my door.

"Does that kind of thing happen a lot?" I ask. "People being rude?"

His head tilts, letting me know it happens more than he cares to admit. "Usually, it's more subtle," he says. "Like I'm invisible or something. A waiter won't ask me directly what I want to order. Instead, they ask someone I'm with. Like I've lost my ability to talk or something like that."

"You don't seem too bothered by it."

"I was for a while, but I'm not anymore," he says. "I figure if I act right, then the next time they come across someone in a chair, they'll know better."

"That's a good way to look at it," I say, unlocking my door.

"Ainsley," he says. "You never answered my question before."

"Which question?"

"If you've been seeing anyone? Dating?" he says. "I saw you changed your status online, and I'd like to know."

I lean back against my door. "I went on one date with this guy Skye works with. The whole date lasted about five minutes."

"That good, huh?"

"It was me. I wasn't ready. Then there was this other man." I look into Rhett's pale blue eyes. "It was after I saw you at the rehab center. I stopped at a hotel bar. I was looking for trouble."

God, he looks so disappointed. I have no reason to feel guilty, but I do.

"Guess you found it," he says quietly.

"Finding it was easy," I say. "Going through with it was harder."

His eyes dart to mine, and I shake my head, letting him know nothing happened. "Goodnight, Rhett," I say.

"Same time tomorrow?" he asks.

This is the exact way we started. Are we starting over?

"Tomorrow," I say.

# CHAPTER THIRTY-THREE

Remember my love.
A. Rose

## RHETT

I SHOULD'VE BEEN knocking on Ainsley's door with Sadie at least thirty minutes ago. I can't stand her up. It's just a walk with Sadie, but I can't do that to her. It's just been a shitty day—all the reasons I pushed her away before, coming back with full force.

It used to be my routine to have a preventative jerk off before our walks. If only that were my biggest problem these days. I still get to hold my dick a lot, only now it's to cath myself. Yep, every four to six hours, I get the pleasure of inserting a catheter and emptying my bladder. If I go too long, I can leak or worse, get infections. I usually get up at least once a night to go, but there's still a hospital pad under the fitted sheet on my bed just in case.

Sometimes I think the bladder and bowel management that goes along with my injury is worse than not being able to use my legs. It's humiliating. I hated being in the hospital when the nurses would do it for me. It's not like I enjoy doing it myself, but if someone has to stick their finger up my ass, it's gonna be me. Yep, I get to do that, too. It was a special day when Ainsley let me do that to her. Unfortunately, it's now part of my bowel management routine.

I've got my gut pretty much trained. I go every other night with the use of mini enemas, plastic gloves, and my finger.

I don't want this for her. I don't want her to see me like this. It's the same old shit. The same feelings I had in the hospital, right after I was hurt. God help me, if I ever get her back into my bed, I don't want her sleeping on a piss pad or worse, waking up wet because I've leaked.

I love her. I don't want that for her.

Then there's sex and children and all the ways I can't fuck her anymore. I should've listened to my instinct after my accident and left her alone.

It's been so long since I've had sex. I lost count around the three-hundred-day mark. I still remember the last time. It was that night. The night I was hurt, before I left to go to Brody's bachelor party. I came out of the shower, finding Ainsley on my bed, doing something on her phone. She had her own party to get to, but she wasn't ready yet. The only thing she had on was one of my old shirts. When I pounced on top of her, her giggles filled up the room.

Most people probably don't consider when they are having sex that this could be the last time. I guess we take it for granted. I won't do that again. I'm thankful I remember.

Yesterday, having her at the game, the restaurant after, and having ice cream, I was on such a high when I got home. But having to manually stimulate yourself to take a shit has a way of humbling a man.

This isn't romantic or sexy. I should just take Sadie for her walk by myself. I know there are couples that don't so much as pass wind in front of each other. Women who don't let their guys see them without makeup. I can't hide this. It's part of my life, but I don't want it to be part of hers.

Same shit, different day.

My phone dings. It's probably Ainsley wondering where I am or telling me to go to hell for keeping her waiting. I look at her message:

*Swamped at work. Probably be here most of the night. Rain check?*

I send a quick response that it's alright then look at the clock. It's almost eight, which means she's already been working close to ten hours. I know Ainsley, she'll stay until she finishes. She could be there until the early morning hours. The idea of her walking the streets of Charleston alone—no fucking way. It's only a few blocks from her shop to the condo, but still. I don't care how charming and pristine our town can be, I still don't want her walking the streets alone. Not sure how threatening I look these days, but I'd roll over the fucker who tried to hurt her.

Putting Sadie's leash on, I head out the door, fully aware that this could just be her blowing me off. I don't think so. At least, I hope not. Ainsley isn't the type. If she wanted to get rid of me, she'd tell me upfront. And even if she is trying to ditch me, I'm not going without a fight.

First, I need to arm myself, stopping by a local sandwich place, picking up her favorite. Sadie and I then make a beeline for Ainsley's shop. Her lights are still on, shining brightly on the street, and I see her inside at her dress form, hands on her hips, head tilted, like the fate of the universe depends on what she does next. I love that about her—her passion. I used to be on the receiving end of it. I miss that.

I stop pushing the wheels of my chair, sitting on the sidewalk. I'm literally and figuratively at a crossroads. I could go back home, leave her alone. Twenty minutes ago, I was debating doing just that. Now I'm sitting across the street from her shop.

If I do this, make this play for her, try to win her back, then I can't go back. I can't let my demons and doubts back in. I can't play with her that way. Sadie looks up at me, whimpering a little. I'm not sure if she's anxious to see Ainsley, or if she just wants a piece of the sandwich.

Placing my hands on the wheels, there's only one direction for me to go, the direction I should've always been going—toward her.

Suddenly, I can't get across the street quick enough. Sadie can barely keep up. I reach for the door handle, but it's locked, my attempt to open it creating a little rapping sound. Looking through the glass, I see Ainsley's cute little confused smile. Hopefully, I'm scoring some points with my small gesture.

She places her sewing needle down, walking toward the door. She's got on a long, flowing dress that moves when she walks, her hair in a knot on top of her head. She unlocks the door, opening it. "What are you doing here?"

"Dinner," I say, holding up the sack with her sandwich. "Sadie needed her walk anyway, and I thought you probably hadn't eaten, so we decided to drop something off for you."

"We?" she says, bending down to give Sadie some love. Where's my love, I wonder? "You didn't need to do that. I could've just ordered something to be delivered."

"You could," I say, "but would you have?" We both know I've caught her. She would work through without so much as a snack break. "What's got you working so late?"

She opens the door wider, inviting me in. Well, at least I made it through the door. She starts telling me about this bride who she's doing a rush order for because the fiancé is in the military. Originally, the bride didn't want any beading, so Ainsley thought it would be a little easier, but then the design changed, and now she's totally stressed out trying to finish on time.

I hand her the sandwich bag, saying, "Looks beautiful the way it is."

"I think that's my problem," she says. "I don't think it needs anything else, so every time I try to place a bead on it, I hate it." She twirls the dress form around, showing me the back, or lack thereof. "I was thinking maybe lining the scoop of the back." She holds up a string of crystals then tosses them aside. "Oh, I don't know."

"Maybe you should eat," I say. "Don't look at it for half an hour then see what happens."

She nods, collapsing down onto a little sofa, facing away from the dress. "Thanks for dinner," she says, tearing open the wrapping. Sadie tries to jump up on the sofa but doesn't quite make it, panting heavily. "Oh, poor thing," Ainsley says, helping her the rest of the way up. "You had a long day, too. Didn't you, girl?"

"A long day of napping."

"Don't listen to him," Ainsley says, taking a bite of her sandwich.

I motion to the dress in her front window. "That's a replica of your mom's?"

Ainsley doesn't know that I know that's the dress she designed for our wedding. I'm not trying to make her uncomfortable by pointing it out, but I want her to remember how happy we were together, plus I'm more than a little curious to see if she'll be honest with me.

"Yes," she says, finishing a bite before adding, with a sad look in her eye, "It was supposed to be my dress, too."

"When did you make it?"

"While I sat on your parents' front porch hoping you'd see me."

Fuck me! Why the hell did I open this wound for her? I wanted her to remember the good times, not the horrible ones. My instinct is to tell her I'm sorry again, but last time I did that, it wasn't received so well. "I'd like to see you in it," I say. "Would you try it on?"

She places her sandwich down, staring at me. I have no idea what's running through her mind. Most guys don't know what a woman is thinking, but this is beyond that. I'm sure Sadie knows her thoughts. A dog can tell everything about a person with one sniff—illness, pregnancy, how they're feeling. I've got all five of my senses working and don't have a damn clue.

"I've never had it on."

"Why not?"

She simply whispers my name, ever so softly.

"Aren't you curious? Don't you want to know what it looks like on?"

She glances at the dress, getting to her feet and walking toward it. Gently, her fingers run over the fabric, the pale roses at the bottom. "It feels like it would be bad luck."

The old wives' tale says the groom shouldn't see the bride in the dress before the wedding. Does she still think of us as the potential bride and groom?

"I think we're way past bad luck."

She eyes the dress, whispering, "It's not like I'm ever going to wear it."

Hearing her say that fucking hurts. In her mind, I suppose we are really over. I wonder when that happened. I know it wasn't when I threw her out of my hospital room. Was it when she stopped waiting on my parents' porch? Was it when she came to see me in Atlanta? When was it exactly that I lost her? Does it really matter at this point? It's over for her.

But in my heart, she will always be mine.

She removes the gown from the stand, her hands slowing undoing each button, one-by-one, until she's carrying the dress across the shop and disappearing into a fitting room in the back. I'm not sure what I said that convinced her to try it on, or if it was even anything I said. I suspect she always wondered what the dress would look like on her, and perhaps the little nudge from me was the excuse she needed.

Staring at the fitting room door, I try not to envision her naked, what color panties she has on, if her bra matches.

"Rhett," she says, opening the door a crack. "I forgot getting in and out of a wedding dress is a two-person job. I can't fasten the buttons in the back."

"Open up," I say. "I'll do them for you. I still have use of my hands."

"That's what I'm worried about," she teases, giving me a smirk.

"I'll keep them to myself."

She hesitates for a moment before opening the door. Her back is to me. She's holding the dress up with one arm and yanking the skirt on it forward with her other hand, making room so I can wheel close enough. The perfect skin of her back is exposed, not a bra strap in sight. What I wouldn't give to lightly trail kisses down her spine.

Instead, I reach up, careful not to touch her skin at all, and begin to fasten the delicate white buttons, one at a time. I don't rush the moment, having not been this close to her in so long. When the last button is fastened, I roll backwards out of the room. I want the full view when she turns around. I want to see her walking toward me like I should've seen her from the altar.

She turns, taking her first steps toward me. If I was ever going to regain use of my legs and stand up, it would be right now. She's absolutely glowing, sexy, sweet—all at once. Her hair messy, no makeup, no veil, and it's exactly the way I would've wanted to see her.

She does a slow spin, showing me the back. When she turns around again, her eyes are right on mine. There is absolutely nothing unlucky about this moment, about seeing her in the dress. I haven't lost her. She can say there's no hope, but that's definitely hope in her eyes.

My eyes wander down the curves of her body, the soft color of the roses catching my attention. When I saw the dress through the window before, I thought I noticed the color coming from a faint handwriting, and now I know I was right. I lift the skirt slightly to try to get a better look.

"Did you write on your dress?" I whisper.

"Calligraphy," she says, holding my gaze.

"*I won't ever let go. A. Rose,*" I read aloud, making out the script.

"My vows," she says softly. "Each rose is a vow. My promises to you."

She's literally sewn her wedding vows to me into her dress. There must be close to a hundred roses. I pick up another, making out her words to me, my heart in my throat. All the things she wanted to say those nights she waited and waited for me are right here. All the love that I denied captured forever. She takes hold of the dress, pulling it slightly, so it falls from my hand, her promises literally slipping through my fingers.

"Almost every stitch was made through a tear," she says, looking at me. "But I still love it."

Am I like the dress? Does she still love me after all the tears I made her cry?

If I could use my legs, this would be the time I pull her to me and kiss her hard. But paralysis has seriously affected my game. So I take her hand, holding her eyes, urging her to me. Slowly, she moves closer, bending down slightly. I'm not playing fair, having her dress like she was supposed to marry me. I knew that would stir feelings in her, but I'll do whatever it takes.

We inch toward each other, and her eyes land on my mouth. Christ, I want to rip her out of that dress, pull her into my lap, and bury myself deep inside her. Even if I can't feel it, she can still feel me.

Here's the thing about being paralyzed—my brain isn't. All the desire is still there. I still daydream about sex. I still have all the drive that I always did. I still want her as much as always. Plus, I have all the memories. That part of the body doesn't shut off or even lessen in any way.

My hand slips to her waist, moving her closer. Suddenly, she stops. "I know what I want to do."

"Me, too," I say, trying to pull her back to me.

"The dress," she says, ignoring me. "I know what to do about my bride's dress!"

I force a smile. "Great," I say, feeling anything but.

Lying in bed, I stare down at my erect penis, making a tent in my sheets. Seriously? To think when I first got hurt, I thought he was dead and gone. I guess I shouldn't complain at this point because, depending on your level of paralysis, some guys have a harder time than others achieving and maintaining an erection. I'm lucky.

It's just at present, I need to get to sleep, so laying here horny as hell isn't helping. I stayed with Ainsley for several hours, handing her beads, encouraging her, keeping her company. I made sure to see her back to her condo, but that was over an hour ago. Even Sadie has gone to sleep, choosing to isolate herself to a corner of my bedroom, surely irritated that I'm keeping her awake.

If this were before my accident, I would've rubbed one out and gone to sleep, but it's different now. I know I can get hard, but orgasm and ejaculation are different stories. No one knows what an orgasm will look or feel like for me now. Everyone is different. I've been told that, for most men in my situation, ejaculation is almost non-existent. Sperm count is still good, but if I ever want to have children, it most likely won't happen the old-fashioned way. All that knowledge has led me not to try.

Honestly, I'm afraid to try. So what used to be a daily occurrence—jacking off—has now become the thing that scares me the most. I don't want to know if I can't. I don't know what that knowledge would do to me. Would it send me into some dark hole again? It's hard to admit I'm afraid, especially of something involving sex. Men are trained to deny their fears. We aren't supposed to openly admit them. Still, Sadie's the only one here, so I guess my secret's safe with her.

But I don't beat off because even on a great day, it doesn't hold a candle to being with a woman. I figure my best odds for succeeding are to be with a woman, at least the first time. That's part of the reason why I asked Ainsley that day at the rehab facility. I knew I could trust her. If anything could get me off, it's her. Not to mention, I love her more than anything.

I've heard all the lectures about how you have to "redefine" intimacy. Be open to new ideas, toys, and so on, but more than anything else about my situation, this is what scares the piss out of me. I'm a man. I'm sorry, but a man is supposed to get hard, fuck hard, please his woman. That's just the way I see it. I can't seem to get over that notion.

I try to remind myself how lucky I am. One poor kid I met was a virgin when he was paralyzed. Another had to have a penile implant.

My eyes close, remembering the feel of Ainsley's mouth on me, the way her head moved up and down as I watched her. We've all seen and heard about women who can have a "mindgasm," think themselves off, but it doesn't work that way for men. Sex might be just as mental for women as it is physical, but for men, it's all physical. We don't need to love the woman. Hell, we don't even need to like them.

But that's not what I want. If it was, I would've had Jay hook me up with one of those women that have wheelchair fetishes.

My phone dings, lighting up my bedroom. It's the middle of the night. Middle of the night calls are either tragedies or booty calls. I see it's Ainsley, so hopefully it's the latter.

*Are you awake?*

Screw this! I'm not texting her back. We need to *talk*. I dial her number. She picks up, her voice soft and quiet. I can never figure why the night makes people speak softer. I guess the darkness holds more secrets, more things to whisper about.

"You almost kissed me," she says.

Oh, I thought we were pretending that didn't happen. Guess not. "*You* almost kissed me," I reply.

"Rhett, if we are going to hang out, be friends, I can't handle that kind of intensity."

If she could see my dick right now, she'd realize I can't turn it off, but I got myself into trouble in Atlanta by trying to move too quickly. I've learned my lesson. "I didn't tell you how beautiful you looked in the dress," I say.

"Thank you," she sighs, and I wonder if compliments are too intense. "I can't sleep."

"Want to come sleep with me?" I ask, already knowing the answer, but unable to resist the urge to flirt.

"You are impossible," she says. "Just talk to me, okay?"

"Okay," I say, trying to think of something light to talk about. "Tomorrow after work, I've got basketball practice. So I won't be able to take Sadie for her walk with you. I'll have to take her when I get home. I'm not sure how late I'll be."

"Why don't I walk her?" she asks. "I can take her after I close the shop."

"You sure?"

"I miss her," she says, a little yawn escaping.

"You still have your key?" I ask, hoping she still does, like that would hold some special meaning.

"Uh huh," she says.

Lowering my voice, I continue to talk to her about nothing important, nothing intense—silly stories from work, the latest basketball play we're practicing. I glance at the floor of my bedroom, knowing right below me she's falling asleep. I hear her breathing slow. She's fading. I don't ask her any questions, wanting my voice to be the last thing she hears before she falls asleep.

# CHAPTER THIRTY-FOUR

## AINSLEY

THE ELEVATOR DOOR opens. I haven't been to the floor above me, Rhett's floor, since he broke up with me. I haven't stepped through his door, either. While he was gone, I could've gone inside—I had the key—but I never did. Why surround yourself with memories of someone you can't have?

The cold metal of the key hits my skin. I'm dog sitting. That's it. That's the kind of thing friends do for each other. Rhett already texted me once today, questioning whether I remembered my half-asleep offer to walk Sadie tonight.

I wonder if his place looks the same. Does he still have the same sofa, the one we made love on more times than I can count? Does he have any pictures of me? He never did before, since we were hiding from Brody, but he had some at the rehab facility. Did he bring those home with him?

Unlocking his door, I step inside, expecting to be bombarded with doggy kisses. Instead, I'm greeted by Diane, standing in her son's kitchen, the refrigerator door open, grocery sacks spread all over the countertops.

She looks surprised to see me here, but the smile on her face tells me she's reading more into this than there is.

"I told Rhett I'd walk Sadie for him," I say, looking around for my furry friend.

"Cliff is doing that," she says, "while I finish up."

She's got dozens of casserole dishes lining his refrigerator and freezer. It looks like enough food to feed him for a month.

Taking a few more steps inside, I glance around his condo. It's the same, yet it's different. The furniture is more spread out, less cluttered. The sofa is the same. It still feels like Rhett, and I feel the same being here. It feels like my second home.

Diane watches me as I roam, peeking my head in the workout room, which is brand new. I don't peek in his bedroom—too many memories in there.

"Why'd Rhett want me to walk Sadie, if you and Cliff were coming over?"

"Oh," she says, coming closer, but I step back a little. "Rhett doesn't know we're here. I knew he had practice and thought it would be okay to drop off a few things. I didn't expect anyone would be here. I would've never let myself in."

"I keep telling her," Cliff says, coming in with Sadie. "If you wouldn't have done it in his old life, you probably shouldn't now."

Her eyes scan all the food she's stockpiled. I sense she knows her husband is right, but she's a mom. She's protective, and she worries.

"Rhett will appreciate it," I say, giving Sadie a little pat. "You've got Sadie taken care of. If I'm not needed, I guess I'll go."

"I would say Rhett needs you very much," Diane says.

"Is that why you arranged for dinner the other night?" I ask.

"Seems like it worked," she says, smiling.

"Diane, I think we've always had a good relationship. You know I love you," I say. "I admire how you've handled Rhett's injury. You can fill his refrigerator, renovate his apartment. I know you're doing all that out of love for your son . . ."

"That's sweet of you to . . ."

"But you cannot fix Rhett and me."

A long silence follows. The awkward kind where no one knows quite what to do or say next. Sadie slinks to the floor.

"Diane," Cliff says. "Maybe we should go."

"What are you afraid of, Ainsley?" she asks. "It's obvious you two still love each other."

My eyes flip to hers. How dare she?!

"You should listen to your husband," I say, sharper than I should. "You didn't interfere in Rhett's relationships before, so you shouldn't now."

She draws a quick breath, like I just struck her with a knife, my words cutting her just as deep. She quickly finishes up in the kitchen. Cliff then places his arm around his wife and escorts her out, his eyes apologetic. The door closes behind them, and I let out a loud grunt, wishing everyone would butt out. Falling back onto the sofa, Sadie jumps up beside me.

"I wanted to kiss him," I whisper.

I tried to blame it all on him, but it wasn't all him. I still have feelings for him. I can't deny that. Apparently, everyone around me sees it, too, but I'm afraid. I'm afraid of getting hurt again. I'm afraid of losing him again. I bury my head in Sadie's fur, using her as a snuggle partner. She softly snores. I envy that about dogs: they can fall asleep within a few seconds.

"I miss him," I confess to Sadie.

I think about Cliff's words, that we should treat Rhett the same way. He's not the first one to say that. If Rhett were never hurt, would I give him another chance if he broke my heart?

I know I wouldn't. So why am I even considering it now? It's not out of pity. It's out of love. I hate the way he treated me, but I do understand why he pushed me away. Understanding doesn't take away the pain, but it does make me wonder if there's a way back.

I feel like I'm stuck. I can't imagine letting him go, but I also can't imagine trusting him with my love again.

# CHAPTER THIRTY-FIVE

You made me who I am.
A. Rose

### RHETT

MY GIRLS CURLED up on the sofa. That's the sight that greeted me when I got in from basketball practice last night. It was a little after eleven when I got home. Instead of jumping in the shower, I watched Ainsley sleep. Instead of going to sleep myself, I placed a blanket over her. Instead of wondering how I was going to win her back, I thanked God she was here.

I know it had to be an accident on her part. She'd never fall asleep at my place on purpose, at least not these days. How did this happen? What kind of divine intervention is this? Whatever it is, I'll take it. She's obviously still comfortable enough here to let her guard down a little bit.

The morning light coming through my windows, I want to kiss her good morning to wake her, but I won't, settling for making her breakfast. Sadie jumps off the sofa, the smell of bacon enough to jolt her from the deepest slumber. She used to be such a good watch dog, barking at the slightest thing. Now I can come in the house, and she barely lifts her head. Most mornings, I have to force her out of bed for her morning walk.

Sadie shakes, the jiggle of her collar ringing. It's like Ainsley's personal alarm clock, causing her to start to wake. This is hardly the morning after, but I know Ainsley's going to flip out like she's waking up after a one-night stand. I come armed with bacon, toast, and orange juice.

I see her stretch, her eyes still closed, a little yawn. She snuggles down deeper into the cushions, like she's hoping for an extra few minutes. Then her eyes flash open, realizing where she is.

"Morning," I say, grinning at her.

She immediately lifts the blanket, checking to see if she's dressed, like she could forget us sleeping together.

"Um."

"Found you on my sofa when I got home," I say, rolling over and handing her some juice.

She takes the juice, her skin turning a bright pink. "I had a fight with your mom. Well, it wasn't a fight, exactly."

I look toward the kitchen. I knew my mom had been here, but I didn't know when. I texted her to thank her once I got home, and she never mentioned in her reply that she saw or talked to Ainsley. "What about?"

"You," she says, putting her juice down.

Ainsley doesn't need to say another word. I already know how that conversation went. My mother needs to stop interfering. From the look on Ainsley's face, it's not helping. "I'll talk to her," I say.

"Why does everyone think they get a say in what happens between me and you?" she asks.

"I think everyone just wants to finally see us both happy again."

She looks up at me from under her lashes. "I was happy the other night after we left the restaurant, and we just talked and had ice cream like we used to."

Brushing her hair off her face, I ask, "That's what you need?"

She nods, and it looks almost sad. She doesn't want to hurt me. She doesn't want to get hurt again, either. That's what I have to prove to her—I'll never hurt her again.

"Okay," I say softly.

Closing her eyes, she leans forward, her forehead resting on mine. I let my eyes close, soaking her in, the feel of her hair brushing my cheek, her sweet smell. Is this some sort of test? She just told me what she needs, and it doesn't involve us kissing. But that's all I want. Just one kiss.

One kiss to show her how I feel. One kiss to erase all the pain and hurt. One kiss so she can remember all the ones that came before.

She pulls away slightly, her eyes opening. Reaching out, she places her hand on my cheek. "Walk Sadie and ice cream," she says. "Tonight?"

"Every night," I say, giving her hand a squeeze.

I'll give her as much time as she needs.

# CHAPTER THIRTY-SIX

## AINSLEY

OVER THE PAST few weeks, my shop has become Sadie's second home. She now has a dog bed in the corner, a water bowl in the back, and a treat container on my counter so all my customers give her a little nibble. On the nights that Rhett goes to basketball practice, Sadie stays with me. It's like we're divorced and have shared custody of our child. Only Sadie's a dog, and we aren't divorced. In fact, I see him every day. Sometimes it's to walk Sadie. Other times, it's when he's dropping her off here to me. Sometimes, like tonight, she stays the night with me, and I take her to the vet clinic in the mornings. Totally like those divorced couples you see exchanging their kids in a fast food parking lot.

This is probably the most he's ever been apart from Sadie, except when he was in the hospital. Sometimes I wonder if he isn't letting me watch her as a way of keeping a little piece of him with me.

"Hello," Skye's voice chimes out as she enters my shop, carrying a huge white garment bag.

I made her wedding dress, so I know it doesn't weigh more than five or six pounds, but she still looks like she's being buried alive.

Rushing over to help her, I feel butterflies flutter in my stomach. I'm so excited that she and Brody are having a redo of their wedding reception. I can't wait to see her all made up in her dress, veil, shoes, makeup, hair—the whole bit. It's been a long time coming. Today we're doing a fitting just to make sure that everything still looks perfect before the celebration next week.

"What's Sadie doing here?" she asks, hanging the dress up in the fitting room.

Sadie barely even acknowledges we have a visitor, simply rolling over a little, looking for a belly rub, which Skye happily provides.

"I've been watching her for Rhett some," I say.

She raises an eyebrow. "First, it's dog sitting. Then before you know it, you're sitting on his face."

"Oh my God, Skye!"

"Don't tell me you haven't thought about it."

Playfully, shoving her shoulder, I say, "Go get your dress on."

She flashes me a look over her shoulder before disappearing behind the door. I look over at Sadie. She's the only one that keeps her opinion about Rhett and me to herself. Pulling out my phone, I snap a picture of her all curled up on her bed, sending it to Rhett.

*Not missing you at all!*

Figuring he's on the basketball court, I put my phone down, not expecting a response, but it immediately dings.

*How about you? You miss me?*

Okay, so we totally flirt with each other all the time. Usually, it's sweet, fun, and not very serious. I told him I need space and time, and he's respected that. You always hear people say they need space and time, and now I'm one of them. The thing is, I'm not sure *why* I need space or time. It's like I'm waiting for something to magically happen, something to make me less afraid.

I think the flirting is his way of letting me know that he hasn't given up. I don't have as good an excuse for my role in the flirting process. Quickly, I reply.

*Parts of you.*

I hit send before realizing he could read that the wrong way, thinking I'm referring to his injury in some way. I'm frantically typing my lame explanation for what I meant, when his response comes through.

*You can have any part of me whenever you want.*

Relieved, I start to respond when Skye opens the door a little, putting an end to our playful banter.

"Ainsley," Skye says, holding her dress up in front. "I don't think it fits. I don't understand. I'm only two pounds heavier than I was then."

I hear her voice crack and realize she's on the verge of tears. Skye's always had this hang-up about her size, and her weight fluctuates with whatever crazy diet she's on. Taking hold of the back of the dress, I begin to lace up the corset. I do this for a living. The corset design is pretty forgiving. You can tighten and loosen as needed, but she does have to be able to breathe. I can tell the dress isn't fitting like it did originally. By the time I get her all laced up, she's worked herself into a tizzy.

I reach for a box of tissues, preferring when a bride is moved to tears for happy reasons. "I can always let it out. There's time."

"Look at my boobs," she says. "It's obscene." There is definitely a cleavage situation happening, but it won't do me any good to make a big deal out of it. She pulls at the dress. "I can barely breathe."

"Let me loosen it," I say, reaching for the back of the dress. I start to unlace it when an idea hits me like a bolt of lightning. I stop in my tracks, frozen.

"Ainsley?" Skye says, turning her head to look at me. "If you have to cut me out of this dress, I swear I'm going to lose my mind."

I hold her eyes. "Maybe the dress not fitting has nothing to do with your weight."

"Then what . . ." She turns all the way around, her eyes wide. She knows what I'm hinting at. "The test I took was negative."

"Yeah, but that was weeks ago."

She starts to chew on her nail. "My period was late last month, and it was lighter than normal. Maybe?"

"You work in a fertility clinic, for God's sake," I say, laughing. "How could you miss this?"

"I don't know. I know women can confuse spotting during pregnancy for their periods, I just thought I'd know the difference."

She looks at herself in the mirror. "The ribcage expands first. My boobs definitely look like I need to be milked. Oh God!"

"Do you have another stolen pregnancy test in your purse?" I ask.

"SKYE'S GOING TO be a mom," I whisper to Sadie, curled up beside me in my bed at home.

Skye swore me to secrecy, but I figure Sadie's not going to tell anyone, and I needed to say it out loud to make it real. I don't know how I'm going to keep from telling Brody and Rhett, but Skye decided she wants to make the announcement at their do-over reception. She wants the photographer to catch my brother's reaction. I can't wait to see that myself.

I'm so excited for them. I'm not sure how I'm going to sleep tonight. I can't imagine what Skye's feeling right now. How she's going to keep this to herself until next week, I'll never know. As for me, I may need to talk to Sadie about it daily.

My phone rings, and I know who it is without looking.

"I'm on my way home," Rhett says. "Want me to come get Sadie?"

"That's okay. I'll keep her tonight. We are curled up together in my bed. She's a good snuggler."

"I'd like to take her place," he says.

Flirting is a lot easier and safer via text. Once we move into phone flirting, my skills vanish. God forbid he flirt with me in person, I basically go to mush.

"Sadie's irreplaceable," I say then whisper, "But so are you."

"You sure you don't want me to come over?" he asks, his voice low and hungry.

"Not tonight," I say, unsure why I'm saying no. "I'll bring Sadie to the vet clinic in the morning before I go to work."

His groan is so low, I know I'm not meant to hear his frustration. "Good night, then," he says.

"Rhett," I say, stopping him from hanging up. Drawing a deep breath and hopefully some courage, I ask, "I was wondering if you would go with me to Brody and Skye's reception?"

If smiles had a sound, I'd be hearing his right now. "A. Rose, are you asking me out on a date? Do you know what that means?"

"What does it mean?"

"It means there's the possibility of a kiss at the end of it."

I giggle like a little schoolgirl. Before I hang up, I say, "A possibility is not a guarantee."

# CHAPTER THIRTY-SEVEN

I love you. I want you. I need you.
A. Rose

## RHETT

I'VE BEEN BACK in Charleston well over a month now. I'm back to working full days at the vet clinic. All in all, things are good. The adjustment hasn't been as bad as I once thought it would be. If only I'd made as much progress with Ainsley.

We're back to walking Sadie together most nights. It's been weeks and weeks of the same routine. She doesn't come into my place, and I don't go into hers. I tell her goodnight at the door, and that's it. We flirt like it's an Olympic sport. Sometimes she calls later, and we talk. Usually, she falls asleep. She won't say it, but I don't think she sleeps well unless I'm with her in some way. Some nights, like when I have basketball and know I'll be late, she's even started keeping Sadie at her place.

She hasn't missed one of my games, and I've spent every all-nighter she pulls in her shop with her. We have all the makings of a relationship, except the physical. I'm beginning to wonder if her hesitation has more to do with my situation than she wants to admit. It's one thing to be friends with a paraplegic, it's another to date one.

Or maybe that's just my shit rearing its ugly head again.

I look up at the clock in the operating room of the vet clinic. I've had back to back surgeries this morning, but I find the day passes faster when I'm in the operating room. It's easier than seeing patients all day. The surgical table is low enough that I can maneuver around quite easily. We don't do any high-risk surgeries at the clinic. We have the occasional emergency, but it's mostly spays, neuters, cyst removals, dental stuff. Things I can do blindfolded. I have the odd pet that doesn't do well, but for the most part, things go smoothly during and after surgeries I perform.

The door opens, and Brody sticks his head in. "How long until you finish up?"

"I'm putting in the last stitch or so." I look up at Brody, seeing tension on his face. It's not like him to check up on me. He did the first few days I was back, but not anymore. Something must be up. I lower my surgical mask. The look on his face is making my stomach churn. "What's up?"

"Ainsley's here. She brought Sadie," he says then leaves.

A sick feeling hits my stomach.

You ever just *know* something's wrong? That's exactly what this is.

On the nights Ainsley watches Sadie, she always drops her off here in the morning before opening her shop for the day. It's been our routine. Brody's never thought to come and get me before. What's going on now? I finish the stitches as quick as I can then rip off my surgical gloves.

When I open the door, Brody is leaned up against the wall, waiting. "Ainsley's in room two," he says. "She . . ."

"Is she alright?"

"It's not her."

I fly through the door, finding Ainsley on a bench with Sadie's head in her lap. She looks up at me with tears running down her cheeks. I stroke her cheek and pat my dog. "What happened?"

"She was whimpering." Ainsley sniffles. "She wouldn't get out of bed, not even for a treat."

"Her arthritis has been acting up," I say. "Did you give her the pill in some peanut butter?"

Ainsley looks up at her big brother. Brody softly shuts the door. "It's not arthritis." He turns off the lights and puts up an x-ray of Sadie's chest.

"No," I say, immediately seeing the problem, all the telltale signs of an enlarged heart. I've seen it before, had to deliver bad news to families, but this time it's my dog. There's nothing that can help her. My head starts to shake, refusing to accept what's right in front of me.

"She doesn't have long," Brody says.

"No," I say again.

"She's in pain," Brody says quietly.

I should've seen this coming. I'm a vet, for Christ's sake. She's not a young dog. She's getting old. She's been lazier than usual. But I haven't seen her in pain before, certainly not recently. I would've dealt with it had I noticed that. I could've prepared myself a little bit.

Sadie lifts her head slightly, licking my hand, then places her head onto my lap. I lower my head and sit quietly for a minute.

"I can't," I say.

Brody kneels and gives a tiny, sad smile to his sister. "I know. I'll do it," he says.

"No," I say. "What's the name of that vet who specializes in canine cardiology?"

"Rhett," Brody says. "He's all the way in Columbia. She won't survive the drive."

My mind goes into warp speed. "Diuretics can help, and there's . . ."

"Her case is very advanced," Brody says. "She's been like this for some time now."

"Maybe we can take her home," Ainsley says, tears running down her face. "She should be at home."

"Rhett," Brody says, his hand landing on my shoulder, giving me his best bedside manner. "She's suffering."

I nod my head, and Brody picks up Sadie, taking her to an exam table. He sets up a few things, the medicine, the needle. I know what's coming.

I've done it myself, but it's completely different when it's your animal. Knowing that Sadie won't suffer is the only consolation my medical knowledge provides me. Ainsley takes my hand and kisses the top of my head. Slowly, we approach Sadie, and Ainsley steps forward first.

"I love you, girl," she says, sobbing. "You're the best dog . . ." Her voice gives, and she can't continue. I put my hand on top of hers and lean down, wrapping my arm around Sadie, burying my head in her fur.

Sadie shifts her head so that she's resting on my and Ainsley's hands joined together. I look up, and Sadie holds my eyes. I swear she smiles at me. In that moment, I know she hung on to life for me, to see me through, to make sure I was okay, to make sure someone else would love me unconditionally like she does.

That's the special thing about a pet. They're always happy to see you. Wouldn't it be nice if your partner greeted you with the same enthusiasm each time you walked through the door, no matter how short of a time you've been gone? Imagine being given that kind of love. The world would be a very different place if everyone was loved like that.

Ainsley loved me like that, even at my worst. She's always been there for me, happy to see me. How different would my life be now if I had allowed her to continue to love me? Not been such an asshole to her?

"It's time," Brody says.

Drawing a deep breath, I nod. He gives her the shot, the medicine seeping into her veins.

Everything Sadie has given to me runs through my mind. Dogs don't get enough credit; they are wise animals. They play every day. They live in the moment and jump for joy when their loved ones come home. They don't hold their emotions inside. When they're scared, they look for love. They don't run from it.

I've run from it. I hate that I did. Sadie knew better than me.

"Thank you," I mumble into her floppy ear, trying to hold in tears.

# CHAPTER THIRTY-EIGHT

## AINSLEY

BRODY INSISTED RHETT go home after Sadie passed. I closed my store so I could be with him, leaving a note on my door and a message on my voicemail that I had a family emergency. Sadie was my family, just the four-legged, furry kind. Perhaps those are the best family members. They're always good listeners, don't mind our bullshit, and never have a bad word to say.

Rhett hasn't had much to say, either. He's just been sitting on the sofa. And aside from the few tears at the clinic, I haven't seen him cry. All the silence is starting to drive me a little crazy. His condo seems eerily quiet without the sound of Sadie's paws tapping along the hardwoods, her tail rapping against something.

We haven't really hung out in each other's places since Rhett's been home, aside from Skye's pregnancy test incident and my accidental nap on his sofa. Now, here we are, together again, in his place, where we spent so many nights before. It's kind of sad that it took Sadie dying to bring me back here. I guess, even in death, Sadie brings Rhett and me together.

"Would you like me to pick up Sadie's things?" I ask Rhett. "I could take them to a shelter, donate them."

He shakes his head. "I'll take care of it later."

Taking a seat beside him, a few tears fall from my eyes. "I'm so sad, and she wasn't even my dog."

"Yeah, she was," he says, looking over at me. "I know how much you loved her."

"I'm really sorry," I say.

Holding my eyes, he says, "No more walks with Sadie."

He doesn't say it like a question, but I know he's asking one. That dang dog was the reason he kissed me the first time. She brought us together. All those walks—we fell in love on those walks. "Guess you'll just have walks with me, then."

His pale blue eyes cut right through me. "It's going to be okay," he whispers.

I'm not sure if he's talking about Sadie or us. "I used to whisper that in your ear in the hospital," I say. "When you were unconscious or sleeping."

"I know." He strokes my cheek. "You'd softly kiss me and whisper to me. I heard every word. I felt every kiss."

"I wanted so badly for you to promise that back, that it would be okay."

"It will be okay," he whispers again, leaning in just a little.

For weeks, we've been spending time together. Since those initial few days he returned to Charleston, he's backed off a lot, giving me the time and space I so desperately needed from him. Through that time, we've been playful, flirty, fun, but my guard has still been up. Maybe it's because I'm too emotionally drained to fight it anymore, or maybe it's just that it's time, but suddenly, it seems that Rhett and I have had too much space and time apart. "You have to kiss me," I say.

Without a moment of pause, he pulls me to him, parting my lips, his tongue greedy for mine. I don't know what I expected—maybe soft and sweet, but there is nothing soft or sweet about this.

His hand grips my hair. My hands cling to his shirt, neither one of us able to get close enough. It feels a like a battle against all that we lost, all the time, all the moments stolen from us. He shouldn't feel this good. I shouldn't want him this much. His kiss shouldn't still do this to me. My body knows what it wants, even if my heart is still scared.

He pulls me into his lap, straddling him. The fear that's in my heart spreads to my body, and I jerk away, harder than I mean to. As soon as my eyes catch his, regret fills me. "I didn't mean to . . ."

"I get it," he says, transferring from the sofa to his chair. "This isn't going to happen, is it? I was right in the hospital; you don't want me like this."

"Rhett!" I cry. "That's not true."

"All this time we've been spending time together, I thought you were still hurting, and just needed time. I thought if I was just patient enough . . . but now I see that's not it at all." His eyes lower to the ground. "You never pulled away from me. Now you've done it twice. First in Atlanta, and just now."

"That's what you think?" He simply stares at me. I know that look. I've seen it before, right about the time the bouquet of flowers flew past my head. "Let's get it all out. Once and for all," I say. "We never really did that. Bits and pieces, but we never had it out—all of it."

"Fine!"

"This just didn't happen to *you*!" I scream. "It happened to *us*. You never understood that."

"I understand that my cock doesn't do it for you anymore."

"If you believe that, then you haven't changed one bit."

"Why don't you just admit it?" he asks. "Admit you don't want me like this."

"I don't want you like this," I say, stepping closer. "But it has nothing to do with the chair."

"Keep telling yourself that," he bites out.

Unsure what comes over me, or what gives me this crazy ass idea, I stand right in front of him and grab his hand. He resists, but I don't let go. His pale blue eyes watch mine, unsure what I'm doing. I'm not quite sure myself.

Guiding his hand under my dress, he jerks back, but I hold firm. "Touch me, Rhett," I say.

Shocked, confused, pissed, thrilled—I have no idea the emotion going through his eyes, but he does what I say. He doesn't wait a moment. His hand drifts higher, his fingers grazing the flesh of my inner thighs.

"Feel what you do to me," I whisper. "What you've always done to me."

Gently, his finger slips under my panties, finding me wet and open. My muscles clench. It's been so long. "Just your kiss does that."

His eyes close. I know I've proven my point and step away, my body screaming at the loss of contact.

He whispers my name, sounding like an apology, but I'm done listening. It's time for him to hear me. "I'm scared, Rhett. I'm scared of losing you again. I left the gym that day because I was afraid you'd get hurt in the game. I came back because I couldn't stand the thought of me not being there if you were. But I can't be there if you won't let me."

"Ainsley," he says, reaching for the chain that hangs around his neck.

"No," I say, holding up my hand. "I pulled away just now not because I don't want you, but because it scares me how much I do." I feel my tears welling up and suck them back down. "You want me to be honest?"

"Always."

"Of course I'm afraid to have sex with you again. It's been a long time. And I don't know what I'm doing. I mean, logistically. Can you be on top? Do I just straddle your chair? I know there's some sort of sex swing that's supposed to help."

"How do you know about the swing?"

"Google," I say.

"You've Googled sex with paraplegics?"

"And wheelchair sex. And sex toys for . . ."

He busts out laughing, interrupting my cyber-stroll down memory lane. "Did you buy anything?"

He thinks he's being cute and funny, but I'm not laughing. "We aren't going to work," I say softly. He stops laughing, his head shaking, and I can see the arguments forming behind his eyes. "If you don't stop putting the chair between us, we don't have a chance."

"I don't."

"You assume everything is about you being in that chair, but it's not. I pull away, and you assume I don't want you. What's it going to be like if I don't want to have sex one night? Are you always going to assume it's about you? Maybe I just have a headache."

"Tell me you have a headache, and then I'll know."

"But will you *believe* me?" I ask.

"A. Rose."

I shake my head. "No, Rhett. You're always going to think I'm sacrificing something to be with you. You can't see everything you give me, and that's no way to have a relationship."

"Ainsley, what can I do?" he asks.

"Get over yourself," I say. "Or get over me. It's your choice."

# CHAPTER THIRTY-NINE

When you kiss me, my toes curl.
A. Rose

### RHETT

"DUDE, I THINK Skye's gone off the deep end," Brody says, sitting at his desk across from mine in our joint office.

"Why?" I ask, trying to act interested, but I've got my own woman problems to contend with.

"You'll see when she gets here," he says. "She's stopping by with some lunch. She's just not herself. Like the other day, the florist called to say tulips are out of season, and you know, that's Skye's favorite flower. She designed the whole wedding around that flower, basically. And Skye just smiled and said we'll have baby roses instead."

"That doesn't sound like her. Must be something in the water with women these days."

Brody looks over at me, holding his hands up. "You know I can't get in the middle."

"I understand, but I need to ask you one thing," I say. "I need you to be honest. Ainsley's your little sister. Would you have any hesitations if she and I got back together?"

I know he knows what I'm asking. I don't have to spell it out for him. He wasn't exactly thrilled when he found out about our relationship, and that's when I wasn't stuck in this chair. He has to have given this some thought. Would he want his sister to spend her life with me? Is he concerned she'll end up being a nursemaid? Concerned about what she might be giving up to be with me?

Brody leans back in his chair, looking straight at me. "Not one."

His support means a lot to me. When I first started dating Ainsley, I really didn't care what Brody thought, or at least I told myself I didn't, but having his blessing this time is important. "Appreciate that."

"I've seen you around here, on the basketball court, how you're handling things. I have no doubt you will take care of her, love her."

"So we have your permission this time?"

"You asking for it this time?"

"Hell, no," I say, chuckling.

Skye walks in with a couple sacks of takeout. "What's so funny?" She gives Brody a kiss on the cheek.

"What's that I smell?" he asks, giving me a look. "Is that fried chicken?"

"Yep," she says, unloading food onto our desks. "That okay? I'm starving."

Brody's right. Skye has been abducted by aliens. I haven't seen her eat fried chicken since college, and even then, she took the skin off.

"So what was so funny?" she asks again, licking her fingers.

"More Rhett and Ainsley drama," Brody says, flipping me the bird.

"Oh, the kiss," Skye says.

What the fuck? Girls don't follow the "don't kiss and tell" policy, I guess. Obviously, Skye knows the whole mess. Well, Ainsley's side of the mess. Which, let's be honest, is probably the more truthful side.

Brody's eyes dart to mine, and I shake my head. "It's nothing."

Skye points her chicken leg at me. "You know, one of these days, Ainsley's going to stop giving you chances."

"Babe," Brody says. "Maybe it's best to not . . ."

"What if Ainsley got paralyzed?" Skye asks me.

"Okay," Brody says, getting to his feet. "I don't want to hear about my sister being hurt, fictional or not. I'm going to go check in with Brenda." He walks out, making a crazy sign by his head.

"So?" Skye prompts. "What if Ainsley was in a wheelchair?"

"So now she and I are both paralyzed?" I ask.

"Yep," she says, grabbing another piece of chicken.

Not wanting to have this conversation with her, I joke, "I guess I'd do a lot of motorboating."

"There you go," she says, taking me totally seriously. "Ainsley feels the same way."

Sometimes female logic isn't so easy to follow. Why is that? It's like they go from point A to point Z in one step. Perhaps that means they are the smarter sex, after all. "I'm missing the point of this whole thing."

Skye puts down her chicken and looks up at me. "The point is, you'd still want her. You know everything that comes with being in that chair. And even knowing all that, you'd *still* want her. You wouldn't care about any of it. You wouldn't stop wanting her because she needed a catheter or couldn't walk down the aisle to you. You'd still want her because you love her that much."

"I would."

"Then you need to start believing she loves *you* that much."

Skye goes back to her ravenous attack on the poultry population, and I just sit quietly, thinking about what she said.

Love is a belief, a faith. I've never thought about love as faith before, but that's exactly what it is. To have faith is to trust someone else totally. That's what love is at its core.

They say you can't have love if you don't have trust. That's what love is.

Love is faith.

It's long past time for me to become a believer.

# CHAPTER FORTY

## AINSLEY

*Pick you up at seven.*

I've been staring at Rhett's text for a solid five minutes. Brody and Skye's party is tonight. Rhett and I planned to go together, but we haven't really talked since our post-kiss argument the other night. I just assumed our date was off, although I never officially told him so. It's a good six hours until we need to be there. I could let him sweat it out, but instead I type.

*No, I'll see you there.*

His response is immediate.

*Then I need to see you before. You don't have to talk to me. I'll do all the talking, but there's some things I need to say to you. Just one more chance.*

There's that charming little *just* word he loves to throw around. I don't respond to his message, but I can't ignore him. My heart won't let me, no matter how much my brain says that's the best course of action. I don't know how long this little saga of ours can go on, but I know it's not over. Not yet.

Slipping on a pair of sandals, I head one floor up to his place. I don't know what he's about to say. All I know is that Sadie won't be barking at my arrival. That's a first. And it makes me sad. Taking a deep breath, I knock. After a quick moment, he answers. I can tell he's surprised to find me at his door, probably thinking I was ignoring him, since I hadn't answered his last text.

There's a look in his pale blue eyes I don't think I've ever seen before. It's intense, almost an urgency, but at the same time a hesitation. I can't put my finger on the emotion. The feeling as I walk inside his place is: *this is it.*

This is the moment where we either let go of each other or grab on and never let go again.

"I don't want anything between us," he says.

"Okay."

"Not this chair. Nothing," he says, and I nod. "I want to show you some things."

He moves toward his spare bedroom, and I say, "Rhett, I've been in your place. I've seen your workout . . ."

"Please, Ainsley," he says.

Exhaling, I nod then follow him into the room now set up as his personal gym. He tells me how the equipment works, what it's designed to do, his workout regimen. He even shows me a couple of the moves. It's interesting, but I'm not sure what it has to do with anything. The same holds true for the tour he gives me of his kitchen, showing me how everything is stored in the lower cabinets now, explaining how he does the laundry, the dishes.

Does he want a gold star chart? I never doubted his ability to live on his own, be independent. Whatever this is, I'm missing the point.

Next, he takes me into his bathroom. I haven't seen this room since he's been back. It's the one room that looks the most different—newly installed grab bars and shower chair. He reaches for a bag that's always attached to his chair, pulling out a small tube in some wrapping.

His chest inflates as he takes a huge breath. "You were in the hospital with me in the beginning, but there's some stuff you missed. I'm not sure how much you know about what my daily life looks like now."

I see a tiny shake in his hand as he holds the package, and the emotion I couldn't place before becomes glaringly obvious.

Fear.

Rhett is scared. My Rhett. The bravest, strongest, toughest man I know is scared.

I take what he's holding, realizing it's a catheter. Quietly, he starts to tell me about his daily routine. I knew all this, but honestly, I haven't given it much thought, and I'm not quite sure why he's going through it all with me now.

He rolls out of the bathroom, going over to his bed, and pulling back all the bedding, even the fitted sheet. "If I'm not really careful, sometimes at night . . ." his voice cracks.

I see the pad on the bed. I know what it's for.

"If we ever were to share a bed again . . ." He stops, looking up at me, and my heart breaks.

He's the sexiest man I've ever met in my life, and he's sitting here telling me he could possibly have an accident in bed with me.

Does he think any of this changes things for me? Does he think I care? These are the reasons he pushed me away before, and now he's laying it all out for me to see. Does he think this might make me love him less? It really makes me love him more.

I want to tell him I don't care, but he keeps talking, and I feel like if I interrupt him, he may never get everything out he needs to say. Using his arms, he scoots forward slightly in his chair.

"Stand behind me," he says. I move, then he lifts his shirt up, the long, jagged scar from his spinal surgery coming into view.

I've seen it, but not in a long time. My reaction when I saw it in the hospital was gratitude that he was alive. Now looking at it, a lighter pink color, no longer fresh from surgery, I'm filled with the same emotion.

Gently, I reach out, running my fingers down it, feeling the small, jagged ripples. Rhett looks back at me over his shoulder, our eyes meeting, and I know more is coming. Slowly, I move away, allowing him to sit back comfortably in his chair.

"Why are you showing me all this?" I ask, sitting down on his bed, facing him. "None of it changes anything for me."

"I'm showing you because I love you," he says. "And I need to make sure you know all of it. I'm showing you because I don't want to put the chair between us anymore. I'm showing you and asking you to love me anyway."

My hand flies over my mouth, tears rushing down my face. Finally! This is what I waited for all those nights on his parents' porch. It's long overdue.

"I'm so sorry, Ainsley. You have no idea how sorry I am. I won't ever hurt you again," he says, wiping my face with his hands. "I want your love back."

"You never lost it," I whisper, leaning my forehead on his. His fingers glide through my hair, both of us whispering *I love you* to each other.

There were times I never thought I'd hear him say those three words to me again, and there were times when I was sure I'd never believe them from him again, either. I thought I'd given up on Rhett's love, but now I know he never really gave up on me. He just needed to learn how to love me from a new perspective.

I lean in to kiss him, but he pulls back, saying, "One more thing."

I know what it is. The biggest hang-up for him. "Sex," I say.

Nodding, he says, "It's not going to be the same."

"No, it's not," I say. "But why do you assume it's going to be worse?"

He shakes his head at me, the smallest hint of a smile on his lips. "I have no idea how it will be," he says, looking away from me.

"But you've . . ." I take a deep breath. The only way we can work through this stuff is to be honest and open. "Pleasured yourself, right?"

Not making eye contact with me, he shakes his head. In all the years I've known Rhett, I've never seen him like this. So unsure, so vulnerable.

"Where's the cocky guy I fell in love with?" I ask playfully.

He turns my way, a mischievous grin sneaking out. That guy is still very much alive.

Taking his hand, I say, "We'll figure it out together."

His eyes drift to my belly. "Having a family isn't impossible, but it's not a guarantee, either."

"It's not a guarantee for any couple," I say quickly.

"But the odds of me being able to get you pregnant naturally are really low."

"So we get some help, then." Holding his eyes, I take both his hands in mine. "Rhett, I know it will be different now."

His eyes close tightly. "The patio, our first time . . ."

He brought the same thing up in the hospital all those months ago. It was great sex, but I'm not sure why he obsesses over that one time. I move to his lap, running my fingers through his hair. "So we can't have sex standing up anymore. There are plenty of other positions."

Interrupting, he whispers, "That was the only time we ever had sex without a condom. The only time I ever really felt you." His eyes close. "I'll never . . ."

He'll never feel me again.

We both knew that, but in this moment, the reality of it hits him hard. Both our hearts break at the same time. I lower my forehead to his, and for the first time since tragedy struck, we cry together.

Tears stream down both our faces until I'm not sure which are his and which are mine. His arms coil around me tightly, and I cling to his shirt. We cry for everything we lost. For all the things we'll never have again. We cry for all the harsh words that passed between us, and all the love we didn't share. We cry for what should have been, and what will never be.

And when the tears slow, he wipes my cheeks, and I wipe his—both of us realizing this is what we needed, and realizing we still have each other.

Our tears are soon replaced by smiles. Smiles for everything we still have, for all the things yet to come. We smile at all the memories of friendship and love between us, for all we shared. We smile for all that will be, and for what's to come.

Sliding off his lap, I stand in front of him, this man that I love more than anything in the world. This man who I just had the most intimate moment of my life with, and it had nothing to do with sex. This man who I want to share everything with.

Staring into his blue eyes, I lift my shirt over my head, dropping it to the floor, revealing my white cotton bra. If I'd known today was the day for this, I would've thrown on a little lacy number, but basic white cotton is what we've got. Slipping out of my pants, I'm grateful at least my panties match. His eyes slide over me, and I know he doesn't care one bit.

"Get over here," he says, grinning at me.

Biting my bottom lip, I do a quick study of his wheelchair, determining the best way to straddle him. He helps guide me, his hands sliding up my back and unhooking my bra. Before I have time to breathe, he pulls my breast into his mouth, sucking down on me, the pleasure shooting right between my legs.

Pulling away sharply, I look down at him and see concern in his eyes, but he gently strokes my back with his fingers.

"Rhett," I say. "I don't want to pressure you, but I really need you to make me come."

The biggest grin comes over his face, and he pulls me to his lips, his tongue invading my mouth. One hand at the back of my neck, he kisses me hard. His other hand slides down the back of my panties, gripping my ass. The muscles between my legs clench. His mouth moves to my neck. I can't remember us ever having sex in a chair before, and right now, I'm wondering why the hell not. His fingers slips between my legs, and I cry out at the contact.

"Fuck, baby, you're so wet."

Letting my hand slide down, I feel him, wanting to make sure he's ready. I know there will be times his body doesn't respond, but Rhett has manual and oral skills that will work just fine in those situations. Right now, though, his dick is responding perfectly.

Slowing down for a second, I slip off my panties then reach for the waistband of his pants. Our eyes meet, and for the first time, I feel like we're nervous, clumsy virgins. I guess in some ways we are. He uses his arms to lift himself up for a second, while I slide his pants off. I reach for his shirt, but he grabs my hand.

"Leave it," he says, pulling me by my waist back into my straddle position.

I feel him hard between my legs. Except for our first time, we've always used condoms. The odds of him getting me pregnant aren't very high, and if he did, both of us would consider it a blessing. But that's not the only reason I don't want to ask him to wear one. I don't want to do anything to jeopardize his experience, and I'm not sure whether a condom would. It's not worth the risk to me.

"Talk to me," he whispers, sensing I'm overthinking. "We have to talk for this to work."

"No condom, okay?" I ask softly.

"Okay," he says, taking hold of himself. His eyes on mine, he glides inside me. My toes curl, my muscles tighten, everything about my body remembering him.

"Christ, you're beautiful," he groans, his hands slipping to my ass, encouraging me.

I know it's not going to take me long to finish. It's been over a year since I've had an orgasm, but I want to make sure this is good for him, too, although I'm not sure how I'm going to know that. If he can't finish, how can I tell? The orgasm is usually the finish line, the goal. What's the goal now?

He pulls me to his lips, kissing me. "Does it feel okay?"

I thrust my hips slowly. "Perfect."

"I love watching you," he moans, glancing between our bodies, watching his dick slide in and out.

My body starts to tremble, building up. "How do I know when to stop?"

He grins up at me, giving me a hard smack on my ass. "We stop when you can't come anymore."

I giggle, and he places his hands on my hips, using the strength of his upper body to help slide me up and down, hitting just the right spot.

"Ride my dick, baby," he groans.

If he keeps doing that, this is going to be over really quick, and I'm not ready for it to end. Before, I didn't give much thought to

Rhett finishing. He's a young, strong, healthy man. I took his ability to orgasm for granted. I know he might not be able to now, but I have to give it my best shot.

Slowing down, I lean into him, letting my breasts rub against his chest, lowering my mouth to his neck. Teasing him, I lightly kiss his neck, the lobes of his ears, feeling his muscles tighten. I've kissed his neck a thousand times. I know it turns him on, but am not sure it will be enough. The last thing I want is to work him into a frenzy without a release.

His hands wind in my hair, pulling me back to his lips. "Come for me, Ainsley."

His voice sounds like he's begging. He needs to know he can still make me orgasm. He might need to know that more than he needs to know whether he can. But this can't just be about me. I know my satisfaction means more to him than his own, but this is about us.

His hand slides to my face, making me look at him. His pale blue eyes are alive with happiness. His finger grazes my lips. My mouth opens, slipping his finger inside, and I suck down. His whole upper body goes rigid.

"Fuck," he groans, biting down on his bottom lip.

Running my tongue around his finger, I suck again. That earns me a "holy fuck."

His eyes are on fire. I know that look. I've seen it many times, usually when I was on my knees. I haven't given a blow job in a very long time, and never to a finger, but how different can it really be? I remember reading something in those early weeks after he was hurt about exploring new erogenous zones. We often get stuck thinking about dicks, vaginas, and forget that our bodies are full of uncharted territory. Perhaps I just discovered the new sexual holy land for Rhett.

He watches his dick slipping in and out of me, all the while I'm sucking, nibbling, and slowly running my tongue around his finger.

"Ainsley," he cries out.

His head tosses back, his hand grips my hip, and his groan is so loud, I wonder if the neighbors can hear us.

Did that just happen? I've never been so happy to give a man an orgasm in my whole life!

Eyes wide, he looks at me. I'm not sure which one of us is more surprised. "What the hell?" he pants. "I'm not supposed to finish first!"

I bust out laughing. "First, you're worried about not finishing, and now you're complaining you came first?"

He smacks my ass, pulling me into a kiss. "Kinky little thing, aren't you?"

"I have a few tricks up my sleeve," I tease.

"Me, too," he says, slipping his now wet finger between my booty cheeks.

# CHAPTER FORTY-ONE

I'm your rose.
A. Rose

### RHETT

"Oh God," she cries.

I've missed being buried between her legs. I thought she might want a break after our chair fun, but we moved to my bed, and I've had her straddling my face ever since.

"Don't come yet," I order, holding onto her perfect ass.

Her muscles clench over and over again, desperate to come, but I'm not ready for this to be over. Working her over with my mouth, she grabs the headboard, thrusting against me. My greed for her gets the best of me, and I won't finish her.

"I love you. All of you," I say, giving her a long, slow lick.

Tiny goosebumps cover her skin as she begs, "Please."

"More," I beg back, devouring her.

I've missed the taste of her. I've been craving her for months, and now I have her again, finally. Her body starts to tremble, and I slow down just a bit, planting sweet little kisses along her folds. She releases a little frustrated groan, and it's my undoing. I can't deny her any longer, no matter how much I don't want to stop. Her whole body tightens before she comes, screaming out my name.

I pull her beside me, resting her head on my chest, and stroke her hair just like I used to. I have her back in my arms, where she should always have been. How could I have been so stupid, pushing her away, letting her go?

Never again.

She looks up at me and smiles. "We're going to be late for the party."

"Their parties are lucky for us," I tease.

She giggles, getting to her feet and raising an eyebrow at me. "Let's shower together. It will save time."

I laugh, using my arms to push myself up until I'm braced against my headboard. I capture Ainsley's hand, looking at her, stark naked in the middle of my bedroom. I'm so lucky. I haven't felt lucky in a long time, but I am. To be the man that gets to see her this way. To be the man in her life—the one she chooses. I'm not sure what I did to deserve her, but I'm damn thankful.

After my accident, I had a serious case of "why me?" I wanted to know why this happened to me, when I had the girl of my dreams, when everything was going so well. What did I do to deserve it? Why did this have to happen? Months and months of self-pity, and I didn't get any answers to those questions.

I can still ask the same question. Why me? Why did Ainsley fall in love with me? Why do I get to be the man in her life? So in a weird way, the questions are kind of the same, but the answers are different. I really don't have the answers, but the bottom line is, I'm damn lucky. I'd much rather spend my life focusing on that.

When most people meet me, lucky probably isn't the word that comes to mind. As soon as they take a look at the woman beside me, I'm sure that changes.

It's great having her back in my bed. I'm not going to lie—it's also a relief. That this part of our relationship still works. Yes, it's different, but Ainsley was right. Different doesn't mean worse. Of course, I miss banging her up against the wall, but I'm not going to spend my life focusing on all the things we can't do anymore, missing out on all the things we can still do. I just wish I'd realized that sooner.

This afternoon with her has been better than I could've imagined, but it's not quite complete. There's still a missing piece. I reach for my shirt, lifting it over my head. I hope this is the right move. I reach for the clasp of the chain that hangs around my neck, unhooking it.

"My ring," she whispers.

"I carry this with me every day."

"You kept it?"

"When I start to feel angry or depressed, I reach for it," I say and hold the ring out to her. "Reminds me what anger cost me."

"Oh, God."

"I can't get down on one knee this time," I say, smiling.

WHEN WE GOT to the party, Ainsley pulled Brody and Skye aside to tell them our news. She wanted to do it in private, not wanting to steal their moment, even offering to take her engagement ring off. But they told her she was crazy, both of them thrilled for us. Ainsley then floated around the party, showing her ring to anyone and everyone.

Turns out, Brody and Skye had a big surprise announcement of their own to make. Looks like Ainsley will be an aunt in the coming months. Of course, Ainsley already knew. I can't believe she kept that from me. I'll make sure to give her a smack on her ass for that later.

Brody and Skye certainly know how to throw a party. This one is at a farm just outside Charleston, a barn the site of the reception. White roses cover everything in sight. Everyone's dressed casually except Brody and Skye, who donned the traditional wedding attire and are posing for photographs. This day is a long time coming for them. I'm glad they are finally getting what they deserve, and I'm happy to be here to celebrate with them.

"You might want to save your bride-to-be," my dad says, walking up beside me. "Your mother has her cornered, going over wedding plans already."

Shaking my head, I spot Ainsley with my mom. "Ainsley doesn't want a big wedding," I tell my dad.

"Good luck telling your mother that," he says.

I laugh, knowing my mother is impossible. On our drive to the party, Ainsley told me she wants something small, the exact opposite of what she wanted before. I don't care either way. She just wants the people who are closest to us. Her dress is made, and she will wear it even though I've seen her in it. We're not giving stock to the bad luck theory.

I hear my cell phone ring. It's Jay. I'd left him a message about Ainsley and me. My dad motions for me to answer it, nodding his head toward the door, away from the noise of the party.

I go outside just in time to hear Jay say, "So you put a ring on it?"

Chuckling, I say, "Is that your way of saying congratulations?"

"That's my way of asking if you knocked her up."

"Not yet," I say.

"I like that," he says. "There's hope in that."

# CHAPTER FORTY-TWO

## AINSLEY

STROLLING AROUND THE party, I can't stop smiling. Hopefully, this time next month I'll be Mrs. Ainsley Bennett. I don't want to wait to marry him. We've waited long enough. I just want to start my life with him. That's what I've always wanted—a life with Rhett.

I truly can't wait to exchange our vows. For most people, the wedding vows you take about sickness and health are abstract, something you don't really think about. At most, it's something far off in the future that might happen when you reach old age. But for Rhett and me, it's our present. When we take our wedding vows, it won't be with some vague notion of growing old together. We know our life can turn on a dime.

And I don't want a big wedding. I may be the only wedding dress designer in the history of the universe that doesn't want a big wedding. I will wear the dress I made. But everything else I thought I wanted the first time around, it just doesn't seem important now. A simple bouquet, some photos, surrounded by our family and dear friends in his parents' backyard—that sounds totally perfect.

As long as I'm Ainsley Rose Bennett at the end of it, I don't care about the details. I love the way that full name sounds. I feel like a schoolgirl doodling my new name in her notebook.

Resting my elbows on a bistro table, I run my fingers over the petals of some long stem roses in the center of the table, admiring them, how fragile they are. I think to myself how we cherish the petals—even when they fall of the stem. And even when they crumble and break apart, they're still beautiful.

"I see you're learning to love them again," a man says.

I look up, finding the doctor from Skye's office, the one I had a five-minute date with, smiling at me.

"I am," I say, knowing we are talking about more than flowers.

"Good news about Skye," he says.

"Very," I say, glancing around and looking for Rhett.

"And congratulations to you," he says, motioning toward the ring on my hand. "I saw you with your fiancé earlier."

"Thank you," I say. "Guess my breakdown makes a little more sense to you now."

He smiles, saying, "I hope this isn't out of line, but I have a friend. A doctor friend of mine. We went to school together. He specializes in helping couples with different levels of paralysis. If you and your fiancé ever need help when you start to think about having a family, I can put you in touch."

"That's very nice of you," I say.

"I wish you the best of luck," he says. "It's admirable what you're doing."

I hate that people assume I'm some sort of saint by being with Rhett—that his being in a wheelchair makes me special in some way.

"No, it's not," I say. "It's just love."

# EPILOGUE
## THREE YEARS LATER

### RHETT

"I THINK I finally found it!" my mom screams so loud I have to hold the phone out from my ear.

After we got married, Ainsley moved into my condo, and we're still here, mostly because neither one of us wants to give up our easy commute to work. We want to build our own home, design it specifically for our needs, but finding land in Charleston close to work has proven difficult. Space is at a premium.

Since my mom is in the real estate game, she's been helping us look, knowing we are quickly outgrowing condo life. I listen to my mom rattle off details of the property she found, the square footage of the lot. Apparently, there's an abandoned house that could be torn down. I zone out when she starts talking about some tree ordinance.

I pick up a wedding photo that sits on the nightstand by our bed. Our anniversary is coming up. I can't believe it's been three years. This is my favorite one of all our wedding photos. It was taken right after we said, "I do." Ainsley's in my lap, and I'm rolling us down the aisle. Her dress is so big you can barely see our faces. It looks like we're lost in a sea of lace roses, but the photographer managed to capture her smile.

The smile that captured me.

"Text me the address, and Ainsley and I will go check it out," I say, ending the call with my mother.

Placing the photo down, I go into the den to tell Ainsley about the latest prospect, finding her parked on our sofa, mesmerized by her laptop. Her little baby bump is finally noticeable. She's five months along now. We had some medical help to make it happen, but seeing her like this—all glowing and happy, growing our child—it was worth every penny, every trip to the doctor, every embarrassing question and procedure.

Our little mixed breed stray, Josie, thinks Ainsley's pregnant belly is the perfect place to rest her head. After Sadie, I wasn't sure I'd get another dog for a while, but a patient brought Josie in, having found her on the side of the road with a broken leg. I fixed her up, but then she had nowhere to go. We couldn't just abandon her. What was supposed to be a night or two recovering with me and Ainsley happened to turn into several years.

"What are you doing?" I ask Ainsley.

"Shopping for your anniversary gift," she says, lowering her computer screen so I can't sneak a peek.

Tradition says that for the third wedding anniversary, you should give a gift of leather, to symbolize durability in a relationship. I looked it up. Ainsley thought a leather flogger sounded like the perfect gift. I knew there was a reason I fell in love with her. So she came up with this idea that every year for our anniversary we should purchase a new sex toy. That was my crazy wife's suggestion, and frankly, maybe the best idea she's ever had.

"I thought we said we were only exchanging sex toys?" I laugh.

"A little extra something," she says, giving me a naughty smile.

Reaching out, I pat her pregnant belly. "I think you're already doing enough."

Not only is she pregnant, but she works insane hours at her shop. Word has spread through Charleston, the entire Southern United States, and up the Eastern Seaboard about her one-of-a-kind dresses. Currently, she has a yearlong waiting list just to get a design consultation. My A. Rose is a regular mogul.

She has plans to slow down once the baby is born, having watched Skye struggle to manage working full-time and raising two kids. Once Brody and Skye got started, they had two boys back-to-back, and she's currently pregnant with their third.

Ainsley won't do it alone. I'm shortening my work week to four days, so I'll have our baby girl all to myself one day a week. Of course, my parents are itching to help, too. We don't have all the details worked out yet, but we still have a little time.

"How's my little rose petal?" I ask, talking to her belly.

"Rose petal?" she asks.

"Yeah, you're *my rose* so she's my *rose petal*. A little mini part of you."

She leans over and kisses me tenderly on the lips. "Did we just name our daughter?" she asks. "Rose Petal Bennett."

I'd only meant it as a nickname, but damn if it's not perfect. "I think we did."

# ALSO BY PRESCOTT LANE

A Gentleman for Christmas

All My Life

To the Fall

Toying with Her

The Sex Bucket List

The Reason for Me

Stripped Raw

Layers of Her (a novella)

Wrapped in Lace

Quiet Angel

Perfectly Broken

First Position

# ACKNOWLEDGEMENTS

THIS BOOK . . . This book is deeply personal to me. I have never cried writing a book before, but this one gutted me more than once. Honestly, I was scared to write it. A romance hero who's in a wheelchair? I was frightened I wouldn't get the medical stuff right. I was scared I wouldn't get his daily routine right. Basically, I stared at my computer for a month, knowing what I wanted to do, but scared to do it. Could I pull this off? In a believable and honest way?

I believe there are things that tie us together as people. Things that, no matter where you come from, we all have in common. These are the strands that bind us. Even if language or culture separates us, certain things are core to every human being. Love is one of those things. It is the reason I write romance. But more than love, it's the desire to be loved and accepted for who we are.

Everyone wants to have someone love their broken parts, the parts we often try to hide. Not so they can fix us, but so we're not alone. The hunger for love and acceptance is universal. Of course, Rhett is literally broken, but the concept is the same.

To my family and friends, thank you for loving the broken, crazy, and insecure parts of me. Thank you for letting me share the parts I try to hide with you.

To my book family—Nina Grinstead, Nikki Rushbrook, Michelle Rodriguez, Michele Catalano—thank you for always having my back in this crazy industry. Your belief in me keeps me going when I doubt I can write another word, let alone a good one.

To my bloggers, thank you so much for pimping my books, yelling from the rooftops about my stories, daily posts, inviting me to takeovers. I know you could be doing so many other things, but you choose to help little old me. I'm so blessed and grateful. There aren't enough thank you's.

To my readers, thank you for reading. Thank you for coming to see me at signings when I've convinced myself no one will. Thank you for your messages—you always seem to know when I need them. Thank you for taking my words into your hearts.

Happily Ever After,
Prescott Lane

# ABOUT THE AUTHOR

PRESCOTT LANE is originally from Little Rock, Arkansas, and graduated from Centenary College in 1997 with a degree in sociology. She went on to Tulane University to receive her MSW in 1998, after which she worked with developmentally delayed and disabled children. She currently lives in New Orleans with her husband, two children, and two dogs.

Contact her at any of the following:
www.authorprescottlane.com
facebook.com/PrescottLane1
twitter.com/prescottlane1
instagram.com/prescottlane1
pinterest.com/PrescottLane1

Made in United States
North Haven, CT
31 March 2023

34858075R00147